ONLY A DREAM?

"Be sweet to me, little one," he whispered.

"Yes . . . oh, yes," she murmured, "I will. . . ."

It was such a lovely dream. She had never had a dream that seemed so real. She could actually feel the man's hairy chest pressed tightly against her breasts and hear his voice, deep and husky, whispering words in her ears—exciting, shocking words.

She held him more tightly and heard his sharp intake of breath, then a ragged "Careful, sweetheart . . . go easy."

She clung to him, wanting and needing, yet innocent to his warning. Her fingers tangled in his hair, their mouths devouring each other. Everywhere he touched her, her body exploded into electrifying sensations.

Then his hand slipped farther down and Hannah suddenly froze as she realized what he was about to do. Even if it were only a dream, he was taking far too many liberties!

PASSION'S CAPTIVE

"Delightful reading." (Five Stars)
—*Barbara's Critiques*

"I loved every minute of it!" (Five Stars)
—Mary Nelson, *Affaire de Coeur*

"A tender, lighthearted romance that guarantees many smiles." (Four Stars)   —*Romantic Times*

SWEET TALKIN' STRANGER

"You can't help loving the characters and enjoying Ms. Copeland's easy-flowing style of writing and her definite sense of humor. We're anxiously awaiting her next historical."   —*Rendez-vous*

FOOL ME ONCE

"Pure fun . . . an utter delight to read. With skill and her special sense of humor, Ms. Copeland has created a book that is a pleasure to read. You'll find yourself laughing out loud and crying a bit, too."
—*Romantic Times*

Also by Lori Copeland

AVENGING ANGEL
FOOL ME ONCE
PASSION'S CAPTIVE
SWEET TALKIN' STRANGER
TALE OF LOVE

SWEET HANNAH ROSE

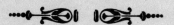

Lori Copeland

A DELL BOOK

Published by
Dell Publishing
a division of
Bantam Doubleday Dell Publishing Group, Inc.
666 Fifth Avenue
New York, New York 10103

ISBN: 0-440-20842-4

Printed in the United States of America

Published simultaneously in Canada

April 1991

10 9 8 7 6 5 4 3 2 1

OPM

"It is not true that a rose by any other name will smell as sweet."

From *Orley Farm*
by Anthony Trollope

1

The door of the towering old Victorian estate house flew open, and a young woman dashed outside and raced down the porch steps.

Angry-looking thunderheads rumbled overhead, promising a good soaking before nightfall.

Glancing fearfully over her shoulder, she bolted toward the meadow, her heart beating against her rib cage like a trapped sparrow.

She sucked in deep drafts of air as her feet flew across the saturated ground. As she ran, her hair escaped its pins and tumbled down her back in long sable curls.

An ear-shattering crash of thunder shook the ground as she ducked beneath the meadow fence in a frantic bid for freedom.

To her horror she felt the hem of her skirt snag on one of the uneven boards.

Her eyes darted wildly back over her shoulder

as she struggled to free herself. A moan escaped her lips when she saw that her pursuer was gaining on her.

Giving the fabric a violent tug, she cursed the billowing skirt that hampered her flight. Panic seized her. In desperation she grasped the button on her waistband and tore it off, then wriggled free of her skirt.

Kicking it aside, she scrambled to her feet and ran on.

A moment later, the man's heavy boots trampled the blue chintz into the mud.

When her feet slipped in the wet grass she fell to her knees, shrieking in despair. Her nails clawed at the wet earth as she tried to pull herself up to keep running again.

He was so near! She could hear his ragged breathing as he struggled to overtake her. His face was white with anger, and she could hear him yelling at her, his deep voice booming above the rising wind.

A cold chill snaked up her spine as she watched him closing in. He was so big—so powerful. Terrified, she bounded to her feet again.

He grabbed the hem of her petticoat, and she felt the fabric tangle around her legs. Tumbling to the ground, she no longer held back her screams.

"Damn you!" he roared.

"No, no!" Her wrenching sobs echoed over the deserted meadow.

Her heart beat wildly as he flipped her onto her

2

back. His face loomed above her, and he was close enough for her to see the murderous gleam in his eyes.

Above him, the heavens split open and sent a jagged fork of lightning to the ground.

While he struggled to hold her, his boots sank into the mire. He tried to steady himself but lost his balance and tumbled to the ground, still trying to hold on to her petticoat.

Jerking free of his grasp, she scrambled to her feet. Her breath came in labored gasps as she forced her legs to run.

She glanced back. He'd pulled free of the mud and he was gaining on her . . . gaining on her. . . .

The ground vibrated as another clap of thunder exploded, and rain began to fall in heavy sheets.

Sobbing hysterically now, the frightened young woman staggered on, turning her face to the sky, letting the rain beat down on her tears of woe. She was no match for his strength. She knew her plight was hopeless.

Her feet slid apart, sending her sprawling to the ground on her stomach. She screamed as she felt herself being jerked to her feet, then lifted and flung roughly over the man's shoulder.

"Pike Brewster, you put me down!" she railed. Hannah's hands balled into tight fists as she pummeled her brother's back, trying to free herself from his mighty hold.

Ignoring her, Pike strode toward the house. He

3

was used to her bossiness *and* her crocodile tears. They weren't gonna work on him, that was for sure! "You are the orneriest, *the* stubbornest, *the* meanest, the downright *aggravatinis'* woman that I have *ever* had the bad luck to meet up with," blustered the six-feet-three, 220-pound youth as he began to lumber back across the meadow.

"You put me down, Pike. I mean it!" Hannah kicked and squirmed for all she was worth, but her slight weight was no match for Pike's powerful arms.

"I'm gonna tell Papa!" She doubled her fists and whacked him between his shoulder blades. "I mean it!"

Gritting his teeth, Pike marched, maintaining a firm hold on her. He knew if she was given half a chance, he'd be a dead man.

He flinched and swore as she dug her sharp nails spitefully into his back.

Whacking her soundly across the backside, he took the porch steps two at a time, wishing she were a man so's he could really sock her a good one!

His heavy footsteps echoed across the wooden floor as he hauled her into the library and stood her on her feet none too gently.

Hannah squealed with outrage and whirled away, refusing to face her brother or her father, who sat watching his children from behind his large cherry-wood desk.

Dripping mud and water on her father's fine

Persian rug, Hannah crossed her arms defiantly and sulked. She would get even with Pike for this if it was the last thing she did!

Sherman Brewster took in the scene before him with pained tolerance.

There wasn't a dry thread on his daughter. She was covered in mud, her skirt was missing, and her hair dripped in soggy ringlets down her back.

"Where is your skirt?" he asked calmly. He knew she'd been wearing one when she'd dashed out of the room a moment ago. Awaiting her answer, he patiently rolled a pencil between his thumb and forefinger.

Turning up her nose, Hannah remained silent.

Sherman sighed. He'd finally reached the end of his rope. Why he should be cursed with a hoyden for a daughter instead of a dignified young lady still escaped him. He'd done everything except jerk a knot in her tail—and he was dangerously close to trying that.

Lord knew he couldn't handle her anymore. He'd sent her to the best schools. She'd been trained properly—no one could accuse him of neglecting his duty with his children.

Oh, he admitted that perhaps over the years he'd been guilty of burying himself in his work instead of sharing personal time with his daughter, but he'd tried, by Jove, he'd *tried* to make a lady out of her.

Now he was forced to face facts. Like her poor,

5

deceased mother—God rest her soul—Hannah Rose Brewster had a strong head on her shoulders.

Lowering his glasses on the bridge of his nose, he peered over the rims at her. "If I may be so foolish as to ask, *what* have you done with your skirt, young lady?"

Sherman realized he was yelling, but his child had no one to blame but herself for his display of anger.

"Pike *tore* it off me!," she lied without batting an eye.

Sherman's gaze shot to his eldest, a strapping youth of nineteen.

"I did not! She's lyin' again! She took it off and threw it on the ground!" Pike declared.

"Did not!"

"Did too!"

"Did not!"

"Did too!"

"Silence!" Sherman bellowed as he shot to his feet and came around his desk.

Laying the pencil on the desk, he resumed the conversation they had been having before Hannah had suddenly bolted out the front door. "Hannah Rose, I'll permit no more of this nonsense."

Hannah lifted her chin belligerently. "I'm *not* going, Papa!"

"Marta has packed your bags, and you will be leaving on the morning stage," Sherman continued as if the conversation was going the way he'd naively envisioned it.

Hannah's violet eyes flashed with fiery resentment. "I will not go to Tribulation to let your brother foist me off on that—that *moron you've chosen for me!*" she declared. She turned her back as if she'd had the last word.

"At this point, we shall *take* what we can get," Sherman assured her wearily.

Lord knew he couldn't buy the girl a husband around here—he'd tried. Her beauty was sufficient, but her temper and rapier-sharp tongue were known in four counties!

Fortunately, his brother Hamilton had assured him there was a man in Tribulation—a solid, upstanding man of the community, who'd make Hannah a suitable husband. Hamilton had given his word that he personally would see to it that his niece snared—er—was properly wed to Edgar Huckett.

Across a distance of eight hundred miles, word of Hannah's small imperfections had not reached Tribulation, and with any luck at all they wouldn't —until it was too late.

Hopefully, Edgar would be so smitten with Hannah's beauty that he would rush her to the altar before it could dawn on him that beauty wasn't everything.

Ordinarily, Sherman wouldn't sell Edgar Huckett—or any other man, for that matter—downriver this way, but dad blast it, what was a father to do?

His daughter was turning into a hooligan whom he could no longer control. She needed a man's firm hand, and, at this point, Sherman wasn't going to be picky about whose hand it was. All he asked was that the man be a decent, God-fearing Methodist.

Edgar Huckett was his last hope. Sherman would see that Hannah was on that morning stage, come hell or high water.

Sherman eyed his daughter as sternly as he could. "Your uncle has graciously arranged the wedding ceremony. It shall be a quiet one. Upon your return to Iowa, we will hold an open house so all our friends and neighbors can meet your new husband. Your cousin Kamen is visiting your uncle, and I feel it would be—"

"It is rude of *you* to marry me off to Edgar Huckett!" she accused. Her back stiffened with renewed determination. "I shall *die* before I become Hannah Huckett."

Hannah didn't approve of what her father and uncle were trying to do. She'd read the letters those two schemers had been firing back and forth. It was ridiculous that just because she was eighteen and unmarried, they should assume that she was doomed to be a spinster.

Well, she didn't care if she was. She'd yet to meet a man she'd spend an entire day with, let alone an entire lifetime! She didn't *want* some cranky old man around the house. She didn't want

8

to have to cook meals for him, wipe his children's noses, and wash *his* old dirty drawers!

"There's nothing wrong with the name Hannah Huckett!" Sherman reasoned.

"Oh, no? I vow to you, Father," Hannah's voice took on a most ominous tone, "if I am forced to marry Edgar Huckett, your first grandson shall be named Puckett Huckett!"

Sherman shrugged. He would not allow her to intimidate him. "I've heard worse."

Hannah's eyes widened with disbelief. "It's positively wretched!"

Well, Sherman *would* have preferred something a little more euphonious for his grandchild, but the way he saw it, beggars couldn't be choosers.

"Now, Hannah, dear, from what my brother tells me Edgar is quite a dashing young man," Sherman coaxed. "He will make you a fine husband."

"He runs the *funeral parlor* in Tribulation. The funeral parlor, Papa! He sounds to me like a perfectly dreadful old man!"

Hannah vividly recalled her uncle's description of Edgar in his last letter.

Edgar Huckett may not be handsome, but he is a man of high morals. Twenty-five years of age, quiet-spoken, slight of build—but in acceptable health, he commands a firm grasp on reality. He should prove excellent in providing our dear Hannah with a guiding hand and a dependable income.

"Old?" Sherman blustered. "He's only twenty-five!"

"That's positively ancient!" Burying her face in her hands, Hannah sobbed.

Pike glanced at his father with one of his why-are-you-putting-up-with-this-looks. "She ain't gonna listen to you, Pa."

"Edgar Huckett is a fine man." Ignoring his son, Sherman went on to soothe his daughter. "You will find him quite palatable."

"I will find him as exciting as *paste.* Please don't make me go to Tribulation, Papa. *Please,* don't make me marry an undertaker!"

For the first time in Hannah's young life, her pleas fell on deaf ears. Seating himself, Sherman took a deep breath, then repeated quietly, "You will be on that stage in the morning, Hannah Brewster. You will marry that nice Edgar—"

Sherman ducked just in time as his prized Ming vase whistled through the air and sailed over his head, shattering against the wall.

Straightening, Sherman counted to three before he continued, "You will marry Edgar and make a suitable attempt to find something you like about the man—"

Next, a painting of his dear deceased wife came flying across the room. Sherman dodged adeptly as he went on, "Now, then. Your brother will escort you to your room where you will make yourself presentable for dinner this evening. Judge Reinhier and his lovely wife, Portico, will be joining us—"

Sherman broke off in mid-sentence as an ashtray sailed by his ear and hit the wall behind him.

"No, Papa, *No!"*

Shrieking, Hannah held herself stiff as a poker as Pike scooped her up in his arms. She shrieked again, "I won't do it!" She crossed her arms mutinously. "You can't make me marry Edgar Huckett!"

Pike carried her unceremoniously out of the room, kicking the door closed behind him as Sherman sank back onto his chair.

Pulling out his handkerchief to mop his forehead, he muttered, "Thank *God* she wasn't twins."

The bright yellow Wells and Fargo coach bumped along the barren countryside in a cloud of boiling dust. Hannah stared out the window stoically, disgusted by the whole ridiculous turn of events.

Before she could say boo, she'd been trussed up like a Christmas turkey and hauled off to Tipton, where she was put on the Butterfield Overland coach to Texas, to marry that old *geezer*, Edgar Huckett!

"Are you all right, young lady?"

Hannah glanced up, startled by the sound of Hezziah Broadwrust's voice. Hezziah leaned forward in his seat, his forehead etched with concern for the young traveler.

"I asked if you were all right, young lady?"

"Yes, thank you," Hannah returned.

Lifting a handkerchief to her mouth, she dabbed nervously at the perspiration above her upper lip. She glanced out the window of the coach at the endless array of cactus and tumbleweeds.

Hell's bells! If this wasn't a fine mess. She was on her way to Tribulation to marry a burying man.

"I'll run away," she murmured. "The moment I get there—or maybe even before I get there—I'll just run away and join a convent."

Glancing back at Mr. Broadwrust, she blurted, "Is it necessary to believe in God in order to become a nun?"

Hezziah went blank for a moment. "Why—er—I believe it would certainly be to one's advantage."

"Oh." Settling back on her seat, Hannah thought about that. It wasn't that she didn't believe in God. She did. She was just put out with Him for not preventing her father from shipping her off to Tribulation. *Tribulation!* She winced. If the town was anything like its name, even God wouldn't want to go there.

But maybe she'd be lucky and find a convent before she got to town that would accept her right away.

Hezziah could tell that something was troubling the girl. Leaning forward, he tried to console her with a paternal pat on her hand. "I know you must be weary, but it shouldn't be much longer before we reach Tribulation."

The young lady looked near exhaustion. Though she had kept to herself, saying very little during the long journey, Hezziah had taken a liking to her. She was such a pretty little thing, with that mass of riotous blue-black hair and eyes the color of wild orchids.

Hezziah couldn't imagine why anyone would let this young woman travel the dangerous back roads unescorted. Why, there were all manner of threats lurking by the wayside to endanger this delicate creature: highwaymen, society misfits, not to mention Indians.

Hezziah knew that there would be nothing that he or the driver could do to protect her if they should meet up with those red heathens.

Unaware of Hezziah's concerns, Hannah stared out the window as the old coach bumped its way along the rutted road. She was weary of the journey and even more weary of thinking about what she would find waiting for her at the end. The thought made her slightly ill.

Edgar Huckett.

Shuddering, she exhaled a long sigh that made Hezziah lift his brows with concern again.

Hannah conceded that there was little she could do about the misery her father had thrust upon her. She would go to Tribulation and meet Edgar Huckett . . . because she had no other choice.

But she didn't have to be gracious about it.

No, she planned to make Edgar Huckett's life a living hell until he was forced to send her home.

Yes . . . A sly grin formed on her lips. She'd create a black, funereal misery that he'd be only too happy to escape.

Smiling, she suddenly felt much better. She wouldn't have to join a convent. She would be back home within the week. If the little burying man liked gloom and doom, he'd find himself in a nest of it.

She would make poor old Edgar *so* miserable that he'd be only too glad to buy her a one-way ticket back to Iowa on the first available stage.

Laughing aloud, she reached up to adjust her hat. She noticed Hezziah's puzzled look and she smiled smugly at him.

There wasn't a man on *earth* who could match Hannah Brewster's cunning frame of mind once she had her sights adjusted.

Not *any old* man.

2

The Kincaids hated the Brewsters.

The Brewsters felt the same about the Kincaids —only they hated them even more.

Neither family was proud of it, but the feud between the two had gone on for longer than anyone in town cared to remember.

And that covered a lot of years.

Old Luis Pedrero could tell you all you wanted to know about the feud because Luis had been just a *Chiquito* when it all started.

Luis had turned ninety last January, and he could say that he'd never seen anything like the way those two families bickered with one another.

Fact was, the feud was a downright disgrace to the townsfolks.

The people of Tribulation liked to think of it as a peaceful town. The population, which numbered only thirty-six—mostly Mexicans and Indians, with an occasional Anglo thrown in—never cared much for trouble. But like most towns wedged on the border of west Texas and Mexico, fate had dealt them their share.

But no one in Tribulation could stir up the kind of misery and downright aggravation the Brewsters and Kincaids did.

The fuss those two families made over one piddling acre of land that ordinarily wouldn't have amounted to a hill of frijoles was enough to make a grown man want to sit down and cry.

Trouble was, this one particular insignificant little acre had water running smack through it; clear, bubbling spring water as sweet and pure as Juan Gomez's old-maid daughter.

Now this disputed piece of ground just *barely* nipped the northwest corner of Thatcher Kincaid's property.

However, it just *barely* nipped the southeast corner of Hamilton Brewster's property, too.

And that's what was causing all the ruckus.

Hamilton Brewster's great-grandfather had contended by all that was holy that the Brewsters owned the disputed acre.

Thatcher Kincaid's great-grandfather had contended that the Brewsters didn't own any such thing—only it was rumored he hadn't used terms quite that polite.

At a time when boundary lines were ambiguous and cattle had the run of the land until they were sorted out at spring roundup, a man would have been hard pressed to say where Kincaid's property ended and Brewster's began.

The feud just kept passing from generation to generation, and no one knew how to resolve the controversy.

Since both Thatcher and Hamilton were cattlemen, like their fathers and great-grandfathers and great-great-grandfathers before them, and since water was one of the most precious commodities in these parts, neither man took lightly to the idea of sharing.

In fact, it downright galled them both.

When he was riled, Thatcher was known to be as hotheaded and stubborn as a jackass. And Hamilton? Well, you could ask anyone, and they'd tell you that when Hamilton took a notion, he was a real pain in the neck.

And the unfortunate townsfolk of Tribulation were caught square in the middle of the fracas.

Since the Kincaids owned half the town, and the Brewsters owned whatever was left, the citizens tried not to take sides in the matter. The shopkeepers didn't want to lose the business of either family, and besides, most anybody would be quick to point out that Hamilton and Thatcher were easy enough to get along with—providing the other one's name wasn't mentioned in conversation.

So, who actually owned the disputed piece of land?

Well, Hamilton had a deed that stated he did,

17

and Thatcher had one that claimed that he was the sole owner.

No one could say for certain how that had happened, but Hamilton's lawyer thought the mistake was made by a tipsy surveyor when Hamilton's great-grandfather had staked his claim nearly ninety years before.

Unfortunately, that had been about the same time Thatcher's great-grandfather had been staking his claim, too.

Because of too much rotgut whiskey, two deeds had been issued, each showing that that one acre belonged to both men.

The Brewsters and the Kincaids had been at each other's throats ever since.

The members of both families were hardworking, honest, law-abiding citizens who got along with nearly everybody except the people in the other family. You didn't dare mention a Kincaid to a Brewster or a Brewster to a Kincaid unless you wanted yourself a peck of trouble.

So after ninety years the feud between the two families still raged on, but it was beginning to get pretty old—to everyone. . . .

On a windswept stretch of flatland, a crow called to its mate, the shrill cry interrupting the uneasy silence that had suddenly come over the riders.

In the distance, the crow's mate called back.

A hot sun bore down on the eighteen men as they sat on horseback lined up facing one another.

Hot and worn out, the eighteen dust-covered riders sat like pieces on a chess board, their tempers already frayed by ten hours in the saddle.

The reins resting in their callused hands appeared deceptively lax. Shirts were stuck to their backs and sweat was beginning to roll from beneath their hat brims.

Eighteen broad-shouldered men squared off against one another—with only a thin strand of wire between them.

There were nine on either side.

Nine of Brewster's men.

Nine of Kincaid's.

Brows lowered, eyes narrowed as occasionally a man moved his palm to rest with firm assurance on his leather holster.

A tall, powerfully built man sitting astride the lead horse, his dark eyes filled with aggravation, spoke again in a calm voice. "Cut the wire, Brewster."

Kamen Brewster leaned forward in his saddle, a lazy grin spreading across his youthful features. "Why don't you try and make me, Kincaid?"

Leather creaked as one of the men shifted in his saddle. The overpowering stench of horseflesh, mingled with sweat, filled the men's nostrils as the crow called out again in the still, dry air.

Uneasy gazes rested on the strand of barbed wire strung across the disputed acre. Every man present knew that Lucas Kincaid wouldn't allow it to remain there.

In the distance, the restless herd of milling longhorns bawled. The thirsty cattle were close enough to smell the water.

Luke calmly lifted a gloved hand to his left shirt pocket as he studied the strand of wire. A moment later, he cupped his hand against the wind and lit a cheroot.

Luke's gaze returned to the other man. "I'm not looking for trouble, Kamen. Just cut the wire."

"Can't do that, Luke." The youth's face sobered. Luke Kincaid was a formidable opponent, but Kamen had his orders. And his orders were to block Kincaid cattle from drinking any more Brewster water.

A muscle worked tightly in Luke's jaw as he considered the boy. How old was Hamilton's nephew now? Fifteen? The boy's smooth jaw showed a hint of peach fuzz, so Luke knew that guess couldn't be far off.

Bringing the cheroot back to his mouth, Luke drew on it, then said quietly, "You seem mighty young to me, boy."

"I'm old enough," Kamen assured him.

Luke's eyes took on a coldness. "You sure this is what you want, Kamen? Dying at an early age?"

The boy shrugged, then sat up straighter, trying to add height to his lanky frame. "Ain't no Brewster afraid of dyin'." Luke could see the boy's Adam's apple working up and down nervously.

Shifting in his saddle, Luke surveyed the herd. Damn, he was tired. He'd been in the saddle since before dawn, and there wasn't a bone in his body that wouldn't verify it.

When he'd been a kid Kamen's age, he could have ridden another six hours and never blinked an eye. But Luke wasn't sixteen anymore, and he didn't need the date on a calender to remind him that he'd turned thirty today.

Taking another draw on the cheroot, Luke's gaze returned to the boy. "I've got a hundred head of thirsty cattle. No wire is going to stop me from getting them to water."

Kamen's hand settled around the butt of his pistol more securely. As he glanced over his shoulder, his cocky smile returned. He and his men could handle Luke Kincaid. "Maybe you'd best turn those hundred head around, Kincaid, and go home. Those cows won't be drinking Brewster water."

The heat closed in around the men and horses as they waited. Behind them the cattle milled about, their cries growing more insistent.

Shaking his head wearily, Luke reached up and removed his hat. He wiped away the sweat that was trickling down the sides of his face.

Overhead, the crow suddenly took flight in search of safer ground.

Settling the Stetson back on his head, Luke spoke softly to the rider sitting next to him. "Guess we're gonna have to teach the little son of a bitch a lesson."

Pedro Guares, a small, wiry Mexican, casually leaned around the horn of his saddle, sending a stream of tobacco juice hurtling to the ground.

The rays of the hot sun caught the spittle and dried it instantly.

Righting himself in the saddle, Pedro adjusted the brim of his hat lower. "He is just a *muchacho, señor*. He blows much smoke, but no fire. We should not harm him."

Bringing the cheroot back to his mouth, Luke drew on it again. "I didn't say we were going to harm him." A grin spread slowly across Luke's handsome features. "We're just going to scare the hell out of the little turkey."

Pedro tried to hide his grin as he glanced back at the young boy. *"Sí, señor*. The lesson will be good for his bowels."

The cattle were beginning to shift, easing around the perimeter of the riders. Their thick bodies bumped and wedged against one another in their eagerness for a cool drink from the bubbling stream.

Luke settled his hat more firmly. "Let's get this over with."

"Sí."

Tossing the cheroot aside, Luke casually gathered his reins. "Get out of the way, Kamen. We're bringing 'em through," he said.

Kamen tensed, glancing over his shoulder to assure himself that his men were still there. "Kincaid, don't be a fool—"

The cattle suddenly bolted forward. Luke glanced back, surprised to see that the wire had suddenly gone slack.

The air grew cloudy with dust as the herd broke into a run, angling sharply in the direction of the wire that was lying on the ground now.

Riders on both sides of the fence were forced to scramble out of the path of the stampeding herd.

The confusion grew louder as the cattle surged through the break in the fence, racing toward the water.

"Dammit!" Luke shouted to Pedro, who by now was caught square in the middle of the sudden chaos. "Who gave the order to move?"

The Mexican reined his horse to a sharp right, barely escaping a set of razor-sharp horns. "Not I, *señor!*"

Luke went for his gun as Kamen rode through the herd toward him, his young face blotched with humiliation.

"Kincaid, you fool!" the boy shouted as he waded his horse through the thick of the longhorns. "Uncle Hamilton will have your head for this!"

"Your uncle will have your butt for this," Luke snapped. "Now, get out of the way, Kamen, before you get hurt."

"You'll be sorry," Kamen shouted. "My uncle

will put that fence back up again—only it won't be so easy to cut next time!"

Luke almost felt sorry for the boy. The little numskull was about to get himself killed, and Hamilton Brewster would be to blame. Hamilton should have known better than to send a child to do his dirty work.

And he damn well should have known better than to string a wire across Kincaid property!

Easing his horse through the bawling cattle, Luke could hear Kamen still yelling after him, "You wait—you just wait! Once my uncle Hamilton hears what you've done, you're gonna be in big trouble!"

Reining to the side, Luke glanced back at the boy, barely able to conceal his disgust. "Stop sniveling, Brewster. Go home and tell your uncle that the next time he decides to string a fence on Kincaid property, he'd better send along a few women to help you!"

The boy's face flamed with outrage as he spurred his horse, fighting his way through the noisy herd.

"You gave those cattle their head!" Kamen accused hotly.

"I didn't give the order to move," Luke admitted, "but I would have. Take my advice, kid, if you want to be a man so damn bad, you'd—"

"Mr. *Patrónee* Man! Yoo-hooooo, Mr. *Patrónee!* Oh, yoo-hooooo!"

Luke and Kamen turned to see a small Mexican

24

standing in the middle of the disputed stream. He was merrily flinging water into the air, laughing with delight as the cool water splashed over him.

"Oh, hell," Luke murmured as he recognized Enrique Santos.

"What's *he* doing here," Kamen groaned.

"I have no idea."

Enrique was the town simpleton. Though the townsfolk would be happy to refer to Enrique more kindly, no one had ever been able to come up with anything more appropriate.

Enrique just wasn't bright. Rumor was that his mother had dropped him on his head when he was an infant, but Elena Santos had never confirmed that, and no one had the courage to come right out and *ask* Elena if her son was all there. What was a mother to say?

Why, even Enrique's father admitted that his son was like a house with a candle burning in the window, but no one at home.

But the townspeople had always accepted Enrique as one of their own.

After thirty years, the citizens of Tribulation had grown accustomed to his bizarre behavior. He was allowed to roam at will. No one ever knew where he might run into Enrique, and no one cared. Enrique was loved by all, and his simple, childish innocence was accepted without question.

"Oh, Mr. *Patrónee* Man," Enrique called again, for that was what he always called Luke—Mr. Boss Man.

Enrique idolized Luke. The town knew it, and Luke knew it.

Through some quirk of fate, both Luke and Enrique shared the same birth date. In fact, Enrique never let anyone in Tribulation forget the coincidence. Enrique openly adored Luke, the handsome, half-Kiowa, half-white son of Thatcher Kincaid, and to all who would listen Enrique boasted proudly of his good fortune to have been born on the same day as Mr. *Patrónee* Man.

Luke, on the other hand, seemed to prefer to play down the coincidence whenever someone pointed it out, and someone always did about this time every year.

Luke could hear the merriment filling Enríque's voice as he jabbed his finger excitedly in the direction of the longhorns now happily drinking their fill from the clear, bubbling stream. "The cows— they verrry thirsty, Mr. *Patrónee* Man! Enrique cut the wire and give them a drink!" he stated proudly.

Luke shook his head, forcing back a quick grin. An instant later, he lifted his hat in a salute and called back to the good-hearted simpleton, "Much obliged, Enrique!"

"No thank me, Mr. *Patrónee* Man! Enrique very good, huh?" Enrique was beaming with pride.

Kamen slapped his knees in disgust. "Well, hell! Can you believe that?"

"Very good, Enrique!" Luke called back.

"Happy birthday, Mr. *Patrónee* Man!"

"Happy birthday, Enrique."

Glancing back at Kamen, Luke rested his fore-
arm nonchalantly on the saddle horn. "Well, son,
now that my cattle are enjoying their fill of nice
cold water, guess I'll just be moseying along."
Touching his index finger to the brim of his hat, he
smiled pleasantly. "Be sure and give my regards to
your Uncle Hamilton."

"Uncle Hamilton will have a thing or two to say
about this!" Kamen vowed.

As he picked up his reins, Luke's grin widened.
"Always nice to hear from a neighbor."

Kamen could still hear Luke laughing long after
he'd reined his stallion around, kicked his flanks,
and started to gallop off.

Striding into the hacienda an hour later, Luke
was in a good mood. He found that he was even
looking forward to his birthday party tonight and
all the moronic jokes about getting older that he'd
be forced to endure.

He gave the housekeeper, Luisa's, a sound
whack across her ample backside as he walked
through her kitchen. Mouth-watering aromas
were drifting from all four of the large ovens in the
cocina this afternoon. The household staff was in
full preparation for tonight's festivities.

"How's my *querida?*" he asked.

Luisa's head popped out of one of the large ovens. Her face was flushed, and a lock of salt-and-

pepper hair lay limply across her forehead. "Do not call me your sweetheart, you *pagano!*"

Rolling her dishtowel into a weapon, she flipped him soundly across his backside while his eyes surveyed the stacks of flaky brown pastries mounded high on silver platters.

"Don't even think about it," Luisa warned. "Those are for your *fiesta.*"

"Luisa, my love, you cut me to the core. Would I take one of those cherry tarts without your permission?" Luke chided.

Luisa eyed him sternly. "You would."

"Aw, what blasphemy from such a pretty mouth." Luke's right arm slipped around Luisa's ample waistline while his left hand was accepting the cherry tart offered by one of the young girls wielding a large, wooden pastry roller.

"Go on with you, now. I have no time for your *tontería,*" Luisa ordered gruffly as she tried to escape his hold. "Your *padre* has been calling for you. Go to him!"

Luisa had raised Luke since the death of his *madre* shortly after his birth, so she was accustomed to his good-natured shenanigans. Though she always had a spirited retort for him, she looked forward to the late afternoons when he walked through her kitchen and gave her one of his smiles.

"Uh-oh." Luke sobered. "Must be time for one of his when-are-you-ever-going-to-get-married-Luke speeches again."

Luisa's hands came to her hips. "Does your *padre* not give you such a speech every year on your birthday?"

"Every year," Luke confirmed.

With a wink, he shifted the stolen tart to his other hand. "Let's humor him, Luisa. With your permission I'll tell him you have finally promised to marry me." As he edged closer to the plump housekeeper, he grinned, melting every woman's heart in the room.

"Naturally," he continued smoothly, "we'll forget all about having those *nietos* he wants. I shall expect nothing from you other than a pan of cherry tarts every evening when I get home."

Luisa tilted her head and eyed him sternly. "You have gone *loco,* maybe?"

"Loco?" Luke looked properly affronted. "I am a man of simple tastes, my love. All I ask is to die with my boots on and a stain of cherry pie around my mouth."

Luisa blushed as Luke, leaning over to steal a kiss from her, reached with his empty hand to snitch two more cherry tarts from the silver platter.

"You do not fool me, Luke Kincaid. Some woman will come along someday, and you'll not be making these jokes about marriage," she warned.

Backing away with both hands filled with tarts, Luke gave her a boyish grin. "Just say the word, my love, and I'll send for the *padre*. We'll be man and wife by sundown."

"Get out of my kitchen—no, wait one *momento!* What are you hiding behind your back?" Luisa demanded.

"Me? Hiding something?"

"You—turn around and let me see what you have in your hands!"

Luke backed through the double doors, looking very innocent. "I worry about you, Luisa. If you're accusing me of taking some of your tarts—well, I'm hurt. I may even have to reconsider my earlier proposal." His expression grew grave as he shook his head. "Even my *padre* would not want to see me stuck with a *loca.*"

Luke winked at the pretty *criada* who had slipped him the first tart. The young girl was giggling as she listened to the exchange. At Luke's wink, she blushed, then hurriedly turned her attention back to her work.

The four other young girls helping in the kitchen that afternoon had paused to watch the exchange of lighthearted banter with envy.

From the moment the elder son of Thatcher Kincaid had returned to oversee the running of the ranch, every woman at the hacienda had been smitten. There wasn't one present who wouldn't bake cherry tarts for Luke Kincaid and relish her good fortune.

Leaving the kitchen, Luke started up the winding stairway leading to his father's room.

Three years ago a stray bullet had taken Thatcher Kincaid down in the prime of his life. Though no one could say for certain from whose gun the bullet had been fired, it was openly believed that it had come from one of Hamilton Brewster's men.

Thatcher had survived the ambush but had been left paralyzed from the waist down.

With the same quiet dignity with which he'd accepted all the unpleasant things in his life, Thatcher accepted his fate and sent for his firstborn to oversee the running of *Esperanza*.

Rapping twice, Luke paused momentarily before opening the door to his father's bedroom. Thatcher seemed to sleep most of the day now.

The shades were drawn against the late afternoon sun, and the heat in the small room was stifling. Luke was again filled with compassion for the shell of a man who lay beneath the sheets.

"Are you awake?" he called.

Thatcher opened his eyes slowly, trying to focus on the figure in the doorway.

"It's me, Luke."

Lifting his hand, Thatcher motioned for his son to enter. "Come in, come in, my son."

Luke moved across the room, his boots scraping across the wooden floor. "I thought you might be asleep."

"I sleep very little these days. I was only resting my eyes."

Luke drew the chair closer to the bed, smiling. Thatcher never admitted to dozing.

31

"I hear there was some trouble this afternoon," the older man said.

"Nothing of any importance." Luke removed his hat before settling himself in the chair.

"You know the ranch hands. Anything concerning a Brewster spreads like brush fire," Thatcher said.

"I know."

"What did happen out there today?"

"Brewster had his nephew string a wire across the north section of our land."

Thatcher grunted. "The old fool."

"No harm done." A smile worked at the corners of Luke's mouth as he remembered the look on Kamen's face when Enrique cut the wire to let the cattle in to drink from the stream. "The problem worked itself out."

"Don't let the son of a bitch get away with a thing, boy."

"I don't recall that I ever have."

Pride was unmistakable in Thatcher's face as he looked at his son. Luke had proved to be a chip off the old block. He ran the ranch with a fair mind and a firm hand, and he could handle a Brewster as well as Thatcher himself.

Thatcher often wondered if it was because he had loved Rosy so deeply that he felt such a close bond with this son. He had other children, but Luke was unmatched in his eyes.

Every time Thatcher looked at the dark hair

and black eyes of his tall, handsome son, he saw his young bride—his Rosy.

Her name had been To-weit-che-ki—Rosy Hummingbird. Rosy was a Kiowa. At the age of three, she was taken in by a small roving band of Comanche after her family was massacred by a band of white marauders.

The Comanche had stopped to winter near *Esperanza* the year that Rosy turned fifteen. Thatcher caught sight of Rosy gathering firewood, and even in those brief moments, he felt a stirring deep in the pit of his stomach. There was something different about her—a gentleness, a goodness he'd been drawn to.

It surprised him when on one bitterly cold morning the chief brought Rosy to *Esperanza* and offered his ward in exchange for ten of Thatcher's best horses and five warm blankets, but Thatcher hadn't refused the chief's offer.

The little black-haired, dark-eyed girl had rosy cheeks and the most winning smile Thatcher had ever seen. At twenty-two he wasn't adverse to the idea of settling down; it just went against his grain to buy a woman.

But before he knew what had happened, Rosy had stolen the young rancher's heart.

Thatcher Kincaid took Rosy Hummingbird for his bride the following afternoon, and from that day forward, Rosy was the center of Thatcher's life.

When death took her only hours after Luke's birth, Thatcher was inconsolable.

For years after her death, he refused to look at their son. Luke bore such a striking resemblance to his mother that the ache was more than Thatcher could bear.

Gradually the hurt began to ease, and as Luke grew to be a man, father and son gradually formed a close bond.

After Luke turned sixteen, he left *Esperanza* in search of his mother's tribe. Thatcher gave his blessing, realizing that Rosy would have wanted it that way.

United with his mother's guardians, Luke learned the ways of the red man. By the time Thatcher summoned him home eleven years later, Luke had become a seasoned warrior, a man well versed in the ways of both the white man and the Indian. He had learned good and evil from both.

Thatcher was proud of Rosy's son, and all who had ears were aware of it.

Luke's eyes moved back to the bed, anxious to get the purpose of this summons over with. It was the same conversation every year. He knew without a doubt what was coming.

Luke, take a wife so I can see Rosy's and my grandchild before I die.

I don't want to get married.

Do it anyway.

"Luisa said you wanted to see me?"

"Yes." Thatcher's eyes drifted shut as they did so

34

often lately. "I wanted to wish you a happy birthday, son."

"You're not coming down for the party?"

"Not this year."

"Manuel will carry you—"

"Not this year," Thatcher repeated firmly. He opened his eyes slowly, and his gaze met Luke's. "You will forgive me, but I'd like to be with your mother tonight."

Luke nodded. Rosy had died thirty years ago, but in Thatcher's mind, it had been only yesterday.

Luke knew it would do no good to try and persuade him differently. His response was the same every year. "All right. I'll have Luisa send up a piece of cake," he conceded. "And you'd better eat it."

"I might."

"That all you wanted?"

"That's all."

Luke felt a brief flicker of hope. Was it possible that Thatcher was finally giving up on Luke's getting married?

Luke started to get to his feet when Thatcher's hand suddenly snaked out to stop him.

No, it wasn't possible.

Thatcher gazed up at his son with tears misting his eyes. "You look more like your mother every day."

Squeezing his father's hand, Luke braced himself. *Here it comes.*

"You never even got to see her," his father murmured. "So beautiful, my Rosy . . . so beautiful. Son, you must find you a wife like my Rosy."

"I was married, once."

"That didn't count."

Luke shrugged. It did to him. "I'll get around to thinking about it one of these days."

Thatcher's grip tightened. "No, you *must* think about it now. It's time you took a wife. I don't have much longer to live, and I want to see Rosy's grandchild before I die."

Luke could hear something in his father's voice. A whine. A well-executed, scarcely concealed whine.

Loosening his grip, Luke laid his father's hand firmly back on the sheet. "You're nowhere near gone, and you're just going to have to be patient. I'll get married one of these days—and if I don't, Ginny is fifteen now. She'll be giving you a whole houseful of grandchildren one of these days. And once Pete settles down, he'll—"

"It's not the same," Thatcher interrupted. He'd loved Pete and Ginny's mother, and he'd grieved when death had taken her five years ago, but Luke, well, Luke was *Rosy's* boy.

Here it comes. "I love Ginny and Pete, but I want Rosy's grandchild."

"I love Ginny and Pete, but I want Rosy's grandchild," Thatcher complained, the whine more pronounced this time.

"I know what you want, but you can't just order

something like that," Luke said, impatience beginning to seep into his voice.

"That's what you say every year. You're not getting any younger, boy, and I *am* getting older. I'm fifty-two, you know."

"Fifty-one," Luke corrected.

"And what's next? Fifty-two. Now, why don't you just give it up and marry Ines Potter from down the road? She's a handsome woman, and she's built like a war-horse. Why, she could have a dozen or more kids. Haven't you noticed that?"

"No, I hadn't noticed."

"Well, you take a closer look at her tonight and see if I'm not right," Thatcher's eyes brightened. "Built like one of those threshing machines the woman is . . . thresh you out a baby every nine months, she will. You better give serious thought to Ines. It's not every day a woman built like a threshing machine comes along."

Thank God, Luke thought as he closed the door to his father's room a moment later.

3

— ✦✦❦❦ ❦❦✦✦ —

When the stage rolled into Tribulation an hour early that afternoon, Enrique was sitting on the sidewalk waiting for it.

He always came a little early on Saturdays for fear that just such a thing might happen.

The stage was rarely early, but it would've spoiled Enrique's entire week if he missed seeing it come into town. He was enthralled by the old, dusty-yellow coach with BUTTERFIELD written in pretty black letters across the door.

And someday, the good *Padre* willing, Enrique was going to have himself a ride on it!

The moment the wheels rolled to a halt in front of the hotel, Enrique sprang from his chair and ran to the stagecoach. Standing on his tiptoes, he peered anxiously through a window to see what the stage had brought Enrique for his birthday.

His questioning gaze was greeted by the most

beautiful pair of lavender-colored eyes he had ever seen. Their color nearly took his breath away. Those eyes reminded him of the big old lilac bush in his *madre's* back yard that smelled so good.

Awestruck, he gaped at the cloud of black hair cascading around delicate shoulders. Add to that the turned-up nose and the tiny mouth shaped like a Cupid's bow, and she was just the most beautiful creature Enrique had ever seen!

Enrique truly had never witnessed anything as lovely. Not in his whole life, and he was all of thirty years old. Today. And so was Mr. *Patrónee* Man.

A *pretty woman.* That's what she was.

This week the stage had brought Enrique a *pretty woman!*

With a grin that covered his entire face, Enrique stuck his head through the open window and said brightly, *"Buenos días, mujer!"*

Startled, Hannah drew back when Enrique's smiling face suddenly popped through the window.

"Buenos días, mujer!" Enrique said again.

She gazed at him with glacial contempt. How dare the man address her with such disrespect!

Turning her head, she lifted her nose and ignored him.

Hezziah stepped out of the coach and urged Enrique away. "Move aside, young man. Move aside now."

Enrique balanced on the tips of his toes, trying

to peek around Hezziah's broad shoulders at the woman. She was soooo beautiful!

While the driver tossed luggage down to Hezziah, Enrique ran around to the other side of the coach and stuck his head inside through a window again.

Cupping his hands to his mouth, he made his voice much louder in case the woman hadn't heard him before. *"Buenos días, mujer!"*

Hannah drew back again. With an angry toss of her curls, she gathered her skirt in her hand and climbed out of the coach.

Undaunted by the woman's lack of response, Enrique raced around the coach to help her.

Pushing his hand brusquely aside, Hannah snapped, "Take your hands off of me, you simpleton!"

Enrique immediately did as he was told, enthralled that she had recognized him!

But this pretty woman didn't sound exactly as Enrique thought a pretty woman should sound. Her voice wasn't soft and pretty as he'd always imagined a *really* pretty woman's voice would be. It was surprisingly cold and impatient.

But it didn't matter. The smile returned to Enrique's face. He was but a simpleton, and simpletons couldn't know what pretty women really sounded like.

As Hannah waited, she was aware that the man was continuing to stare. The way his eyes refused to leave her was annoying. She straightened her hat and consulted her timepiece only to discover that he was still staring. Her patience came to an abrupt end. "Are you simple?" she snapped sarcastically.

Enrique grinned from ear to ear as he bobbed his head up and down enthusiastically, *"Sí, señorita!"*

Rolling her eyes in disbelief, Hannah turned her back on him, hoping that if she ignored him, he would go away.

The town was smaller than she'd anticipated. Although Uncle Hamilton had warned her that there was hardly anything to Tribulation, she'd been expecting more than this little anthill in the road.

She glanced around anxiously for a sign of her uncle, but he was nowhere in sight. She wondered if he had forgotten to meet her stage. Consulting her timepiece a second time, she noted that even though the stage was early her uncle should have been here by now . . . unless he had sent someone in his place.

Glancing back at the funny little man who was still staring at her, she asked. "Do you know Mr. Hamilton Brewster?"

Enrique nodded solemnly. *"Sí."*

Sighing, Hannah realized that her uncle must have sent one of his workers to fetch her.

The very least Uncle Hamilton could have done was to send someone who spoke English, she thought wearily. Apparently this man was barely able to comprehend what she was saying. "I suppose you want me to come with you?"

Enrique's eyes widened, and he nodded faster. *"Sí!"*

Enrique decided that this pretty woman had been sent as a birthday present for him! Then he frowned. Since his life was simple, he had no need for such a fine gift. He had a sack of shiny, pretty marbles to keep him busy.

His face suddenly brightened. He would *give* the pretty woman to Luke as a present for *his* birthday. Mr. *Patrónee* Man would be *very* happy.

Enrique's chest swelled with pride. Enrique's present would be the best Mr. *Patrónee* Man had ever received!

"Oh, very well then," Hannah grumbled. Brushing the dust from her stylish brown traveling skirt, she straightened, popped her matching parasol open, and waited for him to retrieve her luggage.

She waited.

And she waited.

When she turned to him, she found the little man gazing at her expectantly. "Well?" she asked.

Enrique shrugged, lifting his shoulders lamely. She appeared to be waiting for something, but he had no idea what it was.

Hannah was beginning to wonder if this little man really understood *any* English even though he'd appeared to understand her earlier question about his being an employee of Uncle Hamilton.

"My luggage?" she demanded impatiently.

The blank look on Enrique's face deepened. "My *el luggo?*"

Enrique frowned. *"El luggo?"*

Hannah sighed, aware that her limited knowledge of Spanish was inadequate. "Well, maybe *luggo* isn't the proper word—let's see—how do you say—" Hannah glanced around helplessly. The stage driver had climbed down from his seat and was already striding toward the local saloon. *"Luggo*—my luggage—up there. See?" She pointed to the two dusty black valises perched on top of the stage. "Can you get them down for me?"

Enrique's puzzled gaze followed her finger, and the grin promptly returned to his face. *"Ah, sí, señorita!"*

Quick as a monkey, Enrique scrambled to the top of the stage and snatched the two valises, and before Hannah knew what was happening, he had dropped back to the ground, landing directly in front of her.

Grinning, Enrique displayed two dazzling gold front teeth as he jubilantly held up the two valises for her inspection. *"El luggo!"*

Startled, she stepped back, her patience sorely strained.

"Bête!" Hannah muttered.

Estúpida! Enrique thought. Removing her handkerchief, Hannah dabbed at her neck and watched as Enrique hopped up on the planked sidewalk, whistling jauntily as he began to walk away with the black valises.

43

Still grumbling, Hannah turned and began to follow him.

She watched with growing dismay as he periodically dropped a piece of her luggage on the sidewalk in order to wave to a passerby.

Each townsperson would dutifully wave back, but Hannah felt the man was making a complete fool of himself! Everyone was staring at them!

Her chin lifted a little more prominently as she realized that no, they weren't looking at him, they were looking at her! She walked along, keeping her back straight and her head held high. Well, it was no wonder. She doubted that the citizens of Tribulation were accustomed to having such finely dressed visitors from the Midwest.

Hannah squared her shoulders and walked faster, silently lambasting her father again for making her come to Tribulation in the first place where she was so superior to everyone else in the rotten little town.

Ohhh, he'd be sorry! She'd make him rue the day he'd even suggested it!

Her lips tightened in a pinched line as she and the odd little man approached a large, impressive carriage standing in front of Bettianne's Thirst Parlor.

Enrique paused to shift the weight of the valises as Hannah moved around him, her long skirt nearly knocking him over as she passed him.

Hannah, assuming that such a fine carriage belonged to her Uncle Hamilton—because who else in this poverty-stricken hellhole could possibly afford one so grand?—stepped up into the carriage.

With a long-suffering sigh, she adjusted her hat, then primly settled the folds of her skirt around her.

Propping the parasol over her shoulders, she glanced back to see what was detaining the man.

"Are you coming?"

Enrique glanced up. Seeing the pretty woman sitting in the mayor's carriage made his face go blank again.

"Good heavens, man," Hannah said impatiently. The sun was blistering hot, and there wouldn't be a prayer of retaining her dewy-fresh appearance if she were subjected to these deplorable, drying rays much longer. "Stop your incessant dawdling and drive this thing!"

"Sí, señorita!" Enrique obliged good-naturedly as he picked up her expensive, hand-tooled valises and pitched them into the back of the carriage like two sacks of grain.

"Do be more careful!" she snapped.

Lifting her nose, she waited as he climbed aboard the driver's box and picked up the reins.

Peasants! How did *Uncle Hamilton tolerate them?*

"Is there *anyone* in this God-forsaken town who repairs luggage?" she asked, turning to peer over the seat at the large chuck gouged in the side of one of her bags.

"Sí."

45

"There is?" Hannah leaned forward expectantly. "Are they any good?"

Enrique shrugged apologetically. "I do not know, *señorita,* they do not give me the time of day."

"Oh?" Hannah frowned, lifting the small chain around her neck and popping open the locket. "Well . . . it's five thirty."

Enrique nodded solemnly. *"Sí. Muchas gracias."*

Settling back, Hannah wondered why she was being so kind. He'd certainly done nothing to deserve it.

A moment later, her head snapped back as the carriage lurched into motion.

"Really—!" Her words were snatched away as her neck snapped forward painfully.

Peon! Bracing her feet against the floor of the carriage, she took a firm hold of the edge of the seat and held on for dear life as the carriage bounced through the center of town.

The mayor stepped out of Bettianne's just in time to see his carriage disappear around the corner. Bounding down the sidewalk, he shouted, "Enrique! Come back here with my carriage!"

Glancing at the small crowd that had gathered along the street, the mayor's face turned a beet red. "Where on *earth* does he think he's going?" Cupping his hands to his mouth, the mayor shouted again. "Enrique! You come back here right now!"

Enrique heard the mayor, but he didn't have time to stop. Today Enrique was a busy man. He beamed with pride, for he was about to deliver a very important birthday gift.

Enrique could hardly wait to see the look on Mr. *Patrónee* Man's face when he saw the *pretty woman* Enrique had for him!

4

"**H**ere's the boss man now!"

Luke smiled and lifted his hand to the sea of well-wishers as he came down the stairs later that evening.

The sun was just sliding behind the mountain range. The scent of honeysuckle, trailing in thick patches up the sides of the adobe building, filled the warm breeze.

The long row of tables covered with bright red cloths sagged beneath the weight of heavy crocks of corn tortillas, frijoles, enchiladas, burritos, chili con carne, and Luisa's famous hot chilies.

Luke worked his way through the crowd as he called back and forth to friends and family with good-natured camaraderie.

Accepting a drink from her tray, he winked at the pretty *criada* with sparkling brown eyes. Her flashing smile and dark Spanish eyes hinted at the

48

pleasures awaiting him later on in the evening. His hand brushed her nicely rounded bottom as he stepped around her to return a greeting from Juan Rodriques.

Threading his way through the gathering, he spotted Emil Potter, who was engrossed in deep conversation with Lowell Anderson on the veranda.

Luke smiled. Knowing Emil, he was sure the conversation would be centered on the renegade stallion that had been raiding their mares for the past several months. The horse had heated a rivalry among the three ranchers. Each wanted the fiery-spirited stallion almost to the point of obsession, but the glossy-maned chestnut had eluded them for months.

Legend had it that the horse had once belonged to the Kiowa before a raiding band of Cheyenne came along and stole him. Later, he was sold to the Ute, who failed to tame him.

That fall, the Snake, enemies of the Ute, mounted a raid after a bloody fight in the foothills of the mountains, and the horse changed hands again. Afterward, the stallion became wild and uncontrollable, killing three Indians who'd tried to ride him.

When the horse escaped, the Indians didn't try to stop him. They were convinced that the horse was possessed by an evil spirit.

But Luke didn't share the Snake's misgivings.

Twice recently the stallion had eluded capture in the foothills near the ranch.

The gleaming horse made a splendid sight: sixteen hands, close-coupled, stockily built, and corded with long, sleek muscles.

The more Luke saw of the stallion, the more he wanted the horse, and he knew he wouldn't rest until he owned him.

Emil glanced up as Lowell moved away and, spotting Luke, he motioned for him to join him. Luke stepped onto the veranda and shook hands with the graying, distinguished older man.

"Emil."

"Luke. Good to see you, son."

From the corner of his eye, Luke caught sight of Emil's daughter, Ines, coming across the veranda.

Everybody in Tribulation assumed that Luke Kincaid would marry Ines Potter. The pretty, dark-haired Spanish girl and the rugged half-breed rancher with a will of iron made a striking contrast—like the rose and the cactus or smooth wine and home-brew whiskey. Once married, their union would amass a sizable fortune in land and cattle.

Luke had done nothing to fuel speculations about his intentions concerning Ines. In fact, the rumors annoyed him. He wasn't totally adverse to the idea of marriage, but he didn't like to be pushed. Especially toward the altar.

Ines Potter was easily the prettiest belle around. Luke was aware of that, and yet something that even he was powerless to explain kept him from asking her to be his wife.

Indecision nagged at him, and Luke was prone to trust his feelings. Yet, watching the dark-haired beauty walking toward him, he wondered if, in this case, he was wrong. Any man in his right mind would be proud to have Ines as his wife.

Ines paused before him, then reached out and took his large hand in her smaller one. She smiled warmly, her large brown eyes drinking in his handsome stature. "Hello, birthday boy," she murmured.

"Hello, Ines," Luke's gaze traveled with lazy appreciation over her full breasts, which swelled provocatively above the décolletage of her ivory gown. She was all woman, and Luke felt his body responding instinctively.

"You're late."

"I fell asleep."

Laughing, Ines turned to smile at her father. "Didn't I tell you?"

Emil chuckled as he motioned for one of the servants to refill Luke's glass.

"I saw the horse this morning," Emil confided. "Near the base of the mountain."

Luke nodded solemnly. "I know. I saw him, too."

Emil glanced to see if they could be overheard, then leaned closer. "I'm riding out at first light. Care to join me?"

51

Lifting his glass in a silent salute, Luke accepted the invitation.

"Oh, pooh, Daddy! Don't you men ever think about anything other than that old horse?" Ines chided.

"Very little," Emil conceded, then gave Luke a conspiratorial wink.

"Ines, my dear." Luke casually set his empty glass on a tray as one of the servants walked past. "The thought that you might like to dance has entered my mind."

"Oh?" Her smile returned.

Extending his arm to her, Luke affected a mock bow. "Miss Potter, will you do me the honor?"

Smiling, Ines snapped open her fan and batted her eyes at him prettily. "I do declare, I thought you were never going to ask, Mr. Kincaid."

"If you'll excuse us, Emil?" Luke drew Ines into his arms as Emil chuckled again and waved the couple away.

Easing Ines into the shadows of the veranda, Luke fitted his lean frame against her soft curves. Her slippered feet began to move to the strum of guitars and violins.

"May I say you look very pretty tonight, Miss Potter."

"You may."

His deep, resonant voice lowered seductively. "Pretty enough to make a man want to pull you into the shadows and steal a kiss."

Ines inched closer, her fingertips sliding up to

tangle into his thick crop of black hair. "You just do whatever you think necessary, darlin'," she drawled with a soft, Texas accent.

Lowering his head, Luke let his tongue trace across the lobe of her ear sensuously. "Don't I always?"

The mayor's carriage pulled to the side entrance of *Esperanza* a little before ten o'clock that evening.

By now, Hannah Brewster was fit to be tied.

Her parasol was covered with a thick layer of dirt, and her brown traveling dress was ruined. *Ruined!*

Shooting Enrique another murderous look, she made up her mind: Although uncommonly sweet of nature, she was going to give her Uncle Hamilton a good piece of her mind when she saw him! Her evening had been a complete disaster, and it was all his fault.

If the *stupid* carriage hadn't lost a *stupid* wheel shortly after leaving town, they could have arrived hours ago! And if it hadn't taken that—that *man* three hours to do what could normally be accomplished in thirty minutes, she wouldn't be in such a fine temper.

And just *what* did the fool think he was doing now?

She glared at Enrique. He had stopped the carriage and was leaning back in the driver's seat enthralled by the sound of guitars and accordions coming from inside the hacienda.

After spitting out the dust between her lips, Hannah called impatiently to him. "Well? What are you waiting for this time? Get down and open the blasted door!"

Enrique's smile dissolved. He scrambled off the seat to help her.

By now, Enrique was glad he had decided to give the woman to Luke. She had not been very nice to him when he was trying to fix the wheel.

In fact, she hadn't been nice at all.

She had screamed and shouted and stamped her foot in the dust, demanding that Enrique hurry up when he was hurrying as fast as he could!

Enrique opened the carriage door and jumped back as Hannah sprang out like a mad hornet.

Shaking the dust from her parasol, she grew even more perplexed when she heard the boisterous sounds of merriment drifting from the hacienda. The sounds of men's and and women's laughter floating above the sound of maracas and strumming guitars filled the air.

Uncle Hamilton was hosting a party on *her* behalf, Hannah fumed, and here *she* was, looking like the wrath of God.

And to top it off, as late as it was, she would have to rush through her toilette in order to make herself presentable, and that was certain to put her in a bad mood for the rest of the evening.

She stamped her foot irritably and crossed her

arms over her chest while Enrique struggled to haul the two heavy valises out of the carriage.

In his haste to please the woman, Enrique let the smaller suitcase fall to the ground, where it broke open, spilling her delicate camisoles and petticoats.

Scrambling out of the carriage, Enrique grinned apologetically as he began to haphazardly stuff the lacy undergarments back inside the valise. *"Perdoname, señorita."*

Rolling her eyes with disgust, Hannah muttered something under her breath that Enrique didn't understand. And at this point, he didn't want to. He didn't like her anymore. Not at all.

A moment later he had the luggage firmly in hand again.

Motioning for her to follow him, he started climbing the long row of steps leading to the second floor of the hacienda.

Ignoramus, Hannah thought irritably, then wearily turned to follow.

"Luke, darling."

Ines took Luke's hand in a discreet effort to prevent him from accepting yet another drink from one of his men. "Don't you think it's time you took me for that walk in the moonlight?"

Luke shrugged Ines's hand aside good-naturedly. "Just one more, then we'll go," he promised.

Lifting the glass to his lips, Luke tried to bring Ines into focus.

Her hand closed over his again. "Luke, please . . . you've been saying that for the past hour. I want to go now."

"In a minute."

Luke could feel his grin going lopsided. Was Ines trying to imply that he couldn't hold his liquor? Surely not. He'd only had two—four—well, he wasn't exactly sure how many drinks he'd had, but not enough to affect him.

"You think I'm drinking too much?" he demanded when her hand came out to block his a third time.

"Have you eaten anything?"

Luke turned, trying to focus his gaze on the blurry long rows of tables sitting across the room. "I must have. There's a lot of burritos missing."

"But have *you* eaten any of them?"

He couldn't remember. But it didn't matter. Luke Kincaid could drink with the best of them, though he would admit that he had consumed more than his limit this evening. Someone had stuck a drink in his hand every five minutes—but it was a party, wasn't it? His party.

Besides, he wasn't drunk. To prove it, he closed his eyes and tried to stop his head from spinning.

There. He flashed Ines a satisfied grin. Steady as a rock.

Swaying, he opened his eyes to encounter Ines's

reprimanding gaze. "Hell, I'm drunk," he confessed.

Sighing, Ines realized that the night was not turning out as she had envisioned. A walk in the moonlight, passionate kisses—a long-anticipated marriage proposal . . .

Another sigh and Ines conceded that Luke wouldn't be proposing anything tonight.

Linking her arm through his, she began to steer him toward the stairway. The birthday boy had celebrated enough. "I think it's time you went to bed."

"To bed! Now?"

"Yes, now." Reaching the bottom of the stairway, Ines turned him around to face her. "Go upstairs, get in bed, and go to sleep," she said.

"But we haven't taken our walk."

Leaning forward, she placed a forgiving kiss on his mouth. "We'll walk tomorrow night."

He leered drunkenly at her, a boyish grin spreading across his handsome features. "You're nice, Ines. Real nice." His booted foot searched for the first step, slipped, then hit the floor unevenly. "Stand still till I get started," he whispered.

"I am standing still."

"Are not. You're weaving."

"Sorry." Smiling tolerantly, she stood perfectly still until one boot was firmly ensconced on the first step.

Grasping the handrail, he began to pull himself up the stairway. "I'll just lie down for a minute or

two. . . ." he murmured. "Don't go 'way, Ines
. . . just need to close my eyes for a minute or
two. . . ."

Ines watched him leave with another heartfelt
sigh.

No, the night just wasn't turning out the way
she'd hoped at all.

Hannah had decided that the room her uncle
had prepared for her was acceptable . . . but just
barely. Rather Spartan, actually, for her taste. But
what would her uncle know about decorating a
room for a young woman of her fine breeding?

Maybe he'd left it up to her to choose her own
personal decor. She glanced around disdainfully. *I
can do wonders with this.*

At least there was a bed, and it looked very
inviting. Her bones ached and she was so exhausted. She felt as gritty as if she'd gotten down
and rolled in the dirt. If it hadn't been for that
simpleton . . . well, no matter. At least there was
fresh water. She would wash, brush out her hair,
and put on something pretty . . . if that . . .
that . . . well, if *he* hadn't ruined everything
she'd packed.

Turning back to Enrique, she dismissed him
with a wave of her hand. "That will be all."

Enrique fled the room, thankful to escape the
ill-natured woman. He wouldn't trade even one of
his marbles for *her.*

Sinking onto the wooden bench in front of the

dresser, Hannah studied her reflection in the mirror and shook her head with dismay. "I look like I've been dragged here by my heels," she muttered.

It would take all her womanly powers to make herself presentable for the guests her uncle had invited to her welcoming party. Eyeing the bed wistfully, she longed to skip the party and just sink into the downy softness and sleep forever. But Uncle Hamilton would surely inform her father that she had been disagreeable and ungrateful, and then her father would insist that she'd have to stay longer.

That was the last thing she wanted.

After a struggle with hooks and buttons, she dropped the dusty dress in a pile at her feet. Her heavy top petticoat soon joined it, then a second one, until she stood in her camisole and pantalets.

Yawning, she began picking the pins from her hair, letting it fall in a heavy cloak around her shoulders.

Gently massaging her scalp, she closed her eyes. She was so tired. If she could only rest for a while.

Her eyes snapped open. No! Her uncle had planned a party, and she would be expected to attend.

Rummaging through the luggage, she found her comb, brush, and hand mirror and sat down on the side of the bed to brush the tangles from her hair.

A moment later, she rose and walked wearily to the small porcelain bowl on the washstand. She filled the bowl with water. As she began to wash her face, neck, and arms, her eyes began to drift shut. Just a short rest would feel heavenly.

Standing in front of the mirror, she picked up her brush again and tried to decide how to dress her hair. She could still hear music coming from downstairs. She hated to be so late, but perhaps she could make a memorable entrance and make them all forget her tardiness.

Oooh, she would have been rested and looked her most stunning if it hadn't been for that silly little man.

It seemed to take forever, but finally all the tangles were gone from her hair. Rummaging through the suitcases again, she located her powders and creams. Heaving an exasperated sigh, she discovered that with all the rough handling her luggage had received, a messy film of white powder was now covering the bottom of her large valise.

Heaving another long, put-upon sigh, she carefully arranged the jars and boxes on the dresser.

There! That was better. At least it was beginning to look like a lady's room rather than that of a bachelor uncle.

Perching on the edge of the bed, she closed her eyes and dabbed her skin with the perfumed talc. Oh, the bed felt heavenly. She found herself bouncing a little to test its softness.

It was *so* comfortable. Perhaps she could just

. . . no, she wouldn't dare. She must dress and hurry downstairs.

She tested the mattress with another tiny, irresistible bounce. Maybe if she rested just a moment, she would be so much more refreshed and might even enjoy the party. Just one moment—that was all it would take.

Peeling back the blanket, Hannah eased her body between the cool, sweet-smelling sheets. The scent of sunshine and fresh air enveloped her as she released a whimper of pleasure, her weary body sinking deeper and deeper into the downy softness.

Just one moment, she promised herself, letting her eyes drift closed.

She just had to rest . . . just for one, tiny, moment. . . .

Luke groped his way to the top of the stairway. As he reached the landing, his eyes squinted to adjust to the dim light in the corridor.

Where was his room? Luisa must have moved the damn thing again.

No—wait. There it was—ten miles down the hallway.

Straightening, Luke started down the hall, his boots echoing against the polished floor. Longest damn hallway he'd ever seen. "I could have gone to the barn faster," he muttered as the sound of his unsteady gait ricocheted down the corridor.

"Shhh," he berated himself. "Making too much noise!"

Pushing the door open to his room, he paused. *Somebody's sleeping in my bed*. He peered intently into the room, straining to see *who* it was.

A woman. In the glow of the lamplight he could make out the outline of a female figure beneath the blanket. Sagging against the door frame, Luke grinned, realizing what had happened. This "lady" was a birthday gift from his men. They had purchased the same gift for him last year. He thought that he had made it clear that he appreciated their thoughtfulness but he preferred to choose his own women.

He grinned lopsidedly. He must not have been convincing.

Fumbling his way across the room, Luke wasn't sure what he should do. In his present inebriated condition, he wasn't sure of anything.

He glanced back at the bed. Who was the young beauty? He didn't recognize her. Must be one of Bettianne's new girls.

God, she was beautiful. He felt himself becoming aroused just looking at her.

No, he decided. He'd better tell her to leave. If Ines found out about the men's birthday gift, she'd get upset—and rightly so. A man thinkin' about marriage shouldn't be accepting such gifts.

Easing onto the edge of the mattress, Luke tried to ignore his present, but his eyes kept drifting back to his gift. Course . . . he was just *thinkin'* about asking Ines to marry him. . . . His hand reached out hesitantly to touch the cloud of dark, lustrous hair fanned across the pillow. The woman's eyes were closed in a deep slumber. Long, dark lashes spread against her flushed cheeks.

She was strikingly beautiful. Luke wondered why a woman with her kind of looks would choose to earn her keep working at Bettianne's.

She stirred in her sleep, drawing a deep breath that made her breasts swell against the thin fabric of her chemise. The soft, white crests looked unusually tempting.

The throb in his loin grew more pronounced as he groaned. He'd have Pedro's *damn* hide for this.

He glanced down, surprised to see his hands slowly beginning to unbutton his shirt. *Oh, no . . . Kincaid, have one of the men take her back to Bettianne's,* something inside of him warned, but his hands didn't hear it.

Jerking the tail of his shirt from his trousers, he peeled it off and tossed it across the room. A second later, his boots and trousers followed. *Just gonna rest for a minute. Not gonna do anything to her. . . .*

Easing back onto the side of the bed, he watched as she sighed and rolled toward him.

Oh, damn.

Gazing at her in the lamplight, he let his hand reach out to stroke her silken cheek. She sighed, her breath warm and provocative against his palm.

Oh, damn!

Appalled, he watched as his fingers began to tug tentatively at the ribbon gathering the neck of her chemise. The delicate fabric slowly parted to reveal softly rounded flesh.

Lord, Kincaid, if you're thinkin' what I'm thinkin', sober up! If he was going to do this, he wanted to enjoy every agonizing moment with this exquisite creature.

But he wasn't going to do it. He rolled to his side, jerking the cover over his head. Ines would be mad as a hornet.

One eye slanted open as he felt his fingers—behind his back—beginning to ease the chemise aside. With a low groan, he rolled over, pressing his lips to her breasts. So warm. Smell so good. His hand gently cupped the pliant flesh, his thumb brushing her nipple. Smiling, he felt it harden against his palm.

Lying down beside her, he pulled her into his arms. "Come here, lovely one."

"Ummmm?" she murmured.

He hushed her with a long kiss, his lips coaxing hers apart.

Her arms looped around his neck as she nestled against him, her legs tangling with his.

"Hello, my lovely," he whispered. His fingers slid the chemise gently over her shoulders, tossing the lacy scrap to the floor a moment later. "You'll have to forgive me, I'm not in full control . . . but we'll make do. . . ."

Stirring, Hannah snuggled closer as his fingers pulled the ribbon to release her pantalets. Easing the material over her hips, he let his hand caress the soft curve of her waist, her hip, and down her thigh.

Hannah murmured, and he stilled her protests with a skillful kiss. His tongue probed and demanded her response as he caught his hand in her hair and kissed her more ardently.

Dazed, Hannah returned the kiss, caught up in a most wondrous dream. She could feel her body come alive as a man's hand roved possessively over her, touching and probing in the most shocking places.

Bracing himself on one elbow above her, Luke gazed down at her, his fingertips brushing the tangled hair back from her face. She was alluring. As lovely as an angel. Her skin was soft and achingly fragrant. He wanted her. Now, and again and again . . .

Murmuring her confused pleasure, Hannah moved closer, her mouth seeking his more aggressively now.

"Be sweet to me, little one," he whispered, nuzzling her lips open to receive his questing tongue. "Be sweet to me."

"Yes . . . oh, yes," she murmured. "I will . . ."

It was such a lovely dream. She'd never in her entire life had a dream so realistic. She could actually taste the man's brandy-scented breath. She could feel his hairy chest pressed tightly against her bare breasts and hear his voice, deep and husky, whispering words in her ears—strange, baffling words that puzzled her, yet made her stomach tingle warmly; exciting, shocking words, words coaxing her to touch and explore his body while his own hands fondled and caressed hers until she was breathless.

She pressed against him more tightly, and her mouth involuntarily opened beneath his. She heard his sharp intake of breath, then a ragged. "Careful, sweetheart . . . go easy. . . ."

She clung to him, wanting and needing, yet innocent to his warning. Her fingers tangled in his hair, their mouths devouring one another as they rolled over. Everywhere he touched, her body exploded into tiny, delicious, electrifying sensations.

His knee came up to separate her thighs, and Hannah suddenly froze as she realized what he was about to do. Even if it were only a dream, he was taking far too many liberties! She must stop him—now! Confused, she began to push him away, but then he touched her again, and she could only surrender with a weak whimper. He kissed her again and again and until she could no longer think, no longer reason.

Hands that had threatened to push him away were now urging him closer.

Thrusting deeply into her, Luke was surprised by her response as she arched and cried out. Stunned, he stilled his passion, pulling back to look at her. "Did . . . I hurt you?"

Her eyes flew open to look at him, bewilderedly.
"Yes . . ."

For one brief moment—one crazy moment—he
wondered if she was a virgin. Was it possible that
she was an innocent and that he was her first cli-
ent? He thought Bettianne employed only seasoned girls.

"I'm sorry . . ." He began to move more easily,
his eyes heavy with passion. He was caught up in
her beauty once more. She mesmerized, be-
witched, and enchanted him. The way she was
looking at him aroused him to a fever pitch. His
mouth caught hers again as she began spontane-
ously moving with him.

When he moved, she moved. When he arched,
she clung to him with a cry of wonderment. Assured now that she wasn't innocent, he became
more exacting, more demanding. She responded,
yielded, hungry for his touch.

Hannah could not fathom the feelings taking
place inside of her. They were new and fascinating. There was pain, elation, wonderment, and a
total sense of unreality.

Luke was no longer thinking. He was only react-
ing now. Grasping her hair, he pulled her mouth
hotly against his, thrusting deeper.

Go slower, Kincaid, make it last! But her
whimpers of ecstasy drove him on.

Suddenly, her eyes flew open again, and her
fingers clawed his back as she gasped, then cried
out.

"No . . . not yet . . . easy . . ." he pleaded.
He hadn't had his fill of this lovely wench!

Hannah cried out, her fingers digging unheedingly into his flesh. What was happening to her?
What wonderful, frightening, miraculous thing
was he doing to her? She was gasping for breath,
her body vibrating with sensations she had never
experienced before.

Her hips shamelessly kept rhythm with his now,
tearing down what little control he had struggled
to devise.

With more of a growl than a groan, he took her,
her body matching the power and speed of his,
until the hunger was filled and they collapsed into
each other, limp and exhausted.

5

Luke's head jerked up as a brisk rap sounded on the door a moment later.

The girl lay breathless beneath him, a tiny smile of wonderment on her lips.

"Luke?" Pedro's voice sounded anxiously through the closed door.

Sitting up in bed, Luke reluctantly moved Hannah aside. "Don't go away, sweetheart." He looked down on her, desire still burning hotly in his eyes.

Confused, Hannah stared up at him, trying to grasp the enormity of what had just happened.

Groaning softly, Luke buried his hands in her hair and dragged her mouth back to meet his.

"Luke!" The knock was more persistent this time.

"Damn it, Pedro!" Rolling off the bed, Luke began to search for his pants. "What do you want?"

"Luke, you'd better get downstairs. There's trouble."

"Can't you handle it?"

"No, *señor*—I do not think so."

Luke swore under his breath. The party was still going on. Music was coming up the stairs, and he could hear the laughter of men and women.

"What is it?" Hannah murmured vaguely. She glanced at Luke, pulling the blanket more protectively against her breasts.

"One of the men has probably had too much to drink."

The veins in Luke's head throbbed. The liquor was beginning to wear off, and he knew that he was in for one hell of a hangover.

Pulling herself upright, Hannah waited for her head to clear. Where *was* she? Her eyes darted about the room, confused. The dream—she *had* been dreaming, hadn't she?

Turning, she watched as Luke stood and pulled on his trousers. But if it had all been a dream, what was the man still doing here?

She winced as she became aware of the ache between her legs. Oh, please—it had been a dream, hadn't it?

She blushed as he glanced over at her. "Don't go away," he warned.

Dropping her gaze, she shook her head sheepishly.

Luke walked to the door, opened it a crack, and leveled a stoic gaze on Pedro.

70

"This had better be important."

Pedro frowned. "Hamilton Brewster is downstairs."

Luke frowned back. "Hamilton Brewster?"

"*Sí.* He's pretty hot under the collar. He's threatening to make a eunuch out of you."

Luke's eyes narrowed. "A what?"

Pedro cleared his throat, embarrassed. "A eunuch, *señor*— you know, one of those—"

"I *know* what it means. What in the hell is going on?" Luke snapped.

"I don't know. You'd better get down there. Brewster's making a real scene."

"All right. Wait till I get my boots." Luke closed the door and walked back to the bed. Reaching for his shirt, he glanced back to Hannah. "I'm sorry. It looks like I'm going to have to go down there."

When Hannah failed to answer, he glanced over his shoulder to find her staring at him.

"You're in no hurry, are you?" he asked.

She shook her head lamely.

Grinning, he winked at her. "Cat got your tongue?"

She shrugged, smiling wanly.

Who *was* he?

She could see his gaze moving hungrily over her body, assessing the outline of her breasts beneath the blanket, and it made her uneasy.

Pulling his boots on, he leaned over and kissed her again. "You rest until I get back."

Nodding, Hannah absently accepted the kiss.

A moment later the door closed, and she dropped helplessly back onto the pillow, stunned.

Who was he?

"Where is that blue-bellied bastard? Somebody better get him down here or I'll go up and fetch him myself!"

The ladies in the crowd drew closer to their husbands' sides as Hamilton Brewster's angry words echoed off the walls.

"By God, I want to see his yella hide!"

Hamilton's furious voice filtered up the stairway as Luke paused to peer over the banister rail. Hamilton was standing in the center of the hallway flanked by ten of his best hands and his nephew, Kamen.

What rotten timing, coming over here now to bicker about the incident with the water this morning, Luke thought irritably.

His head throbbed painfully as Hamilton bellowed again.

"Get that boy down here! Right now! You hear!"

Luke started down the stairs, and Hamilton spotted him. As Brewster strode angrily toward the staircase, it wasn't hard to see how livid with anger he was. "Boy, you hand her back, or I'll turn your rotten hide every way but loose!"

Luke reached the landing. Pausing, he faced Hamilton coldly. "What in the hell is all this bellowing about?"

Hamilton was blue with rage. "What have you

done with her, you low-down, miserable side-winder!"

"*Who* are you talking about?"

"*Who?* My niece! That's *who!*"

Wincing, Luke drew back as Hamilton's words seared through his splitting head. "What would I be doing with *your* niece?"

"Don't pull that on me, boy!" Hamilton thundered. "What have you done with her!"

"I don't know what you're talking about."

Rushing at Luke, the gray-haired gentleman latched onto his shirt collar, dragging him to within inches of his face. "By God, you'd better know what I'm talkin' about!"

Luke was younger, taller, and stronger than Hamilton. He broke the viselike grip with one sudden jerk. His eyes turned to angry slits as the two men squared off at each other.

"What the *hell* has gotten into you, Hamilton?" Luke demanded.

"Oh, *madre de Dios,*" Luisa whispered, hurriedly making the sign of the cross over her ample bosom. There was going to be bloodshed, she just knew it.

Luke glanced at his men, who were standing on the sidelines, their hands resting close to their holsters. "Anyone know what he's talking about?" he asked curtly.

"He thinks you've kidnapped his niece," Sam Sherwin supplied.

Luke turned back to face Hamilton. "What

73

would I want with a Brewster—a *female* Brewster?"

A few random chuckles broke out in the crowd until Luke's icy gaze put a quick stop to them.

"I'll tell you what you want with her," Hamilton accused. "You're holding my niece for ransom. Somehow you got wind that she was coming in on that stage today and you kidnapped her!"

Luke shifted his stance irritably. "*I* kidnapped her?"

You could hear a pin drop in the room. Everyone was waiting. It had been years since a Brewster had been in the same room with a Kincaid.

"That's right. You don't fool me, boy. You plan to hold her until you can get me to agree to deed over that piece of disputed land to you. Well, it's not going to work! You'll never get that piece of land! Never!" Hamilton's face was fiery red, and his hands were wadded into tight, angry fists at his side. No one could remember ever seeing him so upset.

"Hamilton, I don't know what you're talking about," Luke said again. "I haven't seen your niece—"

"Don't lie to me! She was waiting at the station this morning for me to pick her up, but you got to her first!"

"You're crazy."

Hamilton's eyes narrowed. "Think real hard, Kincaid. A lovely, smartly dressed woman, a woman of refined breeding—of course, I guess a man like you wouldn't recognize a woman of fine breeding—now would you?" he sneered.

Luke's eyes darkened at the insult. "Get out of here, Brewster."

"Not without my niece, Kincaid."

The liquor was making Luke fuzzy and light-headed and he was finding it hard to think clearly. But he knew he hadn't seen a "lovely, smartly dressed with refined breeding" woman anywhere today.

"Kincaid, you are a miserable son of a—"

Hamilton cut Brewster off bitterly. "You're still sore about the incident at the stream this morning, aren't you? Kamen made you look bad, so you figured you'd go snatch my niece and up the ante a little. Admit it, you conniving jackass! You took her —you saw her and took a fancy to her and you think I'm gonna sit back and not do a damn thing about it!"

Luke eyed him coldly . . . "You're *loco* if you think I'd touch a Brewster woman with a ten-foot pole."

"You'd touch one all right. My niece Hannah came in on the evening stage, and you sent Enrique to get her."

"I *what?*"

"Admit it, Kincaid! Enrique was *seen* driving her out to your ranch in the mayor's carriage."

"Then you'd better talk to Enrique and the mayor about your niece's mysterious disappearance," Luke said curtly, "because I *don't* know where she is."

The day a Kincaid took a "fancy" to a Brewster woman was the day Luke would eat his hat.

"The mayor doesn't know anything about it. He said Enrique took his carriage without his knowledge. You and Enrique are the culprits!" Hamilton roared.

"You're accusing me of sending *Enrique* to kidnap your niece and steal the mayor's carriage?" Luke asked incredulously. Hamilton had clearly lost his mind.

"Enrique would do anything you asked, including kidnap my niece!" Hamilton accused.

"Damn it, Hamilton, I don't know anything about your niece!"

Kamen edged forward bravely. "You'd better not lay a hand on my cousin, Kincaid, or else you'll answer to me!"

"You stay out of this, Kamen," Luke snapped. "I don't know anything about your cousin."

"You're a bold-faced liar. Never knew a Kincaid that wasn't," Hamilton declared.

Luke had had his fill of wild accusations. "Get out of here, Brewster. Now."

Hamilton glanced up to find that Luke's men were already beginning to separate themselves from the crowd. Their fingers were nimbly loosening their guns in their holsters.

Brewster realized that Luke clearly had him outnumbered.

"You've got till sunup, Kincaid," he warned, jamming his Stetson back on his head. "Six hours to hand over my niece or you've got yourself a peck of trouble, boy."

Spinning on his heel, Hamilton strode furiously through the front door with Kamen and the others following close behind.

Luke turned back to the small group who'd gathered in the entryway and asked quietly, "Anybody know what he's talking about?"

"Not me."

"No, boss. Sure don't."

"We don't know nothing about his niece," Buck Latimer swore.

Glancing back to the guests, Luke apologized for the unpleasant incident. "I'm sorry you had to witness this. I hope it hasn't spoiled your evening."

A few voices called back to him supportively.

"Don't worry about it."

"Sure sorry it happened."

"What's wrong with Hamilton?"

"He didn't appear to be liquored up none."

"I don't know what his problem is," Luke admitted. "But I think it's time we all called it a night."

There was general speculation concerning Hamilton's sanity as the guests began to get their things together in preparation to leave.

"Luke?"

Luke glanced down to find his little sister, Ginny, standing beside him.

"Are you still up, pumpkin?"

"Luisa said I could stay up as long as I wanted tonight."

"Luisa said that, huh?" Luke ruffled her hair playfully. The petite little blonde had had him wrapped around her finger since the day she was born.

"What kept you from knocking that old fool's head off?" Ginny demanded.

Luke wondered that too. If Hamilton Brewster believed that a Kincaid would sink low enough to snatch a woman for ransom to settle their dispute, then the old coot was crazy.

"Forget it, Ginny. Hamilton made a mistake."

"Hamilton Brewster's a wicked, mean, horrible man," Ginny declared. "I hate those low-down, bully Brewsters!"

"You don't be hating anybody." Luke swatted her on the rump. "Now go to bed."

"You be careful, Luke," Ginny warned. Adoration was shining brightly in her eyes. Though she had been an infant when Luke had left to spend time with the Kiowas, she had always known that she had a strong, handsome, older brother she could rely upon. Since the day he'd come back to run the ranch, wherever Luke went, Ginny wasn't far behind. "I don't know what I'd do if anything happened to you."

"Nothing's going to happen to me." He reached out to tweak her cheek affectionately. "Go to bed."

Wrapping her arms around his neck, she gave

him a hug and he hugged her back. A moment later she disappeared up the stairway, still belittling those *"loco* Brewsters."

One by one, guests began to trickle out. Luke stood at the door acknowledging congratulations for his birthday and commiserations about the scene Brewster had caused.

A few jokes passed back and forth about how Hamilton had "lost" his niece and humorous speculations about where he might find her.

When the last guest disappeared, Luke's younger brother clapped him on the shoulder as they turned toward the stairway. "Well, how does it feel to be another year older, big brother?"

"Big enough to whip you."

Pete grinned. "That'll be the day." Pete was only nineteen, but he was already the same height and twenty pounds heavier than Luke.

The two of them started up the stairs, walking shoulder to shoulder.

"What are you going to do about Brewster?"

"Nothing. If he can't keep track of his family, I sure as hell can't."

"I've always told you those Brewsters are nuts," Pete said, grinning. "Well, I guess I'll call it a night. I'm ridin' out at dawn."

"Where're you going?"

"Me and Skeet Wilson's going huntin' for a few days." Pete grinned. "If I see the stallion I'll bring him back for you."

"You do that."

"Bet his niece is as crazy as a bedbug, too." Pete paused in front of Luke's room. "Don't you imagine?"

"Whose niece?"

"Brewster's."

"I wouldn't try to imagine what Hamilton's niece is like," Luke conceded absently.

His mind was on the beauty sleeping in his bed. He had to get her out of the house and back into town before someone discovered her. Now that he was sobering up, he realized he'd never hear the last of it if Luisa found out what the men had done.

"Good night."

"Good night, Pete."

Luke let himself into the room quietly. Hannah stirred and glanced up as he moved quietly toward the bed.

Smiling, he sat on the side, his gaze running over her hungrily.

Stirring nervously, she smiled up at him.

"Hi."

"Hello."

Their eyes met, and Hannah felt a delicious tingle begin somewhere deep inside her. His hand reached out and caught a strand of her hair and let it curl around his finger.

"You are lovely," he murmured.

"Was there trouble?"

"No—just a neighbor."

He leaned down and kissed her, their mouths

lingering. "You smell good," he whispered, feeling his passion begin to rise again.

"So do you," she whispered back. It was true. Though he had sullied her, she couldn't have been sullied by a more exciting man.

They kissed again, long and deeply. She knew that she mustn't let him make love to her again, yet the thought was tempting.

"Is the party still going on?" she whispered as their mouths parted many long moments later.

"It's beginning to break up." Smiling, he sat up and began to unbutton his shirt. Peeling it off, he tossed it on the bed. He knew he should send her back promptly, but he couldn't stand the thought of it. Not until he had had his fill of her . . . and that could take some time.

Hannah lay back on the pillow to watch him undress. She liked the sound of his voice. It was deep and resonant. She liked the way he looked and the way his skin felt—all warm and masculine and firm. Just thinking about the things he'd done to her earlier made her shiver inside. Oh, the things he had said to her—the secret, intimate places he'd touched. He had been so daring . . . so wonderful. She shivered again as she remembered her first glimpse of a man's naked body, so powerful, so bold, so audacious. She sighed. Shocking as the events had been, the course was clear.

Once Uncle Hamilton learned that one of his hands had gotten drunk and stumbled into her room and taken advantage of her, he would insist that the man wed her. But that was all right with her. This man wasn't all that bad, and besides, it was an act of fate. Now she wouldn't have to marry Edgar.

"It seems strange that a neighbor would decide to attend the party at this hour," she mused. Hannah thought it must be very late by now.

Luke stood up and stripped off his pants. "The neighbor is an old fool without a lick of sense."

Hannah's gaze drifted wistfully to the front of his longjohns. He was indeed a splendid, splendid man.

"You sound as if you don't like him."

"I don't."

"Oh?" She rolled onto her back lazily. This must be the way it was when a man and a woman married. They would make love and then talk for a while. "Why not?"

"It's complicated. There's been a feud going on between our families for years. The old fool won't let it lay."

"Oh, what a shame," she said sympathetically. She couldn't imagine anyone not liking this wonderful man. He seemed very nice to her.

Leaning over, Luke brought his mouth down to brush against hers. "Come here, wench," he whispered.

She murmured softly as his large hand found her breast. Pressing her back against the pillow, he kissed her roughly. "Mmmm . . . please." She giggled. "You really must stop."

"You don't really want me to stop, do you?" He drew his mouth along her neckline, kissing her until goose bumps stood out on her arms.

Her hand drifted out to stroke his bare chest. How bold she felt, lying here with him like this. Why, only a few hours ago she had been innocent. She'd never have imagined touching a man the way she was touching him.

But he was different. He took her breath away. His kisses were like warm, heady wine, and they made her feel weak and giddy and bubbly inside. But she mustn't let him do those things to her again until they were properly wed.

Luke drew back as he felt her stiffen and begin to push his hand away. "Easy, sweetheart . . ."

She giggled again, heady with her newfound charisma. The man was obviously smitten with her. "You really do have to go," she said more firmly this time.

For the first time, reality was beginning to rear its ugly head. Her uncle was going to be furious . . . at her . . . and at this man.

It was true the man had enjoyed too much punch at the party and had gotten into the wrong room, but that was no excuse for *her* to act so . . . accessible.

Her mind worked furiously. What was the best way to handle this? Should she lie to her uncle and say she'd tried to fight him off? Yes, that's it, she'd lie. It wasn't exactly true—she hadn't tried to push him away, but she *would* have fought him off had she had her full wits about her . . . but she hadn't. Actually, he had taken advantage of her. The cad.

She would just have to convince her uncle that she'd been sleeping so soundly that she wasn't aware of what was happening until the dastardly deed had already taken place. That wasn't exactly true either—but it almost was.

Before she knew what was happening, he had kissed her and taken off all her clothes and . . . well . . . it had just been too late to stop him.

Or nearly too late.

Yes, that's what she'd better say. It was just too late to stop him.

While marriage was absolutely the last thing she wanted, marriage to this man was undoubtedly better than marrying Edgar Huckett. Anything was better than marrying Edgar Huckett.

Being burned at the stake buck naked was better than marrying Edgar Huckett. She sighed as Luke kissed her again, ever so sweetly. She did so want to be a proper lady, but it was so hard. . . .

As the kiss deepened to frightening intensity, she summoned every ounce of courage she possessed to push Luke away, sincerely wishing she didn't have to. Being a lady could be such a chore. "You really must go."

Luke's gaze ran lazily over her nakedness beneath the thin coverlet. "What's your hurry?" Easing her back against the pillow, he leaned over and ran his tongue lightly over the swell of her breast.

He smiled as he heard her catch her breath in response. "You don't have to get back yet, do you?"

Her hand slipped up his chest and rested at the curve of his shoulder, her fingers digging into his flesh as he began to caress her.

Her body began to react to his hands, his mouth, his soft urging.

Though she tried, she couldn't think straight. His mouth was too warm, too demanding.

Brushing another lingering kiss across her lips, he caught her hand and brought it down to touch him.

Her eyes flew open, and she bolted upright.

"Easy . . ." He smiled and tried to kiss her again, but she pushed him firmly away this time.

"No, you have to go. Right now."

Luke frowned. "I have to go?"

"Yes." Sliding out of bed, Hannah drew the blanket around her tightly. Her hair spilled over her shoulder, and her beauty made his desire flare ever hotter. Lifting her chin, she met his gaze evenly as she pointed to the door. "Go."

He extended his hand languidly to her. "Come here, honey—"

"Don't 'honey' me." Hannah had regained her full senses, and she was appalled at what she'd done—he'd done. She was really going to have to do some fast thinking to talk her way out of this one.

Handsome stranger or not, they were both in big trouble.

She pointed toward the door again. "Go. I'll talk to my Uncle Hamilton in the morning and . . . and . . . I'm . . . I'm sure he'll want to see you right away to discuss when the ceremony will take place."

Luke wasn't listening. He grinned lethargically. She was downright cute standing there half-naked like—Her words suddenly hit him, and he bolted upright. "You'll talk to *who?*"

"Uncle Hamilton." She sniffed, her courage wavering now. "He'll insist that we marry, of course."

Luke's grin began to fade.

"He'll insist that we get married as soon as possible. Of course, I plan to have it annul—"

"Married!" Luke rolled to the side of the bed.

"Of course." Her chin lifted a notch higher. "Surely that doesn't come as a surprise to you."

As he slowly got to his feet, she could see his face drain of all color. "Why would I marry you? Wait a minute." Hamilton's enraged face flashed before him. "You *are* one of Bettianne's girls . . . aren't you?"

Hannah looked at him blankly. "Bettianne? I don't know any Bettianne."

"Oh, hell." He sank back on his bed weakly. Dropping his face to his hands, he braced himself for what he knew was coming next.

"My name is Hannah."

"Hannah what?" he asked sickly.

"Hannah Rose."

"Hannah Rose *what?*" he demanded, afraid he already knew the answer. A chill washed over him, raising the hair on the back of his neck. *God, no, don't let it be Brewster,* he prayed. *Let it be anything but Brewster!*

Hannah stamped her foot irritably. "Hannah Rose *Brewster,* you dolt."

She paused, frowning. "And what, pray tell, might your name be?"

6

***

Hannah Rose Brewster. *Son of a bitch!* Luke's eyes closed sickly. Hamilton Brewster's niece.

Falling back on the bed, he stared at the ceiling. How in the hell had she gotten into *his* room?

"What *is* your name?" she demanded. She had just shared the most wondrous experience of her life with this man, and she didn't even know his name.

"What are you doing in my room?" Luke shot back.

Hannah drew herself up straighter. "I beg your pardon. This is *my* room. You stumbled in here in a drunken stupor and then took complete advantage of me—"

"*I* took advantage of *you?*" Luke winced as a renewed shaft of pain sliced through his head. Lord, he wished he hadn't drunk so much. "I came in here and found *you*—ready and eager—in *my* bed. What did you expect me to do? Say, 'Howdy, ma'am,' and just roll over and go to sleep?"

Hannah gasped. "How dare you! I wasn't in *your* bed! Why, I was getting ready to go down to *my* party when you came in here and . . . and ravished me!" Her cheeks burned with shame at the thought of what he'd done to her.

"Just where the hell do you think you are, Miss Brewster?"

"I know where *I* am. This is my Uncle Hamilton's house, and he's going to skin you alive when he finds out what you've done. Just where do you think *you* are?"

Luke closed his eyes sickly. Lord, what a mess. Enrique. Enrique must've brought her to the ranch. But why? The answer came to him swiftly. Enrique didn't need a reason. "Well, you're wrong. This isn't Hamilton Brewster's house," he informed her coldly.

"You're lying," she retorted. "I'm going to report you to Uncle Hamilton right this minute." She wouldn't wait until morning. The man's behavior was simply inexcusable.

"Go right ahead."

His insolence seared her. She stamped her bare foot angrily, and gave him her best you'd-better-give-in-to-me-or-else look. "What is your name!"

Luke met her gaze evenly. "Lucas Kincaid."

Hannah gasped, drawing back as if a snake had bitten her. "Lucas Kincaid!"

Why, he couldn't be Lucas Kincaid! The Kincaids and the Brewsters had been at one another's throats for ninety years! She couldn't have . . . she just couldn't have handed a nasty, vile-tempered *Kincaid* her virginity on a golden platter!

"Don't you tease me about a thing like that. This isn't funny," she snapped.

"Do you see me laughing?"

Her hand came to her throat. He wasn't trying to be funny. He was *serious*.

"Oh, dear me."

"Yeah. Oh, dear me. How did you get here?"

"Why . . . some strange little man met me at the stage and brought me here. I must say if he's an example of the type of man you employ, no wonder I'm in the wrong house!"

"What did the man look like?"

"Why—he looked like a man . . . just a man . . ."

"Describe him, Miss Brewster."

Sinking down onto the side of the bed, she cocked her head, trying to recall the man's features. "He had dark hair, black eyes . . . dark skin." Her distressed gaze lifted to meet his. "Truthfully, he didn't seem overly bright. He was babbling something about a pretty woman, but I could hardly understand anything he said. He just kept *staring* at me." Her chin lifted defensively. "He was most rude. And then a wheel broke on the carriage, and it took him *forever* to fix it. It just kept getting later and later, and the dust was awful, and all I wanted to do was go to sleep. When we finally arrived here, my party was already under way—I didn't want to have to attend a party—but I guess it really wasn't my party after all if this is your house and not my Uncle Hamilton's, and, oh, everything is all your fault!"

Luke's head hammered and his stomach rolled as she ranted on and on about how her Uncle Hamilton was going to thrash him to within an inch of his life.

Finally he leaned over and clamped his hand across her mouth to stem the flow of words bubbling out like a mountain stream.

Her eyes snapped at him defiantly. "Mhudghl lsdith tedkfo mydfpp Unflsod!" she retorted, her words so muffled that they couldn't be understood.

"Pipe down so I can think."

"Whodkghjd Enrgflsgak!"

"What made you think this was your uncle's house? Any fool would have known . . ."

Peeling his hand away from her mouth, she glared at him. "How was I to know where that man was taking me? I assumed he worked for my uncle!"

"Well, he doesn't."

"Then why did he let me think that he was there to meet me!"

"Enrique's simple."

"Simple?"

"Not very bright, Miss Brewster. Dense. For

some reason he decided to bring you out here. Why, I don't know, but I plan to find out."

Hannah was stunned. The little man was simple? Instantly, she felt ashamed for the way she had spoken to him.

Luke ran his fingers through his hair absently. Simple or not, Enrique had them all in a fine mess. "Haven't you visited your uncle before? Didn't you know this wasn't his ranch?"

"No, I've wanted to visit Uncle Hamilton, but Papa was always too busy to bring me," she said defensively.

"Didn't you think it strange that your uncle wasn't there to meet you?"

Hannah's mouth firmed. "Mr. Kincaid, I expected someone to meet me and someone did. My uncle is a busy man. I didn't find it unusual that he would send one of his employees to fetch me. How was I to know that some simpleton would come along and force me into his carriage!" She sniffed virtuously.

Luke looked at her. "Enrique *forced* you into his carriage?"

She sniffed again. "He surely did." That wasn't entirely true—but almost. Her eyes met his resentfully. "And I certainly couldn't have known that when I got here, I was going to be a victim of your—your lust."

"You were in *my* bed, Miss Brewster," he reminded her.

"Well, didn't you find that a little strange, Mr.

92

Kincaid, or are you accustomed to finding strange women waiting in your bed?"

"I thought my men had put you there as a present to me."

Her brows rose. "A present? A rather unusual gift, wouldn't you say?"

"I made a mistake, okay? I'd had too much to drink, and I wasn't thinking straight."

"No, it isn't okay. Because of your mistake—I—I'm probably carrying your child." She was grabbing at straws, but she supposed that it was possible after what he'd done to her. Besides, she had to convince him that he had no choice but to marry her or she would be stuck with Edgar. "I think you should be aware that not only was I coming to Tribulation to visit with my dear, sweet uncle, but that I am practically betrothed. My doting admirer is going to just die when he hears what you have done to me in your drunken, 'mistaken' state."

Hannah was growing desperate. She didn't want to marry Lucas Kincaid, but of the two evils, she'd take Kincaid and rid herself of him later. It didn't sound as though Edgar would be so easy to get rid of.

Dabbing the hem of the blanket to her eyes, she began to sob softly. "Now I'm . . . soiled. That nice Edgar Huckett will never marry me now—and he's such a wonderful, handsome man who'd make such a fine daddy for my children."

Luke stared at the floor. Damn. He could wring Enrique's neck for this.

"I just know I'm with child." She drew a long, ragged breath. "I'll just never be able to convince my dear Edgar of the terrible mistake you've made, even though he's truly devoted to me." Covering her face with her hands, she tried to gauge Luke's reaction through her fingers. "Oh, Edgar and I planned such a wonderful future together. He would have built me a lovely big home —and children. Ohhh, I know he'd have wanted at least five children—and now, because of you—I'll be a lonely old spinster for the rest of my life." She broke off into sobs again.

Luke shot to his feet and began to pace the floor.

"Of course, Uncle Hamilton will shoot you when he finds out what you've done," she said calmly, dabbing at her eyes again.

"Uncle Hamilton doesn't have to know what I've done," he returned, just as calmly.

Jerking the blanket away from her face, she glared at him. "Yes, he does. I'll tell him!"

"You won't tell him anything," Luke said. "Not until I've had time to think about this."

"I will! You take me to Uncle Hamilton right now!" she demanded.

"I'm not taking you anywhere."

"I'll run away!"

"No, you won't."

Luke started toward her and she gasped, drawing back against the pillows defensively. "You—

you scoundrel! You can't hold me here against my will!" She hadn't once considered that possibility.

"Honey, you'll find out that I can do a lot of things against your will if you push me hard enough," he promised.

Her hand flew up to slap his face but he caught it in midair. "I wouldn't do that," he warned.

Hannah's heated gaze met his glacial one. Her heart tripped wildly. He was serious. He actually meant to keep her imprisoned, probably in this room.

"How dare you—why, my Uncle Hamilton will strip your hide when he hears of this!"

"So you've said."

Running his hand wearily through his hair, Luke surveyed the room. It was late, and he still had too much liquor in him to think straight. He would have to keep her here with him—at least until morning.

Peeling back the covers, he pushed her to one side and climbed back into bed. He couldn't think straight enough to deal with this tonight. Hopefully, his head would clear by morning.

Pressing herself tightly against the wall, Hannah watched him warily. "What do you think you're doing?" she demanded.

"I'm going to sleep. Nothing can be done about this until morning."

"I'm not sleeping with you!" She snatched the quilts, and drew them up around her neck protectively.

Luke jerked the quilts out of her hands and spread them back over the bed. "Do wherever you want, just dry up so I can get some sleep."

Hannah couldn't believe his arrogance. Yanking one of the quilts back, she glared at him as he calmly drew the other one over his tall frame.

Her cheeks flamed as she drew the quilt around her snugly. That barbarian!

Glancing around the room, she saw that there was nowhere else for her to sleep except the floor.

Well, if he thought he had the best of Hannah Brewster, he had better think again.

Crawling over his chest, she mumbled, "When Uncle Hamilton hears about this, you're a dead man. It's bad enough you took advantage of me, but making me sleep on the cold, hard floor is inexcusable."

Luke grunted as she slid off him and landed on the floor.

She tested the braided rug lying beside the bed. Hard as a brick, but it would have to do.

"I'll bet Uncle Hamilton is out looking for me right now," she muttered, dragging the rug a safe distance from his bed. "And, of course, Edgar will be destroyed. Simply destroyed, when he hears what has happened. He'll shoot you, too, you know. Blow your head clean off. He's planned a large house. A beautiful house. Just for me."

Rolling over, Luke slid the pillow over his head to block out her voice.

"He sent for me, you know. All the way from

Iowa. We were going to have a fine wedding. I was going to have a white dress, with a long train. And six bridesmaids—maybe even seven. Edgar doesn't care how many I have. But, of course, none of that's going to happen now because *I'm* carrying *your* child . . . a Brewster carrying a Kincaid." She shuddered. "It's perfectly revolting."

She glanced toward the bed and saw that he had the pillow over his head. "Are you listening to me? I'll be all alone and a burden to my family. Uncle Hamilton will never forgive me! He's such a southern gentleman, you know. He believes a man should treat a woman like a lady. Not like a common . . . trollop. You should be thanking your lucky stars he doesn't know I'm here with you. Once he finds out, well, I wouldn't want to be in your boots, mister."

Falling silent, she rummaged irritably through her valise. A moment later she began brushing her hair.

Luke dozed off, then jerked awake at the sound of her voice.

"Uncle Hamilton looks upon me like his own daughter, you know. That's why I came all the way out here to marry. I could have married any man I wanted in Iowa, but Uncle Hamilton says Edgar will make me a wonderful husband."

"Don't you ever shut up?" he grumbled.

"Am I bothering you?" Hannah asked sarcastically. Well, good! She hoped she *was* bothering him. He certainly didn't seem to give one wit if he was bothering her or not.

Rolling over on his stomach, Luke gripped the pillow more firmly over his head. It was going to be a hell of a long night.

For ninety years the Kincaids and Brewsters had been at each other's throats, but until now there hadn't been one single drop of bloodshed. Luke had a feeling that if she didn't pipe down, all that was about to change.

The sun was just coming up when Luke opened his eyes in the morning. It took a moment for him to focus. A dull throbbing pain was centered somewhere in the back of his head.

Rolling slowly to his side, he groaned as he saw Hannah lying below him. Her hair was a tangle and she was curled up like a kitten, sound asleep.

The events of the night before came back to him in a rush. Swinging his legs over the side of the bed, he paused, waiting for his stomach to stop churning.

Hannah stirred, turning onto her back. Her eyes opened slowly to focus on the ceiling. For a moment, she couldn't remember where she was. Her body ached—a strange, most uncomfortable ache. Shifting drowsily, she saw Luke sitting on the side of the bed, his head in his hands.

Suddenly it all came back to her.

"You are really going to be sorry," she murmured.

Luke's head came up slowly. "Don't start."

Last night she had chattered like a magpie until she'd become totally exhausted. It had been close to dawn before she had given up. Luke couldn't remember a more miserable night.

Hannah sat up, holding the blanket to her breasts. "I demand you take me to my uncle immediately."

"You're in no position to demand anything." Luke got to his feet, and Hannah quickly averted her gaze. The barbarian was intent upon embarrassing her, parading around in his longjohns like some heathen.

"You can't keep me a prisoner."

Ignoring her, he began pulling on his pants.

"You can't keep me here forever. Someone is bound to be looking for me," she told him confidently.

"I can't imagine anyone that *loco.*"

"What?"

"Nothing." Luke reached for his shirt.

"Where do you think you're going?"

"I fail to see how that concerns you, Miss Brewster."

Reaching for her brush, Hannah drew it through her hair, smiling at him. "You're getting nervous now, aren't you? Now that you've had time to think about what you've done, you know that when my Uncle Hamilton finds out that you're keeping me here—"

"Your Uncle Hamilton knows where you are."

The brush paused in midair. "He does? Well—was that what all that commotion was about last night? Was my Uncle Hamilton here looking for me?"

Luke pulled his boot on. "He was."

Hannah frowned. "Then why didn't he come upstairs and get me?"

"I told him you weren't here."

She caught her breath. "You lied to him?"

"I didn't lie to him. I didn't know you were here." He stood up and reached for his belt. "I had no idea Brewster's niece was in my bed."

Hannah's eyes drifted to his broad chest where a thick coating of dark hair was peeping over the buttons of his shirt. She wondered if Edgar had such a nice, masculine chest. Probably not. It was probably snow-white and flabby.

"Well"—she sighed and lay back on the rug—"you now know who I am, and once my Uncle Hamilton learns for certain that I'm over here, he'll—"

"Blow off my head along with other parts of my body," Luke finished for her, adding to himself, *God knows I've heard that prophecy often enough in the past seven hours.*

"Yes, and you'll—"

"Be sorry." He'd memorized that, too.

Striding across the room, he removed a key from a dresser drawer and proceeded to lock a large trunk at the foot of the bed. "You are not to leave this room, do you understand?"

100

Hannah leaped to her feet, tripping on the quilt. Steadying herself, she faced him defiantly. "I'll leave the moment you're gone."

"No, you won't."

Stunned, Hannah watched him pick up her scattered underclothes and stuff them into the valise, then stack her second suitcase on the first and shove both of them in front of the door. Stripping the sheets and the blankets from the bed, he spotted the telltale blood. Wincing, he carried the soiled linens to the door and pitched them into the hallway, angered by the evidence that she had been a virgin.

"You can't get away with this. I'll scream the roof down!" she railed. There had to be others living in this house. They would come and rescue her.

Luke smiled, an infuriating smirk that made her see red. "May I remind you, Miss Brewster, that you have only the blanket on your back. If I hear one peep out of you"—he leveled his finger at her sternly—"one peep, you won't even have that."

She gasped, drawing back, affronted. "You wouldn't dare."

"Don't push me, sweetheart."

Shoving her two suitcases out the door, he turned to face her one final time. "Stay in here and keep quiet."

Hannah gaped at him. He was really going to leave her here in his room with only a blanket to cover her nakedness! The man was inhuman!

101

"What will I do while you're gone?"

"Look out the window."

As the door closed behind him, she waited a moment, then took a deep breath, doubled up her fists, and screamed as loudly as she could.

The door opened quietly a moment later.

Wide-eyed, she drew back as Luke strode across the room. Jerking the blanket from her hand, he turned around and strode out again.

Stunned, she sank down on the bed, trying in vain to cover her nudity with her hands.

Why, the gall of that *imbecile!*

Her gaze shot to the trunk sitting at the end of the bed. She bet there were clothes in there; that must be why he'd locked it. *His* clothes.

Well, it would mean sinking pretty low, but she would wear his old clothes, though the thought of having anything touching her that had been touching him revolted her. To think that only last night she had thought he was the most exciting, handsomest man in the world.

Well, she'd show him! She would get that trunk open, put on one of his shirts and a pair of his pants, and escape through the window.

She would show Lucas Kincaid that he wasn't as smart as he thought he was!

Luisa was in the kitchen when Luke walked through the door. Because of the Brewster woman he had washed and shaved at the bunkhouse this morning.

"Biscuits, eggs, and steak," she announced brightly.

"Just coffee."

"Too much of the fire last night?" Luisa wagged her finger at him reprimandingly as she set a mug of coffee in front of him.

"Since it was your *cumpleaños,* I won't lecture you, *sí?*" Dishing up a plate of steak, eggs, and biscuits, she smiled fondly. "If it hadn't been for Mr. Brewster, the party would have been perfect, *sí?*"

Pedro entered the room before Luke could voice his opinion.

"The *alcalde is* here, *señor.* He wants to know why his *vagon* is out back."

Luke swore, and Luisa snapped his backside with a dishtowel.

"The mayor's carriage is here?"

"*Sí.* So is his horse. They are both out back."

Luke stood up, taking his cup with him. "Where is the mayor?"

"In your office, *señor.*"

José Calebro was pacing back and forth impatiently as Luke walked into the room a few moments later.

"Good morning, José."

José paused and looked at him sourly. "What's good about it?"

"Very little," Luke had to admit. "Sit down, Mayor." Seating himself behind the desk, he opened the humidor and extracted a cheroot.

"Would you like to tell me why my carriage is out back of your hacienda?"

"Not really."

The mayor frowned. "What kind of an answer is that?"

Lighting the smoke, Luke leaned back in his chair. "I really can't say why your carriage is here, José. Someone mentioned they saw Enrique driving it yesterday."

"It was Enrique, all right. I yelled for him to stop, but you know that boy only hears what he wants to hear." The mayor shook his head, exasperated. "What I want to know is who Enrique had with him and why he left the carriage out here?"

Luke drew off his cheroot absently. "I wouldn't know. I haven't seen Enrique since yesterday morning. Did he damage the carriage?"

"No . . . no damage that I know of. He just made it damned inconvenient for me."

"I understand. Sorry I can't shed any light on Enrique's motives, but I'd be happy to have one of my men drive your carriage back into town for you."

"That won't be necessary. I brought a man with me. Just wondered if you had any idea what Enrique thought he was doing."

"Now, José"—Luke smiled patiently—"you know that no one knows what Enrique's doing, including Enrique." Luke stood up and came around the desk to walk the mayor to the door.

104

The mayor grunted. That was the truth. Enrique's bucket didn't reach the end of the well. "You heard about Brewster's niece? Sounds like someone's grabbed her."

"Is that right?"

"Yeah." The mayor grinned. "Word has it you've got her."

Luke nodded gravely. "Of course. She's locked up in my bedroom, stark naked."

The mayor roared, slapping Luke on the back. "You're crazy, Kincaid."

Luke grinned. "Take it easy, José."

As Luke turned to go back into the house, he remembered his appointment with Emil to hunt the stallion this morning.

Luke hailed one of the ranch hands and told him to ride over to Emil's and explain that Luke wouldn't be able to join him today.

The rider's dust was fading as Ines rode up. Luke walked out to meet her and grabbed her horse's reins as she slid out of the saddle.

"Good morning, darling." Leaning forward, she brushed her mouth against his cheek. "Did you sleep well?"

"Not bad."

She eyed him with amusement. "You look in considerably better shape this morning."

Luke smiled and settled his arm around her waist as they began walking toward the house.

"I'm sorry about last night," he apologized.

"I forgive you." Her hand rested lightly on his

arm as they strolled along the flagstone walk lined with Luisa's flowering annuals. "I halfway expected to find Hamilton camped on your doorstep this morning. Rumor has it that you had Enrique kidnap his niece and that you're holding her hostage." Ines laughed, glancing at him hopefully. "Have you ever heard of anything so farfetched?"

"I didn't kidnap the girl, Ines."

"I wasn't accusing you, darling. I find those rumors incredible. Where do you suppose the girl has disappeared to?"

Luke shrugged. "I can't say."

They entered the kitchen and found Luisa bustling to pour Ines a cup of coffee.

Ines took the seat opposite Luke and smiled. "I thought you were going with Father to hunt the stallion again this morning?"

"I was, but something came up here that needed my attention."

Lifting her cup to her mouth, Ines studied him. "You look tired."

"Actually, I didn't sleep well last night."

"I hope that doesn't mean you can't come for dinner this evening."

"No, it doesn't mean that." Luke returned her smile. "I'll be there."

"Well, come hungry. Francisca is preparing rabbit and dressing." Inez winked as she drew on her riding gloves. "And you know the woman is madly in love with you. She spoils you terribly."

Luke rose to escort her outside. When he returned to the kitchen a few minutes later, he sank down onto a chair and rubbed his face wearily.

"You have problems, *hijo?*" Luisa asked, pouring him a fresh cup of coffee.

"Luisa, I need your help."

Luisa's brow furrowed. "What's wrong?"

Luke sighed, stirring sugar into coffee that he usually drank unsweetened. "Sit down, Luisa."

"Oh, *madre de Dios.*" This was bad trouble.

Dropping onto the chair opposite him, Luisa clasped her hands on the edge of the table. "Who have you killed?"

"I haven't killed anyone."

She sighed with relief and crossed herself.

"You're aware that Brewster's niece is missing."

"*Sí,*" she nodded.

Luke's eyes lifted to meet hers. "Hannah Brewster is upstairs in my bedroom."

"*Madre de Dios!*" Luisa gasped, hurriedly crossing herself again. "What have you done?"

"I haven't done anything . . . well, what I mean to say is, I didn't kidnap her," he said defensively. He'd done plenty, but Luisa didn't have to know that.

"Then how did she get into your room?"

"From what I can piece together, Enrique brought her out here and left her there. Until I can find him, I won't know why he did it."

"*Mio Dios,*" Luisa breathed again. "This is *malo.*"

"I know. That's why I need your help. I want

107

you to take her something to eat . . . oh . . . and Luisa." Luke glanced up. "I had to take her clothes away from her to keep her from screaming for help."

Luisa dropped her eyes and crossed herself again hurriedly.

"I have to get her out of here and back to Brewster sometime this morning."

"But how will you explain such a mistake to *Señor* Brewster?"

Luke rubbed his chin thoughtfully. How in the hell *was* he going to explain his part of the blunder? He had compromised the girl's virtue. He couldn't know for certain whether or not she was carrying his child. He had been too drunk to be prudent. But he wasn't going to marry her. There wasn't a power on earth strong enough to make him marry her.

"I have no idea how I'll explain it. But once she's fed and dressed, I'm returning her to her uncle."

"I will pray for you," Luisa vowed solemnly. She stood. "I will go now and light a candle at the mission."

"Better light a dozen," Luke murmured. "I'm going to need all the help I can get."

7

⋯⋯❦❦⦁ ❦❦⋯⋯

Luke glanced up twenty minutes later as a rap sounded at his office door. "Yes?"

The door swung open to reveal Luisa, trying to balance a well-laden breakfast tray.

"Yes?" he asked again when she just stood staring at him.

"Luke . . ."

Luke came slowly to his feet. Luisa was as pale as if she had seen a ghost. "What's wrong?"

"It's Ginny . . . they have Ginny." As Luke's sister's name escaped Luisa, it sounded more like a moan than a statement.

"Who has Ginny?"

Shaken, Luisa set the tray down, then removed a folded piece of paper from her apron pocket. Handing the note to Luke, she watched as his eyes quickly scanned the message.

I have your sister, Kincaid. If you're lucky, she'll be returned unharmed if and when my niece is safely back in my care.

Hamilton T. Brewster

Lifting his eyes, Luke surveyed Luisa's worried countenance. "Where did you find this?"

"In Ginny's room . . . her door was open as I walked by to take Miss Brewster her breakfast. I could see that Ginny wasn't in her bed. . . . Oh, *madre de Dios,* what will we do now?"

"Dammit!" Anger and cold, gut-wrenching fear coiled inside Luke as he crumpled the paper in his hand. He'd like nothing more than to send Brewster's niece back, strapped across the back of a horse!

"Luke, Ginny's been kidnapped," Luisa cried. "You must do something—oh, *madre de Dios* . . ." She crossed herself again. "If your *padre* hears of this . . ."

"No one, Luisa, *no one* is to speak a word of this to Thatcher," Luke warned.

"But he will find out . . . the child visits with him daily."

"There's no reason for him to know—not yet." Luke walked to his desk and reached for a piece of paper. "You will make some excuse for why Ginny doesn't visit him for the next few days—tell my father she's staying with a friend. Then find Pedro and tell him I want to see him—immediately."

Crossing herself, Luisa picked up the tray and

hurried out of the room to find the foreman as Luke angrily scrawled a brief, but precise, message to Hamilton Brewster:

If one hair on my sister's head is touched, you will answer to me.

Lucas Kincaid

Pedro rapped on the office door as Luke was sealing the envelope.

"You wanted to see me, *patrón?*"

Luke glanced up. "The son of a bitch has Ginny."

Pedro stepped inside the room and quickly closed the double doors behind him. He strode over to stand in front of Luke's desk. "The son of a bitch?"

"Hamilton Brewster. He had one of his men snatch Ginny sometime during the night. I want you to deliver this note personally to Hamilton, then get back here as soon as you can."

Rolling the brim of his hat with his fingertips, Pedro waited for Luke to continue. There had to be more. Hamilton Brewster didn't go around kidnapping helpless young women unless he had gone off the deep end.

"Well?" Luke shot Pedro an impatient glance. "What are you waiting for?"

"Hamilton Brewster kidnapped Ginny."

"That's what I said." Luke was mad now. Fighting mad. What in the *hell* did Hamilton think he

111

was going to accomplish by pulling a stunt like this? And how had one of his men gotten into the hacienda?

The answer rose up to haunt him. Whoever Hamilton had sent had gotten into the house and into Ginny's room while he'd been trying to deal with that black-haired she-devil niece that Brewster was so hell-bent on getting back!

"But, *señor,* why would—"

"Just see that Brewster gets the message," Luke snapped. He couldn't explain the mess he was in if he tried. Luke strode across the room and jerked the doors open. In an instant, he was slamming them behind him.

Pedro glanced down at the envelope in his hand and shrugged.

The Kincaids and the Brewsters—they were *muy loco.*

Taking the stairs two at a time, Luke admitted to himself that Hamilton had him backed into a corner.

Thatcher could be protected from the news, but not for long. When word reached him that his only daughter was being held by a Brewster, all hell would break loose.

On the other hand, if Luke gave in to Hamilton's underhanded theatrics and returned Hannah, then he would be, in a sense, admitting that he had planned the abduction of Brewster's niece.

112

Luke was reasonably sure no harm would come to Ginny while she was in Hamilton's protection, and he fully intended to make sure that no further harm would come to Hannah while she was under his own protection, but the longer this craziness went on, the more room there was for error—on both sides.

The only sane course was for him to return Hamilton's niece and try to explain the misunderstanding.

Pausing at the door to his room, he took a deep breath. As far as he was concerned, he couldn't get rid of the little hellion fast enough.

Entering the room, Luke gazed with horror at what Hannah had done in his absence.

She surely hadn't spent her time looking out the window.

The interior of his bedroom was in shambles.

She had ripped both pillows open, and feathers were floating around the room. Perched in the middle of the bed, arms crossed defiantly, Hannah sat glaring at him. Wispy feathers were caught in her hair and matted on the bare mattress.

Leaning against the doorframe, he crossed his arms and stared back at her.

"What?" she demanded.

When she hadn't been able to get that *stupid* trunk unlocked, she had lost her temper, and in a fit of anger she had torn his room apart. At first it had seemed like a justifiable thing to do, but now she was feeling a little foolish that he'd caught her in this humiliating position.

"Well, I see you've been busy."

"No, I've been angry, Mr. Kincaid. *Angry!*" She swatted a feather off her nose, and it flew into the air and floated lightly back to the mattress.

Luke slammed the door, sending another cloud of feathers into the air. Feathers were stuck to everything in sight. It was the damnedest mess he'd ever seen!

"I hope you know you're going to clean this up," he said calmly.

"You'll have to make me." She crossed her arms again rebelliously.

"If I don't, Luisa will, and believe me, next to Luisa, you'll think I'm a saint."

Her chin shot up with defiance. He'd taken her clothes, taken the blanket and the bedsheets, and left her alone for hours! Did he think she was just going to let him get away with doing that to her? If he wanted the mess cleaned up, he could do it himself.

Her gaze locked with his stubbornly. "I want to go to my Uncle Hamilton."

"Get off that bed and pick up every last one of these feathers," he demanded.

"You can't make me." Her chin came up again.

"You will, or you'll be across my knee," Luke warned.

"Try it, and I'll scratch your eyes out!" He started for the bed, and she drew back. "You

114

wouldn't dare—you get away from me, you brute!"

"You get your fanny off that bed and start picking up those feathers."

Hannah sucked in her breath indignantly. No one had ever spoken to her so insolently! "You can't keep me here!" she began. "When my Uncle Hamilton comes to get me—"

"He will find you on your hands and knees, picking up feathers. Now get busy."

She watched as he waded across his room, his boots breaking through the piles of plumes.

"I can't pick up feathers when I'm so hungry!" she cried, wishing she had something to cover herself with. He kept looking at her bare breasts, and she didn't like that. It made her feel as if he were touching her again and, for some reason, she was all weak and mushy inside.

"Do you plan on starving me as well as holding me prisoner?"

"Luisa is bringing you something to eat." Luke picked up a torn pillow and tossed it onto the bed. "I pity you when she sees what you've done to this room," he murmured.

Sliding off the bed, Hannah kept a close eye on him as he moved to the far side of the room. His boots were covered with feathers now.

"This Luisa . . . she won't really do anything to me, will she?"

Hannah hadn't considered the possibility of a third party becoming involved in her anarchy.

"I don't know what Luisa will do to you. She'd shoot *me* for tearing up anything this way." He glanced around the room again. "She'll probably shoot me for letting *you* tear up the room," he predicted.

Luke tried to ignore the bright tears that suddenly sprang to the girl's eyes. For a moment he almost felt sorry for her. She looked like a young, frightened child who wasn't sure what to do next.

His gaze ran over her nubile curves, and he could see that she was trembling. She stared back at him with those violet-colored eyes that were large and clouded now.

Desire jolted him, and he realized that he wanted her again. Damn! That was all he needed!

He turned and walked out of the room, returning a moment later to hand her a blanket.

"Here," he said quietly. "I'm giving this back to you, but don't try anything."

Sniffing, she accepted his act of compassion gratefully. "If you were a gentleman, you wouldn't curse in the presence of a lady."

"If I were in the presence of a lady, I wouldn't be cursing," he returned evenly.

When the blanket was firmly secured around her, Hannah accepted the pillowcase he handed her, then gingerly plucked a feather off the bed. Keeping one eye on Luke, she picked feathers one at a time, carefully stuffing them into the bag. "Just who is Luisa?"

"You'll find out sooner than you care to."

116

Dropping to her knees, Hannah crawled along the floor, intent now on picking up the tiny quills. "You don't think you can keep me locked up in this room forever, do you?"

"No."

"Then when are you going to let me go?"

"Just as soon as I can."

Her face brightened. "You are?" This was wonderful news. Now he would take her to Uncle Hamilton and confess what he'd done to her, and they would be married right away.

"I'm not doing it to make you happy."

"Oh, I know that." He'd made his feelings in the matter perfectly clear.

He walked across the room, sidestepping her. "It seems your Uncle Hamilton has decided to up the ante in this asinine little game."

She paused, looking up at him. "Oh?"

"Yes. Sometime during the night one of his men abducted my little sister. He's holding her until I return you."

Hannah frowned. "Oh, dear."

"Yeah, oh, dear."

"Well, you needn't worry. Unlike a Kincaid"—her eyes slid over him insolently—"a *Brewster* would never compromise an innocent young woman."

A knock sounded at the door, and Hannah's blood froze. Glancing at Luke, she whispered anxiously, "Is that Luisa?"

"Probably."

117

Hannah crawled closer to him. "Don't let her come in yet—there are still feathers everywhere."

Luke glanced down at her sourly. "You think *I'm* going to protect you?"

Moving Hannah aside, Luke opened the door a crack. Luisa frowned when she saw him.

Holding the breakfast tray, Luisa admonished him in a whisper, "What are you doing here?"

Accepting the tray, Luke smiled. "Cleaning up a little."

"Cleaning up a little?" Luisa's hands came to her hips. "What are you up to—where is Hamilton's niece?"

"Hamilton's niece is busy at the moment."

"Doing what?"

"Doing whatever women do. I have your word, Luisa, no one is to know that she's here," Luke warned again.

"*Sí, sí,*" Luisa sighed. "But it is wrong."

Luke balanced the tray on one arm and closed the door with the other. Quietly, he carried the tray over to the bed. "After you eat, I want you to get dressed."

Hannah got to her feet, picking the feathers from between her fingers.

"Are you going to take me to Uncle Hamilton's?"

Luke nodded. "Can you be ready in an hour?"

"Of course." She sighed, then turned her attention to the plate of hot biscuits and eggs. "I'll need my clothes returned, and a pitcher of fresh water."

"I'll tell Luisa."

She glanced up anxiously. "Oh—don't bother Luisa—I don't want to be any trouble." She smiled sweetly. "I'll just make do with what's in the pitcher."

"You are to keep quiet," he warned again.

She smiled again. "I will."

Luke doubted that she would cooperate, but at this point it no longer mattered. She would be gone within the hour.

"I can trust you?"

She sighed wearily. "You can trust me."

She glanced up as she heard the door close a few seconds later.

A sly grin spread across her face smugly. If he believed that, he was crazy.

"Miss Kincaid?"

Ginny Kincaid glanced up to find a young boy about her age standing in the doorway.

"Yes?" She brought the backs of her hands up to wipe the tears running down her cheeks.

"Uncle Hamilton sent me up to see if you needed anything." Kamen entered the room hesitantly.

The girl sitting on the bed was the prettiest thing he'd ever seen. He'd never dreamed that a Kincaid could be so comely.

"I don't need anything." Ginny admitted to herself that she'd been scared half out of her mind

119

when she'd been bound and gagged and carried from her room in the middle of the night by one of Brewster's hired hands, but she was feeling better now.

The household staff had been treating her well this morning, calling her "missy" and telling her that if she needed anything, they'd be happy to get it for her. She was surprised that anyone connected with a Brewster could be so thoughtful.

"You sure? I wouldn't mind fetchin' you a glass of cool buttermilk from the spring," Kamen offered.

"I'm fine, really—but thank you very much." Ginny smiled back at the gangly youth, thinking that he was about the most handsome boy she'd ever seen. The early morning sunlight streamed through the window, catching his blond hair and turning it to a flaxen gold. He had nice, soft, brown eyes, and he was looking her over as if he thought she was nice, too.

Kamen shyly stuck his hands into his pockets. "My uncle won't be keeping you very long, you know. No need for you to be afraid."

"I know." She gazed up at him, making his heart flutter like a leaf in a high wind.

"You're not afraid, are you? Won't no one hurt you," he promised. "It's just this silly feud." He shrugged lamely. "Seems like it keeps gettin' worse instead of better."

"I know—but Luke doesn't have your cousin,"

120

Ginny said. "He wouldn't do a thing like that just to keep a silly old piece of land."

Kamen frowned. "You sure about that?"

"Near sure. He told me he didn't."

"He could've been lying to you."

Ginny shook her head. "Luke don't lie to nobody."

Kamen studied her a moment. She was as pretty as a sunrise on an Easter morning.

"Well," he said, "guess we'll have to leave it up to Luke and my Uncle Hamilton to figure out what they're gonna do next."

"Guess we will."

He started to leave, then turned back. "Sure you wouldn't like that buttermilk? Wouldn't be no trouble."

"Not now, but maybe you could come back and ask me later." She smiled at him, and Kamen thought he was going to faint.

His eyes ran over her small breasts and tiny waist. Why, he could wrap his hands around her middle twice!

He felt a sheen of sweat suddenly break out across his forehead, and his hands began to tremble. "Sure . . . I can do that."

His hand fumbled blindly for the doorknob. She was gonna hear his heart trying to thump its way clean out of his chest if he didn't get out of there!

"Don't you forget to come back now, you hear?" She smiled at him again.

"I won't." He flashed her a quick grin. "Won't forget that, all right."

Letting himself out of her room, Kamen sagged against the door and let out a sigh of relief.

Weren't *no way* he was gonna forget to do that.

8

"Are you *sure* I look all right?" Hannah brushed at the wrinkles in her dress anxiously. "I've never met my Uncle Hamilton, you know. He's only seen a tintype of me."

As usual, Luke didn't answer her, Hannah noted.

Lifting the reins, Luke whistled sharply. The old buckboard sprang forward, forcing Hannah to grab his shirtsleeve for support.

She glared at him accusingly. He was just upset because she'd dallied too long! But she had to look right, for heaven's sake!

Luke's jaw was set in a tight clench as the buggy rumbled out of the yard.

It had taken her a half hour to eat breakfast, then another hour to choose something to wear. She'd discarded half the dresses she'd brought with her because they just weren't "right."

123

He wasn't sure what "right" meant, but she had declared that it had something to do with color, wrinkles, and whether a dress had too many ruffles for morning.

By the time she'd gone through all of that, it was *noon*. Luke failed to see what difference a few ruffles made anyway.

Hannah studied Luke out of the corner of her eye. They were sitting so close their shoulders touched, but not in a friendly fashion. He wasn't exactly in a friendly mood. He wasn't exactly a friendly *man*.

Well, it didn't matter if he liked her or not. She didn't like him, either. She straightened her skirt primly. And he wasn't going to be able to trust her —not one bit. She planned to thwart him every chance she got. But she would marry him so that she could tell Edgar Huckett to go hang. She sighed contentedly. She'd show her father and her uncle that she couldn't be pushed around.

They rode in silence as the old buggy whipped along the country road. Hannah heaved a bored sigh every once in a while, thinking about her wedding.

At least this man would make a handsome groom. And she would be a beautiful bride. Her dress would be . . . white. Of course. No one need know what he had . . . well, her dress would be white, anyway. And there would be at least three attendants. Surely Uncle Hamilton could find three girls who would consent to being her bridesmaids. The wedding would take place as soon as possible. She would have dozens of summer roses in her bouquet. She would pick them from the bushes she'd seen in back of the Kincaid house. Pink roses. And white. Yes. That would be pretty. With pink and white ribbons.

Now. How should she dress her hair? With curls and ringlets. Yes, she looked lovely in curls and ringlets. And someone would play an organ—if this godforsaken place had an organ. Failing that, perhaps she'd request a piano.

And when she walked down the aisle toward Luke, he would gaze upon her, and see that she was the most beautiful bride ever, and he would think how very lucky he was that she would even consider marrying him—however brief their marriage was destined to be.

Her chin lifted defiantly again. Perhaps he'd even fall in love with her. Well, after her behavior this morning, maybe not. But it didn't matter. At least she wouldn't be stuck with Edgar . . . but she mustn't let herself become smitten with a Kincaid ruffian. And she could—oh, she could if she wasn't extremely careful. He was a handsome rascal, even if he was mean to her . . . and that would be terrible. The feud between the two families would make it impossible for her to love him. . . .

She glanced over to see that Luke was lost in his own thoughts as the buggy crossed the creek and rolled up the hill. Somehow he was going to have to come up with a solution that was acceptable to both Hamilton and himself. Luke realized that he would be agreeable to almost anything except marrying this twit.

There would be bloodshed before that happened.

The buckboard hit a bump and lurched to one side, causing Hannah to latch onto his shirt for support again.

"Will you stop that!" Luke grumbled. She'd been squirming and fussing ever since they left the ranch.

"The sun is so hot," Hannah said, fanning herself a little. It wouldn't have occurred to him to offer her a parasol. "Is it much farther? I'll have freckles if I'm out in the sun much longer."

Luke whistled again, urging the horse into a faster gait.

"Is my nose pink? I just know it is," she fretted. The rays were deplorable, and she was beginning to perspire. How indelicate. He couldn't expect her to greet her uncle with perspiration beading her face.

One wagon wheel hit a deep pothole. With a shriek of dismay, Hannah grabbed for the pins that suddenly sprang loose from her hair. Shooting Luke an exasperated look, she braced her feet on the floor and held on to her hat.

The man had positively no breeding.

By the time they approached the gate of Hamilton Brewster's ranch, Hannah was in a full-blown pout. Jerking her bonnet off her head, she let her hair whip free as the buggy rolled into the barnyard.

Luke Kincaid had deliberately made the trip as unpleasant as possible—she just knew it. Thanks to his total lack of gentility, she was sweaty, dusty, and her hair rivaled a wild woman's!

Pulling the horse to a halt, Luke set the brake, then turned to look at her. "You let me do the talking. Do you understand?"

"Perfectly." Her eyes snapped back at him. She couldn't wait to see how he tried to worm his way out of what he'd done.

Luke jumped down from the high seat and rounded the buckboard.

Lifting her off the seat, he stood her on her feet. Hannah refused to look at him. Her chin was stuck up in the air again, and she had that haughty look that set his teeth on edge.

The front door opened, and Hamilton walked out. Luke turned, and the the two men locked gazes.

"I see you've finally come to your senses." Hamilton barked. "I thought you would."

"Brewster, I want a word with you. In private." Hannah could see a muscle working tautly in Luke's jaw.

Hamilton's eyes moved to his niece. "Are you all right?"

Hannah nodded hesitantly, watching Luke from the corner of her eye.

Scooting around Luke, Hannah took her place at her uncle's side. Satisfied that he'd called Kincaid's bluff, Hamilton turned and started back into the house.

Glancing apprehensively over her shoulder, Hannah waited for Luke to stop him.

"Hamilton, I want a word with you," Luke repeated again.

"Get off my land, Kincaid."

"Can't do that, Brewster."

"Uncle Hamilton, shoot him," Hannah ordered. "He's been treating me awful."

Hamilton turned, his eyes sweeping Luke coldly. "You're a miserable low-down, good-for-nothing bastard. If you know what's good for you, you'll get out of here before I lose my temper. One of my men will see that your sister is returned within the hour," he tossed over his shoulder as he began walking away again.

"We have business to discuss, Hamilton. That doesn't make me any happier than it makes you, but walking off isn't going to solve the matter." Luke knew that if he didn't tell Hamilton what had happened, Hannah would.

"A Brewster has no business to discuss with a Kincaid."

Hannah listened to the exchange with growing apprehension. Was it *possible* that her uncle would refuse to hear Luke's confession? Hysteria rose in her throat as visions of living in a funeral parlor the

128

rest of her life rose to taunt her. She couldn't let that happen!

Laying her hand on her uncle's arm, she said quietly, "I think you'd better talk to him." She cast her eyes down demurely.

Hamilton's brows rose. "Has he acted in an ungentlemanly manner toward you?"

Hannah drew a ragged, long-suffering sigh and looked away. The implication of her sigh rang out like buckshot over the strained silence.

Turning back to Luke, Hamilton's eyes hardened. "You have five minutes, Kincaid."

Luke followed Hamilton and the girl into the house. Hannah welcomed the cool interior with a grateful sigh. "I'd like to freshen up," she murmured. She wanted to be presentable when Luke was forced to ask for her hand in marriage.

"Of course, my dear. Your room is upstairs, second on the right. I'll have your things sent up shortly," Hamilton returned. "Is there anything else I can get for you?"

"Yes—I—I would enjoy a nice cup of tea." She slanted a haughty glance in Luke's direction. "It's been so long since I've had the opportunity for—for even small courtesies."

Luke met her glance unemotionally.

"Of course, my love." Hamilton motioned for one of the servants. "My niece would like a pot of tea when she returns."

The servant nodded and hurried out of the room.

129

Turning back, Hamilton motioned Luke and Hannah into the library.

"Sit," Hamilton ordered curtly as he walked to stand behind the massive desk. Removing his watch from the pocket of his vest, Hamilton made note of the time. "You have five minutes to state your position, Kincaid."

"That's three minutes more than I need."

Hamilton glanced up, his wintry gaze skimming Luke. "Why, young man, do I get the impression you're about to make me mad as hell again?"

Luke shrugged. "I don't expect either one of us is going to be rolling on the floor by the time I finish."

Reaching for a cigar, Hamilton studied Luke. He didn't want to admit it, but he liked what he saw. The boy had backbone; Hamilton appreciated that. Too bad he was a Kincaid. "Go on."

"Last night I had too much to drink. When I went to my room, I found a woman in my bed. Thinking that she had been given to me as a birthday present from my men, I . . . accepted the present—"

"You took advantage of me!" Hannah interrupted. "It wasn't my fault, Uncle Hamilton . . . it . . . it was all his!"

"Without," Luke went on, "knowing that Enrique had—for some still unexplained reason—brought your niece to the ranch and left her in my bed!"

"He didn't put me in your bed!"

Luke shot to his feet. "Well, dammit, that's where you were when I found you!"

The two glared at each other hotly.

Wide-eyed, Hamilton listened as the bizarre story began to sink in on him. "Son of a bitch," he finally murmured as Luke and Hannah continued to stare at each other. By now he had chewed the tip of his cigar into a nasty stub.

"My exact thought," Luke admitted as he sat down again.

Shifting the cigar from one corner of his mouth to the other, Hamilton tried to digest this distressing turn of events. "You say Enrique brought Hannah Rose to your place?"

"From what I can piece together, that's what happened. Enrique has disappeared again, so I can't say for certain, but that's how it looks."

"And when you came up to your room, she was half-naked—asleep in your bed?"

Luke nodded gravely. "I thought the men had sent her as a birthday present."

Hamilton glanced up again. "Didn't she say or do anything to stop you?"

Luke colored when he recalled how her passion had matched his and how she had begged him to continue. "She didn't protest."

"I did so!"

"The hell you did."

"Hannah Rose, go to your room," Hamilton ordered.

"But Uncle Hamilton—"

LORI COPELAND

"Go to your room!"

Shaking his head, Hamilton rose from his chair when Hannah had left the room. "Good Lord. What a mess."

"I understand Hannah is engaged to Edgar Huckett?" Luke said quietly.

"Well, you might say that. Her father and I have made arrangements of a sort . . . but Edgar has yet to meet her. . . . He was planning to meet the stage yesterday, but cholera broke out in Livingston. Edgar had to go over there and stay until the crisis eases, so he asked me to meet Hannah."

"Then he could be gone for a week or so?"

"Yes, or longer. They've already lost four adults and three children."

"Then we have time."

Hamilton's brows rose. "Time? For what? Looks to me like you've got yourself in a peck of trouble, boy."

"Not necessarily," Luke said. "I think that I've come up with a way we can settle this misunderstanding with the least possible embarrassment for your niece."

"I think in view of what you just told me, the way this 'misunderstanding' is settled goes without saying. *You* will marry Hannah Rose," he said impatiently. The thought of Hannah's marrying a Kincaid galled him, but he couldn't have her shamed!

Luke met his gaze evenly. "Think about it, Hamilton. Do you really want your niece mar-

132

rying a Kincaid? Even if a mistake of this magnitude has been committed?"

Hamilton turned back to the window to think about it. A moment later, he turned back pensively. "What are you proposing we do?"

"Hannah will go on with her marriage to Edgar Huckett as if nothing has happened. No one knows about the mistake, except you, me, and Luisa, and even Luisa doesn't know the full extent of it."

For a moment there was a stunned silence, then recovering, Hamilton whistled beneath his breath. "Are you suggesting that we cuckold Edgar Huckett?"

"No. We just don't mention the events of last night to him."

"We'd never get away with it," Hamilton declared. "Hannah would tell Edgar what took place."

"Not if it would be to her advantage not to tell him."

"But suppose she's carrying your child—"

Luke didn't want to suppose that. The thought made him ill. "If she is, then Edgar will never be the wiser if they marry within the next week. For all practical purposes, the child will be his."

Hamilton began to pace in front of the fireplace, his arms locked tightly behind his back. What Luke was suggesting was blasphemy! But a Kincaid married to a Brewster? That would be an even more heinous crime. "Think about it, Hamilton. It's the only sensible way to handle this,"

Luke said quietly. "No Kincaid and no Brewster wants a marriage between our two families."

Luke knew that when Thatcher learned of the situation, the shock alone could bring on a stroke. Luke would do anything humanly possible to protect Thatcher from that possibility—with the exception of marrying the girl. There was no way in hell he was going to marry a Brewster!

Hamilton paused, turning to Luke again. "And if I were to consider going along with such deception?" Hamilton wasn't simple. A Kincaid would never have the audacity to ask a Brewster to make such a concession unless he was willing to make a sacrifice of the same magnitude.

"If you do, then I'm prepared to hand you over a clear deed to the disputed piece of land," Luke said simply.

Hamilton's jaw dropped. "You're willing to deed the land over to me. Lock, stock, and barrel?"

Luke nodded. "Lock, stock, and barrel."

"But the water? Your father?"

"That particular piece of land is ideal to water my herd," he admitted, "but there's nothing to prevent me from moving my herd to the east range. Thatcher is bedridden now, and not likely to ever find out if we keep this a gentleman's agreement." Luke considered the tradeoff a small price to pay for his blunder.

"Well, I'll be damned." Hamilton sank slowly into his chair. The Brewsters had tried for ninety years to buy a clear deed to that land, and to no avail.

Now, Luke Kincaid was offering to give it to him.

Upstairs, Hannah hurriedly went about her toilette. The past twenty-four hours had been exhausting, and she would welcome a cool compress to her forehead and a long nap. But she didn't dare.

She wanted to be present to see the look on Luke Kincaid's arrogant face when Uncle Hamilton demanded that he marry her. She wanted to see the worm squirm.

Of course, Edgar would be notified of the change in plans immediately.

She started as a tap sounded at the door.

"Yes?"

"Your uncle would like to see you in the library, Miss Brewster."

Smiling, Hannah dabbed water on her sunburned nose. "*Sí,*" she called, triumphant in the knowledge that she was already becoming so adept in Spanish. Of course, Papa had always told her that she was exceptionally bright. "Tell Uncle Hamilton I'll be right down."

And Luke Kincaid thought that he could bully her.

She flipped her curls over her shoulders sassily. *Ha.*

* * *

When Hannah hurried downstairs a few minutes later, Hamilton was pacing. Pausing at the door to the library, she knelt to peek through the keyhole.

Luke was sitting quietly in a large wingback chair, drawing slowly on a cheroot as he watched her uncle stride back and forth across the woven rug.

Hamilton's face was a pinched mask as he paced, mentally reviewing the dilemma.

Enrique drives Hannah to the Kincaid ranch. For some reason, she thinks she's at the Brewster ranch. She goes upstairs, undresses, and crawls into Kincaid's bed.

Hamilton paused and shook his head.

Silly twit! Damn that girl's hide! What was she thinking! Kincaid is drunk, and being drunk and being male, why, he naturally assumes that Hannah is one of Bettianne's new girls—why, even I can see how a man could make a mistake like that!

Hamilton began pacing again.

Kincaid beds her, then when he discovers who she is, well, the damage is already done. But the boy is trying to do the right thing, I've got to hand him that. He brings Hannah back, and he is facing up to what he's done like a man. It's the right and proper thing to do. And the boy is offering a clear title to the disputed acre as restitution. Granted, Kincaid wants to save his own miserable hide, but under the circumstances, it's a right fine offer. A right fine offer.

"Even if I was to go along with this," Hamilton began, "my brother tells me that my niece is a headstrong girl."

Luke's eyes narrowed as he took another long draw from the cheroot. "I think you could say that."

Oooooh! It was all Hannah could do to keep from stomping her foot!. The man's haughtiness made her blood boil.

"Well, a man does make mistakes," Hamilton reasoned. "And in view of the circumstances . . . you could be right."

"I'm right, Hamilton. Like it or not, we're going to have to work together on this one."

Straightening, Hannah smiled and turned the doorknob. It was all settled. All she had to do was breeze in and claim the victory.

Hamilton glanced up as Hannah entered the room.

Clasping her hands in front of her, she smiled her prettiest smile. "You wanted to see me?"

Stepping aside, she allowed the *criada* to enter the room carrying a tray laden with tea and pastries.

"Just set the tray on the desk," Hamilton instructed.

"Oh, how refreshing." Hannah moved to the desk to serve. "Please, gentlemen, allow me."

Glancing at Luke, she began to pour tea into

delicate china cups. He seemed remarkably composed for a man who was about to have his precious freedom snatched away.

"Lemon?" she inquired nicely.

Both men shook their head.

"Sugar!"

Hamilton nodded absently.

"One lump, or two?" Hannah asked, tilting a glance at Luke.

Luke brought the cheroot back to his mouth, his gaze meeting hers evenly. "I don't drink tea."

"Oh?" She smiled. "Well, you'll learn."

Taking a seat next to the desk, she brought the cup to her mouth daintily. It annoyed Luke to see her amused eyes peeping over the rim of the cup at him.

"Please, go on with whatever it was you were discussing, gentlemen."

Hamilton cleared his throat, his eyes darting back to Luke for assurance. "Hannah Rose."

Responsibility for this child lay heavily upon him. His brother had entrusted his only daughter to his care with the understanding that Hamilton would assist Hannah in procuring a proper husband. Now his niece had been defiled, and by a rotten, no-good Kincaid.

Hamilton did not relish the unsavory task that lay ahead of him. "Kincaid has informed me of the uhh . . ." Hamilton cleared his throat. "The misunderstanding."

"I'm sure he lied to you about last night. I . . .

138

was a . . . an innocent victim in all of this." Hannah sniffed and rummaged for her handkerchief. In all likelihood, she knew she could assume that Luke had tried to downplay his part in the matter, but it wouldn't take her long to set her uncle straight. "I'm ruined. Edgar will never have me now."

Hamilton awkwardly leaned over to pat her shoulder. "No, Kincaid told me what . . . took place."

Hannah glanced up. "He has?"

"I believe so."

"Everything?" Hannah probed, turning to look at Luke.

Luke nodded. "Everything."

"But you needn't worry. He's offered to make it right."

"Well." Hannah settled back on her chair, breathing more easily now. Luke was surprising her. She would have sworn he'd try to squirm his way out of this, like the rodent he was. She sighed fatalistically, picking at the pleats in her skirt. "I suppose I'm going to have to marry him."

"Oh, no, no, my dear. Nothing so . . . so disturbing as that," Hamilton assured her, squeezing her shoulder.

Her eyes darted up again. "What?"

"Kincaid has come up with a solution—one I think you'll find perfectly acceptable."

Stunned, Hannah let her cup clatter back to the saucer. She glanced over to find Luke grinning at her, and irritation furrowed her brow. "Exactly *what* is Mr. Kincaid suggesting?"

"You'll be relieved to know that the unfortunate turn of events will not interfere with your plans to marry Edgar." Hamilton smiled at his niece as he went on to explain the simple plan: the mistake would go no further than this room. The wedding would go on as planned. On the day of the wedding, Edgar would be taken aside and told that regretfully Hannah had suffered a serious riding accident in her earlier years. Hopefully, Edgar would then assume her lack of virginity was due to the accident.

Hannah listened with growing horror. "No! You can't do this to me!"

"No?" Hamilton's brows shot up. "Why, my dear, it's the only sensible way to handle the matter. We can't have a Brewster *marrying* a Kincaid. That would be unthinkable."

Springing to her feet, Hannah slapped her palm on the desk angrily. "I won't have you bartering my virginity this way!" I won't have it! I won't marry Edgar!"

"But, my dear!" Hamilton sprang to his feet, stunned by her display of belligerence. "If you're with child, you have little choice. I can't permit you to marry a Kincaid!"

She whirled around and pointed her finger at Luke. "Yes, yes, you can. He ruined me. Make *him* marry me!

"Now, Hannah Rose," Hamilton said sternly.

"Nothing can change what has happened. It was a simple . . . well, maybe not simple, but an understandable misunderstanding. It is our Christian duty to forgive." Hamilton could view the situation quite benevolently if it meant purging himself of a Kincaid.

"*Our* Christian duty! You're not the one who's going to be living in a funeral parlor!" She spun around and leaned down to go nose to nose with Luke. "The Good Book doesn't say anything about protecting a Kincaid," she said ominously. "*You* are going to marry me!"

Luke shook his head. "Now, Hannah Rose, you're making another scene."

Jerking away, Hannah began to pace. "And what if I'm carrying *your* child?"

"If you're carrying a child, then Edgar must be convinced that it is his," Hamilton returned quietly. He sighed. "Your position on this surprises me, Hannah. I thought you would be relieved not to have to marry this man."

With her tears blinding her, Hannah couldn't find her voice for the first time in her life. In spite of everything she'd done, she was still going to be forced into marrying Edgar! Whirling, she ran out of the room, slamming the door behind her.

With a defeated sigh, Hamilton sat down. "Dear me. My brother warned me she had a temper."

"She does. Don't let her anywhere near a pillow." Leaning forward, Luke stubbed out his smoke, then reached for his hat. "You'll contact

Huckett and arrange for a quick wedding. In the meantime, I'll contact my lawyer."

"Agreed. And on Hannah and Edgar's wedding day you will hand over the deed to the disputed land."

"I'll hand over the deed when my sister is returned."

"I'll arrange to have the transfers take place simultaneously."

Luke stood, and the two men shook hands.

"I will expect Ginny to be treated as a guest in your home until the matter is fully resolved," Luke reminded him.

"You have my word on it."

The men shook hands again. Luke hated to admit it, but he was beginning to respect Hamilton Brewster.

But not much.

9

Luke was bone-tired. The ache in his lower back had reminded him of that as he rode back to the hacienda later that afternoon. After he left the Brewster place, he headed straight into town to talk to his attorney, Ben Jackson. The old lawyer had been surprised at Luke's request and had argued the wisdom of that decision. Luke could see that Ben thought he had clearly lost his mind and rightly so in view of what Luke was asking.

But the promise of a clear deed to the disputed land was the only sure trade Luke figured Hamilton would find acceptable in exchange for his niece's virginity. Luke winced as he admitted to himself that he'd been damn lucky to talk Brewster into that.

Ben found Luke's decision surprising, considering the intensity of the feud, but by the time Luke left Ben's office, Ben agreed to have the deed drawn up and ready for Luke's signature no later than Saturday.

As a matter of fact, Luke was relieved to have the matter between Brewster and himself settled. Hannah would marry Edgar, Luke would be free from responsibility, and the feud would finally be laid to rest.

He planned to sleep like a baby tonight.

Sliding off his horse, Luke tossed the reins over the rail in front of the house. For a moment he toyed with the idea of canceling supper with Ines, then changed his mind. He'd go, but he'd make it an early evening.

As he was striding toward the side entrance to his house, he heard hoofbeats fast approaching. A galloping horse was kicking up a thick cloud of dust as his rider reined him into the yard.

"Kincaid!" the man shouted.

Luke turned. "Yes?" Letting the screen swing shut, Luke walked to the edge of the veranda.

"Message from Brewster." The rider leaned down and handed Luke a folded piece of paper. "He says it's important. The old man's upset."

"Brewster?" Luke opened the note and scanned the message briefly:

You'd better get over here, Kincaid. We got trouble.
Hamilton Brewster.

"Damn," Luke muttered as he crumpled the note in his hand. "What's wrong now?' "

"Boss didn't say. He just said to ride over and get you."

"Tell Brewster I'll be there as soon as I can."

The cowboy spun his horse and rode out at a gallop as Luke stepped into the kitchen. Pots were bubbling on the stove, but Luisa was nowhere in sight.

Taking the steps two at a time he strode upstairs to his room. Pausing in the doorway, he caught the scent of Hannah's powder. He was surprised to feel an immediate reflex in his groin as he remembered the way she had responded to him the night before. She had been warm and giving—then hot and—

Slamming the door, he peeled off his shirt, leaving a trail of dusty clothes as he headed for the tub of hot water he knew Luisa would have waiting for him.

An hour later, Luke dismounted in front of the Brewster house, hoping he wouldn't run into Hannah. He wanted her out of his life and out of his mind.

At the sound of an approaching rider, Hamilton had stepped out of the house to meet Luke.

"What's the problem now?" Luke demanded.

"She's gone."

"Who's gone?" He was hoping Hamilton wasn't meaning Hannah was gone.

"Who do you think?" Hamilton bellowed.

Luke tensed, sensing that he wasn't going to like Brewster's answer. "I don't know, Hamilton. Why don't you tell me."

"Hannah Rose, that's who's gone!"

"Where the hell is she?"

"God knows! All I know is that after you left I had some book work to catch up on. When I finished, I went upstairs to talk to her, and she wasn't there."

"Are her things here?"

"Her suitcases are exactly where she left them. She didn't take a thing. Nary a thing."

Luke swore under his breath.

"You can forget that," Hamilton grumbled. "I've been cursing the girl for over an hour, and it hasn't changed a thing. She's still missing."

"Maybe she decided to go for a walk."

Hamilton drew a deep breath. "I don't think so —not after the way she bolted out of the room earlier. No," he shook his head grimly, "I think she's run away."

"Run away!"

"That's what I think. I think she's made up her mind she doesn't want to marry Edgar, so she took off out of here. You'll have to go after her."

"*Me?* Why me?"

"Because if it wasn't for you, Kincaid, my dyspepsia wouldn't be acting up." To prove his point Hamilton thumped on his chest and belched. Those blasted greens he'd had for dinner were turning on him. "Until the moment Hannah Rose

146

is married to Edgar and that deed is in my hand, we're still in a hell of a mess, boy."

Luke shifted his stance irritably. This was getting ridiculous. He was not going to wet-nurse the wench!

"It's going to be dark soon," Hamilton warned, glancing at the western sky. "We'll have to find her soon. Can't let her stay out all night by herself."

"I wouldn't begin to know what direction she headed in," Luke argued.

"I wouldn't either. The boys said a horse is missing, though."

"Does she know how to ride?"

"I doubt it."

Luke tossed the reins over his horse's neck and mounted again. "Have one of your men ride over to Emil Potter's and let Ines know I won't be coming for supper."

"Where're you going?"

Reining his horse around, Luke muttered through his clenched teeth, "To gather a thorny rose."

The sun was just beginning to set late Friday afternoon as Enrique's donkey cart wobbled down the middle of the road. The warm, golden rays spread a palatial carpet across the earth.

Spending the day with his *abuela,* grandmother, had been fun. The fishing had been good, and Enrique had several fine *pescados* for his mother to fry for supper.

He began to whistle a merry tune as he urged the donkey to move faster. It would be dark soon, and Enrique didn't like the dark. Big green eyes peered at him from behind the bushes when it was dark.

His whistling abruptly stopped and he slowed his donkey. Shading his eyes, Enrique peered at a small figure standing in the middle of the road, waving her arms at him.

Recognizing the pretty woman, Enrique drew back fearfully, his hand fumbling under the seat for the wooden cross his grandmother had given him earlier that afternoon.

He clamped his eyes shut tightly and his hand trembled as he thrust the cross out in front of him and prayed for protection. Enrique did not like the pretty woman anymore. The pretty woman was not nice, and he was afraid of her now.

Hannah waved frantically when she spotted Enrique, relieved to see that it was someone she knew in the cart approaching.

When she escaped from Uncle Hamilton's ranch the day before, she believed that the town couldn't be far away. When she'd ridden quite a while without coming to it, she gotten off to rest a while. But, of course, the horse had other ideas and immediately ran away. Then she walked all afternoon and evening. Finally, when she couldn't have taken another step, she curled up beneath a tree—and went to sleep.

After sunrise she washed her face in a cold

stream and began walking again. She managed to find a few berries to eat, but now she was so hungry that her stomach was aching.

Oh, *nothing* had worked out the way she'd planned. Absolutely *nothing.* She waved at Enrique more urgently now.

As if stumbling into Luke Kincaid's bed hadn't been bad enough, her Uncle Hamilton had thoroughly humiliated her. Well, enough was enough. She would not permit herself to be bargained away like a piece of worthless chattel. She was going back to Iowa and be done with this poppycock!

"Enrique," she called, jumping up and down in the middle of the road. "Yoooo-hooo!"

Trembling all over, Enrique squeezed his eyes shut tighter, trying to steady the cross before him to ward off the evil.

"Enrique!" Hannah called again as she began to run toward the cart.

Enrique opened his eyes and scrambled frantically to the back of his cart as she drew closer. *"Alto! Alto!"* he shouted desperately. But the pretty woman wasn't stopping!

Alto? Hannah's footsteps slowed. Now *why* would he be asking her if she sang alto?

Her feet began moving again. She didn't have time to sing! She barely had time to catch the stage before Uncle Hamilton and that horrible Luke Kincaid found her.

Enrique kissed the cross and placed it beneath

the seat. For some reason, it wasn't stopping the pretty woman. Frantically, he slapped the reins against the donkey's rump. *"Rápido,"* he shouted, *"más rápido!"*

When she realized Enrique was running away from her, Hannah's eyes widened in astonishment, and her heart thumped wildly. Would she be able to make this simple fellow understand where she wanted him to take her?

"Enrique! Stop!" Hannah demanded irritably, reaching out to catch the little donkey's bridle as the cart shot by her. "Where are you going!"

The cart rolled to a halt as Enrique cowered in his seat.

Shooting him an impatient look, Hannah snapped, "Where do you think you're going?"

Enrique grinned lamely and shrugged.

Hannah was in no mood for games. She was hot, tired, and thirsty, and she was certain that her feet had at least a hundred blisters on them.

"Enrique, now listen closely." She held the bridle tightly. "I need you to drive me to Tribulation. This is Friday, so the stage will be coming through again—am I right?" She could only hope he understood a trifle of what she was saying. "The *stageola?*" she said, trying to guess the Spanish equivalent. "Will there be a *stageola* today?"

"Sí," Enrique said, nodding his head submissively.

"Are we very far from Tribulation? Can we get there before the stage leaves?"

Enrique nodded again. *"Sí."*

"Good." She heaved a sigh of relief as she released the donkey's bridle and walked to the cart. "So you do understand what I'm saying."

She climbed into the cart, then paused as she saw dead fish lying on the floor. Wrinkling her nose in disgust, she lifted the stringer gingerly to inspect the smelly catch.

An ebullient grin spread across Enrique's face as it finally became clear to him what she wanted. *Ohhhh!* The pretty woman wanted to go *fishing!*

Well, Enrique had fished all day, but if the pretty woman who belonged to Mr. *Patrónee* wanted to go fishing, then Enrique would take her.

The stringer of fish went flying through the air as Enrique slapped the reins across the donkey's rear, and the cart lurched forward.

Landing with a thud on her backside, Hannah gripped the sides of the cart, seething as it wobbled erratically down the road.

Peon!

The sun was sinking quickly. Hannah kept turning to look over her shoulder as the cart bumped along. If she was lucky, she would make her escape and be halfway back to Iowa before her uncle realized where she'd gone.

The cart suddenly veered off the road and onto a grassy path.

Hannah held on to the sides of the cart and watched as the path became narrower and rougher. A few moments later a lazy stream came into view.

Crawling to her knees, Hannah peered at the stream, then back at Enrique. "How do we get across?" she asked anxiously.

Pulling the cart to a halt, Enrique reached back and handed her his fishing pole with a proud smile.

Hannah stared blankly at the cane pole he'd thrust into her hands.

"What is this?"

Enrique stared back at her, confused. *"Pescar."*

"Pescar?"

Enrique grinned, pointing toward the stream. *"Pescar!"*

Hannah's gaze followed the tip of his finger. *"Pescar* . . . fishing? You're taking me fishing?" Hannah closed her eyes in dismay.

Fishing. He thought she wanted to go *fishing!*

"I don't want to go *fishing!*" she wailed.

Suddenly the donkey's ears pricked up and he moved restlessly. Enrique turned around and looked in the direction from which they'd just come, and his eyebrows shot nearly to his hairline.

"What is it?" Hannah asked.

When Enrique's eyes grew larger with alarm, Hannah turned, hearing the sound of hoofbeats rapidly approaching. Following Enrique's gaze, she feared her own heart would stop when she saw a small band of Indians riding rapidly toward them.

Hannah and Enrique let out a scream at the same time.

"Vamanos!" Enrique shouted, urging his donkey to run.

The donkey, startled by the unexpected commotion, bolted forward, snapping Hannah's head backward. She bit her lip and tasted blood as the cart lurched forward. Grabbing the sides, she hung on tightly as the cart careened erratically across the meadow.

Glancing over her shoulder, she screamed as she saw the dark-skinned braves kick their ponies into a run. They gained on them quickly, overtaking the small cart effortlessly.

Enrique yelped and urged his donkey faster, faster! The little cart hurtled across a ditch, and Hannah tasted blood again as her teeth snapped down on her tongue. She felt the cart lurch and tip, and then she was screaming as she sailed through the air like a rag doll.

The breath was knocked out of her as she tumbled head over heels and slammed to a halt against the hard ground.

She heard Enrique yelp again, then the thudding of feet racing over the ground. She turned her head to see Enrique dart for the long row of scrub oaks lining the banks of the stream.

Sprawled helplessly on her back, her whole body in agony, Hannah lay trying to catch her breath. Staring at a brilliant blue sky, she wondered what she'd done to deserve such a day. If she lived through this—and she wasn't going to count heavily on that—she was definitely going to have to change her ways.

Struggling for breath, she moved her anguished gaze and found five savages astride their ponies poised in a circle around her. The fierce-looking braves made an imposing sight, clutching their rifles, their muscular bodies clad in soft breeches, gay feathers, bright paint, shiny bracelets, and earrings. Their hair was hanging in long lanks. Hannah groaned. *Please, God, for whatever I've done, I'm sorry. Truly sorry. Don't let me die like this. Not out here in the middle of nowhere in the dirt.*

The braves continued to stare at her with grave, expressionless black eyes.

Finally one spoke, and another one answered something back. Hannah couldn't understand what they were saying, but she knew they must be talking about her.

What were they planning to do? Kill her? She'd heard stories of what Indians did to people. To women. She shuddered and her stomach rolled.

Don't let me be sick, she prayed. But a moment later she retracted her request. If they were going to kill her, she had every right to make their job as unpleasant as she could.

The brave with the red feathers finally slid off his horse to land silently on the ground beside her. A moment later, the others followed.

Hannah managed to push herself to a sitting position, gasping as pain shot through her shoulder and hip. She blinked back tears and watched the braves close in on her.

Occasionally one murmured to the others and nodded. Pinpointing her with his dark eyes, the one who seemed to be in charge, the one wearing the red feather, seemed to speak directly to her.

She brought her finger to her chest nervously. "Me?"

He nodded again, motioning for her to stand.

She climbed slowly to her feet, her hands gripping the material of her torn skirt, groaning and almost falling as pain shot through her hip and shoulder. She lifted her chin defiantly and wished she could stand a little straighter. She was afraid to look at her elbow. The way it was hurting there couldn't be any skin left on it, and her leg wasn't much better.

The brave wearing the red feather reached out, and Hannah began easing away.

He gestured sharply, and she immediately froze.

His hand came out again. Closing her eyes, Hannah made herself stand perfectly still. *Maybe he's just curious,* she prayed.

Lifting a lock of her hair, the Indian let his gaze move over the tightly coiled strand admiringly. He tugged at it, and she whimpered. He tugged again, frowning, letting the curl spring back again and then again.

He made a brisk sign, and the other four men nodded and grunted their approval.

155

Hannah sensed that there was something about her hair that fascinated them.

The brave wearing the red feather suddenly grabbed her shoulders and spun her around. Hannah pressed her hands to her mouth, stifling a scream.

His hands went back to her hair again. Hannah cringed as the Indian wove his fingers in and out of the shiny ringlets, murmuring almost reverently.

Oh, dear Lord, before they kill me they're going to scalp me! My hair will be divided five ways and will be hanging from these men's belts by evening.

The leader removed the pins, and her hair tumbled in a riotous cloud down the center of her back. The four other braves began circling her, murmuring among themselves, occasionally reaching out to pull a strand and watch it spring back. It was obvious they'd never seen naturally curly hair and thought it very strange.

After what seemed like an eternity to Hannah, the five men gathered into a tight huddle. Their eyes darted back and forth to her as they talked, their leader's voice rising above the others.

A moment later, he walked toward her drawing a knife from a sheath strapped to his thigh.

Hannah closed her eyes in dread.

She tensed as she felt a brief yank on her hair. Opening her eyes a second later, she gasped as she saw a thick lock of her hair dangling between the Indian's fingers.

A second brave stepped forward, drawing his knife. Hannah drew back, crying out softly as a second hank of her hair came off.

Stunned, her hand came up to feel the right side of her head. Two large locks of hair were missing now.

Tears welled in her eyes as the third brave stepped forward, drawing his knife.

No longer was there any doubt in Hannah's mind. They were going to scalp her. Her curls would be hanging on their belt . . . she could only pray that they wouldn't kill her.

The sun was sinking low Friday afternoon as Luke's horse crested a small rise. Resting his hand on the saddle horn, his gaze scanned the valley below him.

Where in *hell* was the girl? He'd ridden all of last night and today and still had found no sign of Brewster's niece. It would be dark soon, and he would be forced to make camp for the night.

He tensed, suddenly sitting up straighter in the saddle. He shaded his eyes against the sun, and his gaze narrowed as he viewed the scene taking place below.

Brewster's niece stood in a circle of five Indian braves. Her hair tumbled loosely down her back. Her dress was torn, and dirt streaked her face and arms. Luke watched as one of the braves reached out, lifted a strand of hair, and with the flash of his knife, severed the long, curling lock.

Hannah stood paralyzed as each brave stepped forward systematically to claim his prize. Another snip, and another lock of hair was gone.

Swearing, Luke kneed his horse forward. At this rate, she'd be bald before he could get to her.

Tears rolled silently down Hannah's cheeks. Though she didn't want to marry Edgar, she didn't want him to see her this way.

Dead *and* bald.

The tears began rolling faster. Why hadn't she just stayed at Uncle Hamilton's? Why did she always have to do things her way? Why was she so stubborn? Suddenly, Hannah Huckett didn't sound so bad after all. She could have adjusted.

A sob tore through her as the fifth brave stepped forward. Stiffening, she saw a rider kicking up dust as he rode hellbent toward them.

Oh, dear Lord, she didn't have enough hair to supply another one!

As the horse drew near, Hannah's knees suddenly went weak as she recognized the rider. Luke. Lucas Kincaid!

Luke rode into the small group and reined to a stop a few paces away. He knew the braves. He'd grown up with two of them: Stalking Horse and He Who Rides With Darkness.

The braves stood quietly as Luke dismounted and walked toward them, his eyes scanning Hannah briefly. With the exception of her hair, she didn't appear to be harmed.

Luke paused before Stalking Horse, and the two men faced each other. Hannah listened as they exchanged a quiet greeting in Comanche.

Using sign language, Luke asked why Stalking Horse had captured a mosquito. Stalking Horse laughed and signed that the mosquito was fascinating. The mosquito's hair bounced.

Luke had suspected that Hannah's hair had attracted Stalking Horse. The Comanche were accustomed to seeing raven-black hair, but not hair that curled up tight and sprang back at a touch. They obviously planned to take samples back to the village. *"What do you plan to do with her?"* Luke signed.

"We will take her back to the village," Stalking Horse signed back.

Luke's gaze moved back to Hannah. She was crying, but for once she wasn't running off at the mouth. He could see that she was scared, and she should be. If Stalking Horse took her back to his village, she would be available to the brave who won her, or she would be made a slave for one of Stalking Horse's wives.

As tempting as that thought might be, Luke knew that he couldn't let it happen. As spoiled and pampered as she was, she'd never survive.

Shrugging aside his pride, he signed, *"This woman is mine."*

Stalking Horse lifted his brows. Luke could see that the brave questioned this. Luke Kincaid had never claimed any woman as his.

"She is my woman. She ran away, and I have come after her," he signed.

"Your woman has run away?" Stalking Horse signed with humor dancing in his dark eyes. *"You should beat her."*

"I plan to," Luke signed.

Stalking Horse looked back at Hannah. White Brother's woman was very beautiful, he thought. He envied White Brother's good fortune. Turning back to Luke, Stalking Horse signed, *"She's your woman. Bring woman to village, and Stalking Horse and White Brother celebrate good fortune."*

"I would like that, but I cannot," Luke returned. *"I must see to my White Father."* Luke knew Stalking Horse would understand responsibility to a parent. *"He is not well,"* Luke explained.

Stalking Horse nodded his understanding. Walking to his horse, he signaled the other braves to leave the crying woman to White Brother. The braves mounted their horses, and a moment later they rode off, each with a curling lock of hair tucked into his scalp belt.

Hannah sank to her knees, staring at the Indians as they rode away. Her gaze went bleakly to Luke, who stood a few feet away, calmly reaching inside his pocket for a cheroot.

"You knew those heathens?" she asked.

"They are my brothers."

"Your brothers!"

"My mother was Kiowa. When I was younger, I

160

left *Esperanza* to live with my mother's people."
He cupped a match against the wind. "Stalking
Horse and I are blood brothers."

"Stalking Horse?"

Luke's eyes raked over her irritably. "Where
the hell have you been?"

She straightened, her fear subsiding. She was
appalled to realize that she felt safe with him, but
she did. She couldn't remember ever feeling so
secure except with her brother Pike. And that se-
curity gave her the courage to stand up to him
again. "Running from you."

"Why did I ask?" he muttered.

Lifting the cheroot to his mouth, he studied her.
She was somewhat the worse for wear from her act
of defiance. Her dress was torn. Dirt and tears
streaked her face, and her hair looked as if the
dogs had chewed it on one side. The haughty
wench who'd awakened in his bed was gone, and
in her place stood a bedraggled waif, grateful to be
alive.

His gaze moved to the donkey, standing quietly,
still hitched to Enrique's overturned cart.
"Where's Enrique?"

"He ran away."

With a sigh, Luke held out his hand to her.
"Mount up. We're going home."

Hannah looked at Luke's hand a moment, then
hesitantly took hold of it. Home didn't sound so
bad now. She'd made her bid for freedom, and

she'd failed. She was doomed to marry Edgar Huckett.

As Luke pulled her to her feet, she wavered, her knees going weak as water. She closed her eyes against a sudden wave of dizziness. She was hungry, thirsty, and completely exhausted.

"How did you manage to get this far from the ranch?" Luke unbuckled his canteen and handed it to her.

"I walked," Hannah said, gratefully accepting the water. As she drank, the water splashed over her chin and down the front of her dress, but she didn't care. The tepid liquid tasted wonderful.

"Slow down. Too much at once will make you sick," he warned.

"I . . . I don't suppose you have something to eat, too?" she asked hopefully.

"No, but I'll shoot a snake or a rabbit for supper. It'll be dark soon. We'll make camp tonight, then ride back in the morning."

"Please . . . try to make it a rabbit . . . if you don't mind."

Snake wasn't her idea of edible food, but right now she'd chew the leather on his saddle if given the opportunity.

"Mr. Kincaid . . ." She reached out timidly, laying her hand on his arm as he was about to walk away. "Thank you. I . . . I really don't know what would have happened to me if you hadn't come along."

He glanced at her slender hand resting on his

arm, and his gaze lifted to hers. "You would be bald right about now, Miss Brewster."

Hannah could have sworn she saw a flicker of amusement in the depths of his dark eyes.

"Oh . . . yes, yes I would," she said softly. "Thank you again."

His eyes sobered, and he abruptly turned away. Sighing, she began to trail after him. "After they cut my hair . . . would they have killed me?"

"I doubt it."

"How do you know?"

"I just know."

Hannah wished he would talk to her more. The sound of his voice was somehow reassuring, but he didn't seem to be a man inclined to bother with small talk.

"I think they would have killed me."

"They wouldn't have killed you." He swung around to face her, his expression grim. "They would have taken you back to camp, and most likely you would have ended up as one of Stalking Horse's wives."

Hannah's eyes widened. *"One* of his wives." Her hands came to her hips. "How many wives does the man have?"

"Depends on how brave a warrior he is." He turned on his heel and started off.

"Well!" She began following him again. That didn't sound fair to her. She certainly wouldn't share her husband with any other woman. Her gaze followed the broad set of Luke's shoulders, and she suddenly wondered if he, being half-Indian, planned to choose his wives in the same manner as his blood brother Stalking Horse.

A painful prick of jealousy stung her, and she felt annoyed. She told herself that she didn't care if Luke Kincaid had five wives. It would take at least that many to put up with him. But then, she argued with herself, Luke couldn't *really* have five wives. That would be absurd. No woman in her right mind would put up with him!

"What did you say to make them let me go?"

Luke was silent so long that Hannah was beginning to wonder if he intended to answer her at all.

"I told them you were my woman," he said gruffly.

"Your woman!" She laughed, and he turned to glance over his shoulder at her.

"Don't laugh. You could be scraping buffalo hide right now, lady. If Stalking Horse had wanted to, you'd be riding belly down across the back of one of those ponies, and there wouldn't be a thing I could do about it."

Hannah's smile quickly faded. "I'm sorry . . . I really am grateful that you came along when you did."

"Yeah? Well, see that you keep it that way."

Luke mounted his horse, then leaned down to catch hold of her arm. He swung her up and set her behind him. Her arms circled his waist, and she leaned her cheek against his back and squeezed him. It felt so good to know he was

there, that he would take care of her no matter
how angry he was with her.

"No squeezing," he grumbled, feeling himself
immediately responding to her touch. It had been
an innocent hug, but Luke had decided that she
had a way of arousing him without trying.

Her grip loosened, but only slightly. "Sorry. No
squeezing."

They rode for a while, until Luke found a protected area near a small creek. Hannah went
down to the creek to wash while Luke started a
fire. She looked at her reflection in the water and
stifled a gasp. Her hair! One side was almost completely whacked off. It was . . . it was almost to
her chin! With trembling fingers she touched the
ragged pieces, then leaned over and bawled like a
baby.

When Hannah didn't return from the stream,
Luke went looking for her. She'd been gone for
over an hour, and he was beginning to wonder if
she'd run off again.

As he walked to the clearing he saw her sitting
beside the stream, crying. Luke felt himself tense.
He hated it when a woman cried. The tears and
the snuffles and the sobs made him skittish. He'd
sent Ginny to her room more than once until she
could get herself under control from one of those
womanly peculiarities, but he couldn't send Hannah to her room. She didn't have one.

"What's wrong now?" he asked as he stepped

through the clearing. He hoped with any luck at all she'd look up, dry her eyes, and deny that anything was wrong.

But she didn't. She looked up and started bawling harder. "My hair," she sobbed. "My hair!"

She'd been proud of her hair. It had been beautiful. Luke remembered how she'd brushed it for an hour the night they'd made love and then again the next morning. Now what was once her crowning glory hung in matted tangles down her back, except for the right side, which hung in ragged clumps at least six inches shorter.

He sighed as he walked over to squat down on his heels beside her. "Well, hell . . . it's not so bad," he lied. "At least you still have your scalp."

Hannah knew he was right. She should be thankful that she was still alive, but she felt so ugly. She leaned against him, and her tears fell faster.

She had wanted so much from life. She'd hoped for so much. Then her father had shipped her off to this godforsaken place like some piece of baggage to marry a man she'd never even met. A stranger who ran a funeral parlor! Then Luke had . . . had done those things to her . . . those terrible, wonderful, exciting things that she shamelessly kept thinking about every time he looked at her, but they had meant nothing to him. He had cheapened the memory of those wonderful moments by trading her off to her Uncle Hamilton for a stupid piece of land.

She sobbed raggedly. She couldn't even run away successfully! She couldn't do *anything* right!

Luke's arm tightened around her, and he drew her closer. She clung to him like a child, sobbing into his shirt as if her heart was breaking. He rubbed her back, the way he'd done with Ginny when she'd been a little girl. He had to admit that it felt good to hold her again. For a moment, he almost wished that she wasn't a Brewster. She was damned aggravating, no getting around that, but he had to admit that if she hadn't been Hamilton Brewster's niece, he might almost be tempted to tame her. Having a woman with her spirit in his bed . . . well, Luke could think of worse. "Look, I can cut your hair and make it look better," he said gently.

"How? They've cut all of it off!"

Tilting her face upwards, he studied the shorn locks.

The tears rolled again when she saw the frown on his handsome features. "It looks awful, doesn't it?"

"It'll be short, but I hear women are wearing their hair shorter now," he said soothingly.

She looked at him, a flicker of hope springing alive in her eyes. "You've heard that? Really?"

"Well . . . not really, but you may start one of those new styles that Ginny keeps talking about."

Sniffling, she watched as he drew out his knife. Studying her right side for a moment, he finally

167

raised the knife to make the first cut. Clamping her eyes shut, she vowed to keep quiet this time.

He made a clean slice, then drew back, recoiling as he looked at the large hunk of hair in his hand. He'd taken more than he'd intended, but there was no turning back now.

Drawing a deep breath, he tossed the lock aside then cut another hank, and then another.

Fifteen minutes later, the dirty deed was done.

"There, that should do it."

Relieved, Hannah finally summoned the courage to open her eyes. She viewed the mound of hair lying beside her. Lifting her gaze back to Luke, she asked, "Does it look better?"

"Yeah, looks fine now," he said, backing away. "Short . . . but fine."

10

Morning painted the sky with the soft footprints of silky clouds and colors of misty yellows and pinks as if some artist had spilled his pastels across the canvas of pale sky.

Hannah opened her eyes slowly, trying to orient herself. The invigorating aroma of coffee filled the air. Rolling to her side, she found Luke squatted on his heels, stirring the fire. *He has a nice, strong face*, she thought dreamily. The face of a man who knows who he is and where he's going. He was a strong man. She knew that instinctively. He would be strong in any matter he undertook in his life.

He had told her that his mother was Kiowa, so that would make him a half-breed. She'd heard unkind things said about half-breeds that had made her afraid, yet this man didn't make her afraid.

At least, not when she behaved herself.

She smiled. She sensed that Lucas Kincaid could be tender—tender and at a woman's mercy when a woman made love to him. She knew, and she cherished the knowledge that he had been at her mercy, at least once.

She noticed that he was gazing at something in the distance now. Intrigued by his preoccupation, her gaze followed his. On the horizon, a horse was silhouetted against the sun. A magnificent horse. As they watched, the animal reared on its hind legs and spun, racing up and down the ridge as if taunting the man who sat quietly observing him.

"Oh, he's beautiful," she breathed. "Who does he belong to?"

Luke's eyes never wavered. The stallion held him mesmerized. He had never wanted anything as badly as he wanted that horse.

"No one."

There was something different in Luke's voice. It was barely discernable, but she'd detected it.

"He's free?" She sat up and wrapped her arms around her knees.

"He is right now, but I plan to change that one of these days."

Hannah glanced from the horse to Luke, then back again. "Oh, no. He's too beautiful. He should belong to no one."

Luke tossed the remains of his coffee into the fire. "The horse is wild. He raids mares and tears down fences."

"Then why do you want him?"

170

Pouring himself a fresh cup of coffee, Luke fell quiet. Why did he want the horse? Was it the thrill of the chase or a true desire to own such an animal? "I'm not sure. I just know I'd give my eyeteeth to own him," he finally admitted.

Hannah watched the stallion prance on the horizon, his beautiful neck arched, his hooves dancing. "He shouldn't be owned by anyone," she murmured. "No one should be *owned.*"

Luke studied her. "What difference does it make to you what happens to the horse?"

Her gaze traveled back to the horizon. The sun was up now, and the horse's coat glistened in the morning rays. "Because he should be free if he wants. He shouldn't be imprisoned in a corral just because someone wants to own him."

Luke could tell by an undercurrent in her voice that she was comparing the horse's plight with her own. Her eyes had turned on Luke accusingly more than once this morning.

"Being captured may be the best thing for him. He'll be taken care of, fed, groomed. In the winter, he'll be warm and safe from irate ranchers who don't take lightly to him stealing their mares," he reminded her.

"Oh, pooh. That's not enough. The horse obviously relishes his freedom."

He handed her a cup of coffee. Their hands touched, and Hannah felt a shiver race up her spine.

"When you lived with the Indians, were you happy?"

Luke glanced away, his gaze returning to the horse. "I suppose so. It was my mother's life, and I wanted to know more about it."

"Why didn't you stay?"

"When my father took ill, I had to come back to run *Esperanza*."

"But you liked your mother's people?"

"Yes," he admitted. "I did." He had liked the freedom, the war games, the gaining of his manhood.

They sat watching the horse who stood at attention on the horizon. *At least Luke was given a choice of where he wanted to live,* she thought. She was not being given the same choice.

"I wonder what the horse is doing way out here?" Hannah didn't know exactly where they were, but it seemed very remote.

"I wouldn't know," Luke said absently. "I'm not sure what his range is. There's an old scar from a loose saddle on him, so someone owned him at one time. But he's elusive now. He comes down out of the mountains to raid the mares, then he's off again."

"Why does he need so many mares?"

Luke glanced up, smiling at her innocence. "He's building a harem, Miss Brewster."

She looked back at him. "Harem?"

Luke smiled. "A tally of mares to service."

Her cheeks colored. "Oh . . ." She dropped her

172

head and drank from her cup, nearly choking on the scalding liquid.

"Careful, it's hot."

"Thank you," she murmured, sipping more prudently now. "It's awfully early, isn't it?"

"Yes. Did you sleep well?"

"Better than the night before."

"Where did you sleep then?"

"Under a tree." She grimaced. "But I didn't sleep much. There were too many strange sounds." The night creatures had chirped and croaked and howled all night long.

"What happened to your horse?

"I'm not sure. He ran away," she admitted reluctantly. "I suppose my uncle will be worried when the horse comes back without me."

"I imagine he will."

"Well," she said with a sigh, "I guess I shouldn't have run away, but I was angry. It wasn't right for Uncle Ham to trade me off the way he did." She met Luke's gaze evenly. "And it wasn't right for you to suggest it."

"I didn't see any other way to handle it."

Wincing, Hannah threw the blanket aside to examine her feet. They were still puffy from the long walk, and multiple blisters dotted the bottoms of her soles. "I met Enrique on the road back into town and asked him to take me into Tribulation, but he misunderstood. He thought I wanted him to take me fishing."

Luke laughed out loud. "Fishing?"

173

Hannah's mouth firmed. She didn't find any of it amusing. "I don't know how he got such an idea, but that was apparently where we were heading when the Indians attacked us. He tried to outrun them, but the cart tipped over and threw us both out. I don't know where Enrique disappeared to, but the last I saw of him he was headed over the hill." She picked her cup up again and sipped her coffee thoughtfully. She'd forgotten all about Enrique. "I hope he's all right."

Luke chuckled again. "Enrique can take care of himself."

"I guess you'll be taking me back today?" Hannah still wished that they didn't have to return. Going back meant marrying Edgar Huckett, and though the marriage now seemed inevitable, she wasn't in any hurry to meet her fate.

"No, we'll rest today, then start back tomorrow." Luke knew that she was in no condition to start back, even though she would be riding. Her feet were a pitiful sight and it was obvious that when the cart tipped over she'd gotten quite a jolt. Every time she moved she groaned and muscles pulled in the fall made her walk bent over like an old woman.

"Thank you." She wriggled her toes with relief and winced when a muscle in her leg protested. Luke wasn't so bad. In addition to cutting her hair the night before, he'd doctored her feet and made some kind of ointment to dab on them from a plant he'd found near the creek. The medicine had stung and made her feet sticky, but this morning they didn't hurt quite so much. However, she still couldn't get her shoes on and walking was almost impossible. One whole side of her body was bruised and sore.

"Are you hungry?"

Feeling better, Hannah grinned. "I'm hungry. What's for breakfast?"

"You'll know as soon as I do." He winked at her, and she thought her pulse would hammer its way out of her throat. This was a side of him she hadn't seen before. He was actually being *nice* to her and she liked it. To her surprise, she was even beginning to like *him*.

"I'll go see what I can scare up." Luke rose, reaching for his hat. "Stay close, and don't let the fire go out."

"I'm not likely to go anywhere," Hannah conceded. "I'm just wondering if I'll ever walk again." She examined her feet and grimaced, then attempted to stretch out one leg. "Probably not."

"You're a pessimist, Miss Kincaid. Those feet will be as good as new in a few days."

"Maybe, but I'm not so sure about the rest of me," she murmured skeptically. She'd never been so sore and aching in her life. Not even when she fell off the barn roof when she was ten years old.

Hannah watched Luke as he walked over to his horse, saddled it, then rode off.

As the silence closed in around her, she suddenly felt alone again—not frightened, the way she'd felt when she'd spent the night alone beneath a tree—but alone. She found Luke's presence comforting. Though he didn't like her, though he considered her to be nothing but an annoying nuisance, she realized that he was all she had at the moment.

She realized too that it would feel strange, after she and Edgar married, to bump into Luke at church socials or Sunday picnics and remember the night they had shared together. Would he remember that night? She doubted it. He had probably shared many such nights with other women.

She sat for a moment, sipping the coffee; then, deciding that while Luke was gone she'd better see to her morning duties, she rose slowly. Leaning against a boulder, see cautiously tested her feet. Not too bad. Walking gingerly so her blisters wouldn't break again, and very carefully because each step made her muscles scream in protest, Hannah tiptoed into the edge of the scrub brush.

Afterward she explored a little, forcing her muscles to function by walking along the edge of the small stream. As she limped about, Hannah absently plucked at pieces of grass and the small yellow flowers that were delicately sprinkled in among the clumps.

As she approached a small clearing, she paused and listened. Her gaze followed the sound, and she caught her breath. The stallion was standing upwind at the edge of the water, drinking from the stream.

She held her breath, afraid she would frighten him away.

He lifted his head and looked at her, studying her for a moment.

"Easy, boy," she whispered, "easy."

His ears pricked forward as he listened, watching her.

"Easy, now . . . I won't hurt you." She spoke gently, praying that she wouldn't frighten him away.

He stood quietly, his muscles quivering, his ears twitching. He was so big, so extraordinary. He was absolutely the most beautiful animal she'd ever seen. He didn't appear to be afraid of her, but seemed to sense that she wouldn't hurt him.

"Would you like a taste of this?" she whispered, holding out the grass tentatively.

When he didn't move, she took a tentative step forward. He watched, his ears twitching with curiosity.

Hannah took another step, then another, the grass and flowers held out in both hands toward him. Two more steps and she would reach him. One more step.

The horse suddenly whirled, and trotted off.

Disappointed, Hannah watched him. He had been so close. So close!

Kneeling beside the stream, she washed her hands and face. Lifting the hem of her skirt, she patted her skin dry. A soft whinny made her whirl around. The horse was standing at the water's edge again.

"Well, hello. Did you decide to come back?"

Getting slowly to her feet, she limped toward him. Warm whuffs blew from his nose as he watched her approach.

"You shouldn't be so careless," she told him. "You must keep your distance from strangers. There are those who mean to catch you and put you in an old pen, and that would be terrible."

As if he understood her, the horse turned his head, exposing his neck to her. She longed to touch his shiny coat, but she knew he wouldn't permit her to come that close.

He turned again and looked at her, then to her surprise began walking toward her.

Standing perfectly still, she waited until he stood a few feet away from her.

His liquid brown eyes stared back at her curiously.

Extending her hand, she watched as his lips hesitantly extended to nibble the tender shoots of grass.

"That's right," she whispered. "I won't hurt you. You can trust me."

He whuffed again and she tensed, but he kept eating. In a moment the grass was gone, and he was nosing her hands for more. Laughing, she picked a few more clumps, and he ate them.

"I have to get back to the camp," she finally told him. "I hope we see each other again."

When she stepped back the stallion snorted, then wheeled and trotted off.

She watched until he had safely disappeared upstream, then turned and made her way as quickly as she could back to the camp. She'd just seated herself next to the fire when Luke arrived.

"I hope you found a rabbit?"

He nodded, holding up a nice, plump one.

"Want me to do anything?"

"Not a thing."

She watched as Luke carried the rabbit to the stream. Ten minutes later, he brought the dressed meat back to the fire. He thrust a stick through the meat and hung it over the flame. It wasn't long before the aroma of roasting meat filled the air.

It seemed to take forever for the rabbit to cook, but when it was finally done, Luke tore off a leg and handed it to her. "It's not fancy, but it's food."

"I could eat rocks," Hannah admitted, accepting the meat gratefully. "My father and brother wouldn't believe it if they saw me now."

"You have a brother?"

"Umhum." She took a bite and sighed. "Pike. We fight all the time."

Luke didn't find that hard to believe. Glancing toward the west, he poured himself another cup of coffee. "Looks like rain."

"Rain?" Hannah turned to follow his gaze. The sun was shining, and the sky was a cloudless blue. "When?"

"Not before morning."

"How do you know?"

"I just know."

"Oh . . . one of those obscure Indian powers I've heard about?" she said with a note of sarcasm.

He shook his head, quietly amused. "Yeah, strange powers."

"Well, I hope you're wrong." Hannah couldn't imagine anything worse than sitting in the rain, eating rabbit.

"I'll look around. There should be an overhang or a cave around somewhere. We'll take shelter there."

Hannah kept a close eye on the sky the rest of the day, hoping the rain would pass them by. They spent the time talking about their families, carefully avoiding the subject of their meeting, the land, the tradeoff, Hamilton Brewster, and Edgar Huckett.

Luke cooked another rabbit for lunch, and another for dinner. Hannah wished for some variety, but she wasn't about to complain. She hadn't been eating this well the day before.

At twilight, while Luke dozed by the fire, she returned to the stream, hoping for another glimpse of the horse.

Gathering blades of tender grass, Hannah realized the probability of seeing the horse again was slim. But when she rounded a small bend in the stream, there he stood at the pool, as if waiting for her.

Elated, she moved slowly toward him. "Well, hello, I see you're back again."

He stood very still, watching her.

Hannah approached with caution, pausing a few feet away and carefully extending her handful of grass.

He took if from her, munching the blades contentedly.

"You're very handsome, sir," she said, reaching out to stroke his long neck with her fingertips.

He started, then settled down and continued eating.

For over ten minutes, she fed him grass and he whuffed and stamped and ate. His flesh quivered at her touch, but he let her stroke him at will.

You aren't wild, are you? she thought smugly. *You're just like me. You don't want anyone telling you what to do.*

Well, don't worry. I won't tell Luke about our meetings.

Not ever.

Hannah was gone for over an hour before Luke began to wonder what had happened to her. Adding wood to the fire, he began walking in the direction of the stream, wondering what she could be up to.

At the stream he glanced up and down the bank, then headed upstream. As he approached a small clearing, he heard her talking to someone.

No—she wasn't talking. She was crooning a lullaby. To herself? *Surely not,* he thought as he walked softly toward the sound.

When he reached the row of scrub, he stopped and parted the tall underbrush. He swore softly when he saw what she was doing.

Not only was she humming to the horse, she was feeding him grass.

Luke watched with growing amazement as the stallion allowed her to touch him, stroke his neck, aa he ate from her hands like a foal, carefully lipping pieces of grass from her palm.

It was as if she had cast some mystical spell over the wild beast. Suddenly Hannah and the horse seemed to sense danger in the same instant. Hannah stepped back. The stallion wheeled, sent her one last look, then galloped off. Moments later he'd disappeared into the growing twilight.

Luke let the bushes drop back into place and returned silently to camp, amazed at what he'd seen.

Hannah entered the light of the campfire a few minutes later and sat down. Luke watched from the corner of his eye as she primly adjusted her blanket. He knew without a doubt that she was not going to mention the horse.

"Supper's about ready," he announced quietly.

"Good, I'm starved."

"I found some berries. They're late ones, but still good."

She smiled, absently accepting the handful Luke gave her.

"Where have you been?"

"Down by the stream."

"See anything interesting?"

She glanced up. She wasn't going to tell him about the horse. He'd want to capture it, and she didn't want that. "No."

His brows lifted. "No?"

She smiled. She was getting pretty good at fibbing. "No—why?"

"No reason. I just wondered if you'd spotted the horse again."

She studied the horizon as if searching for the horse. "He was pretty, wasn't he," she said, hoping he didn't ask any more questions.

Luke began to remove the rabbit from the spit. "You'd mention it if you did, wouldn't you?" He handed a leg of the rabbit to her.

"Of course I would. Immediately." She sighed, taking a bite out of the succulent meat.

Hannah slept like a log that night. The next morning they ate rabbit again, and Luke examined her feet. Even though she had been on them very little, they looked worse this morning.

She looked at Luke expectantly. "Are you taking me back today?"

"I don't know. We'll stay in camp this morning so you can walk around more and work out some of the muscle soreness enough for you to ride. Maybe by tomorrow your bruises will be better and the swelling in your feet will go down."

Smiling, she settled down on her blanket and went back to sleep.

When she awoke, the sun was up. Rising, she grimaced as she viewed her rumpled dress. She needed a bath, desperately.

"Do you think I could wash my dress in the stream?" she called to Luke who was lying near the fire, his hat pulled over his face.

"If you think you're a big enough girl to do that," he said wryly.

Shooting him a resentful look, she murmured. "Of course I'm big enough."

Luke smiled. It might be interesting to walk down to the stream with her. He had seen her in various ways—undressed and lying in his bed, crawling around naked on the floor with feathers sticking to her, perched prim and prissy on the seat of the buckboard whining about wrinkles and worrying whether her hair was perfect, and now sitting by the fire, barefoot and dirty, with greasy fingers and a greasy mouth. He had the damndest urge to take her in his arms and—*You're crazy, Kincaid!*

"Well, I suppose I'll go take a bath and wash my clothes."

When Luke didn't answer, she picked up the blanket and ambled off toward the stream.

As she approached the pool, Hannah glanced upstream anxiously. The horse was nowhere in sight this morning. And neither was anyone else. *Silly,* she chided herself. *As if there's anyone out*

184

here to see you. Just Luke, and he's not going to look at you.

She stripped off her dress and petticoats and pantalets, then stepped into the pool, dragging her clothing with her. The warm water felt heavenly. She quickly soaked her clothes and squeezed water through the individual pieces until most of the dust and grime had disappeared. A few of the stains would never leave. Of course, with all the tears and rips she'd never be able to wear it again anyway.

A wave of homesickness flooded her. How wonderful it would be to soak in a tub of hot, fragrant water with her sponge and lilac soap. To shampoo her hair over and over until it was squeaky clean, then step out into a warm, fluffy towel and sit by the fire in her soft, silken gown, brushing her hair until it dried—if she had any hair left! If she ever got back to Iowa, she'd never take those things for granted again.

After wringing out each article of clothing, she'd tossed it up on the bank Ducking beneath the water, she rinsed her hair as best she could, running her fingers through the tangled strands and massaging her scalp. It wasn't as effective as a hot bath and shampoo, but it was definitely better than nothing.

She finally climbed out of the pool and dried off on the blanket. Glancing in the direction of camp, she draped her clothes over tree limbs and bushes, hoping they would dry quickly. Then she tucked the blanket securely around her and walked back to camp.

Luke was stirring the fire as she approached. His eyes darkened with interest when he saw that she was wearing only the blanket.

Hannah hesitated at the look in his eyes, then moved to her place opposite him.

Luke returned his attention to the fire. Damn. Why hadn't he thought about her not having anything to change into? There was no way he was going to sit in camp all day with her half-undressed like that. Every time she moved, the blanket shifted lower, revealing the tantalizing swell of her breasts. Tossing the stick aside, he suddenly rose and strode over to his saddle.

Hannah watched as he dug into his saddle bag, then tossed a bundle toward her. "Here. Put this on."

When Hannah reached to catch the bundle, the blanket dipped lower.

Luke's gaze lingered there momentarily, then dropped away.

Blushing, Hannah held the blanket more tightly as she shook out what he had tossed her. It was a shirt.

"You won't need this?"

"Not as much as you do."

Her cheeks flamed again. "Thank you," she murmured, struggling to her feet.

She disappeared behind a bush and let the blanket drop to the ground, feeling quite shameless.

And yet, as she pulled the shirt over her head, she found herself hoping that he would peek.

He wouldn't, of course, but she hoped that he would. After all, he had taken her virginity, so it wasn't as if he hadn't seen her naked before. Why, according to the Good Book, they were almost like man and wife.

She rolled back the sleeves and buttoned the front of the shirt and then looked down to survey herself. Well, it didn't cover anything below her knees, but at least it was easier to control than the blanket.

She returned to the fire and sat down again. "This is better," she admitted.

It wasn't a hell of a lot better, Luke thought. The blanket wasn't falling off her, but she somehow managed to look very desirable even in a damned oversized shirt. She sat in the firelight combing her hair with her fingers, turning this way and that, her profile taunting him. He shifted uncomfortably. They were starting back this afternoon, he decided.

A low rumble of thunder made him glance up. He studied the horizon, frowning. The storm was moving in faster than he'd expected.

"The rain is getting closer," he said. "Can you smell it?"

Hannah sniffed. The air smelled musky and damp. "Yes, I can."

Luke nodded toward the small grove of scruffy trees. "Just behind those trees is a sandstone bank with a wide overhang. Looks like someone has camped there before. It's not large, but big enough for two people and our gear. I'll tie the horse close by. The stream cuts over that direction not too far, so we should be protected."

Hannah listened to another roll of thunder and shifted closer to the fire. It felt eerie sitting out in the open this way.

A long wavering wail rent the air, and Hannah shivered and glanced at Luke.

"What was that?"

"Coyote."

"Coyote? I thought they called at night." Hannah knew little about this uncivilized land, but she'd heard stories about the wild animals that roamed at night.

"Guess the storm has them stirred up."

Moving closer to the fire, she listened as an answering call came from another direction, followed by a series of yips and another long wail. Glancing at Luke, she moved closer to him, grateful he'd found her before the Indians could take her back to their village, or kill her. It would have been so easy for Luke to just leave her out there to her own devices. He could have told Uncle Hamilton that he hadn't been able to find her.

He would be rid of her, he'd get his sister back, the dispute would be settled. She'd caused him so much trouble that she really wouldn't have blamed him for considering it—yet somehow she knew that he would never have done that.

"Luke," she ventured hesitantly, "may I ask you a question?"

He lay down again, settling his hat over his face. "All right."

"You don't have to answer if you don't want."

"What's the question?"

She picked at a burr on the blanket, shy to meet his gaze. "That night . . ." She found another burr and worried with it. "That first night . . ."

"What about it?" he asked cautiously.

She leaned over, lifted his hat, and looked down at him. He looked back at her warily. "Is it always like that between a man and a woman?"

He relaxed, lowering the brim of his hat again. "Like what?"

Hannah sighed. "Like . . . well, you know. Though I have nothing to base it on, what happened seemed . . . very different."

She could see he was smiling now.

"Don't you dare laugh at me."

"I'm not laughing at you."

They sat in silence a moment. "Well?" she prompted.

"Well, what?"

"Was it different?"

"I suppose it was."

"You suppose? Don't you know?"

"It's not always like that. It should be, but it isn't."

Her nervousness eased. So what she'd felt *had* been special. And he'd felt it, too.

"Why isn't it always?"

"Damn, Hannah. I can't tell you why." He lifted his hat, cradled his head against his arms, and looked up at the sky. "I don't know. I guess some people just . . . fit together better than others."

"Like, maybe they're just made for each other?"

"I suppose," he murmured grudgingly. He didn't lie, and he wasn't going to start now.

Hannah studied him. He was long and lean and all man. She remembered waking beside him, remembered touching him. She wondered what he would do if she moved closer now and asked him to hold her again the way he'd done that night. Would he laugh at her? It would break her heart if he did. She might be spoiled and willful, but she could make him very happy if she set her mind to it.

A jarring clap of thunder suddenly brought them both to their feet. The clouds were dark and rolling now. In the distance a jagged streak of lightning forked across the horizon.

"It's moving in fast," Luke called as he kicked dirt on the fire. The wind sprang up, scattering the embers through the air. "Take my hat and get some water to pour on the fire."

Grabbing the hat he tossed her way, Hannah hurriedly limped to the stream.

Another streak of lightning seared across the sky as she knelt and filled the hat with water. Rising quickly, she turned and started back when her heart caught in her throat.

The stallion was standing beneath the trees, watching.

"Shooo, shoo, go away!" she called, glancing anxiously over her shoulder. "Go!"

But the horse continued to stand as if waiting for the tender shoots of grass he hoped she had.

Thunder rolled and streaks of lightning lit the sky as she ran toward the horse, waving her arms. "Go! You're in danger! If Luke sees you—"

But the words had barely left her when a rope snaked out, settling firmly around the stallion's neck.

Wild-eyed, the horse reared, trying to break free.

Screaming, Hannah whirled, furious when she saw Luke controlling the rope. "Luke Kincaid, you let him go!"

"Get out of the way," Luke yelled.

"No!" Hannah screamed. "You can't have him!"

Rushing him, arms flailing wildly, she pounded his back and tried to loosen his hold on the rope.

"Get out of the way, Hannah!" he shouted, pushing her back to safety.

The horse lunged and reared as the thunder rolled in earnest, sending jagged streaks of lightning to the ground. The sky opened and the rain came down in torrents.

Luke's hands slipped on the rope twice, but he continued to hold tight. The stallion reared and lunged again as Luke took a half hitch around the only fair-size tree around.

Crying out, Hannah scrambled to her feet and started toward him. "No, no!" she cried. "You can't do this to him." Sobbing, she cried out again. Her feet slipped and sent her sprawling helplessly to the ground.

Luke took his eyes off the horse for one instant to see if she was hurt, and, in that instant, the horse charged. In a flash of lightning, Luke went down beneath the stallion's hooves.

Screaming, Hannah watched as he rolled back and forth, trying to escape the slashing hooves. He got up once, but the horse charged sideways, knocking him back to the ground.

Hannah could hear herself screaming, but she was powerless to stop. The rain came in torrents and the lightning forked, striking the ground in loud bolts. Thunder split the sky apart as the horse came back a third time and struck Luke. He was going to kill him, there was no doubt in Hannah's mind.

Struggling to her feet, she ran at the horse, waving her arms, shouting.

Wild-eyed, the horse reared as she continued to shout and wave her arms frantically.

Suddenly the horse spun away, and she could hear him crashing wildly through the thicket as he ran off.

Weeping, she dropped to her knees and crawled to Luke. He lay bleeding and broken on the ground.

"Luke, oh, Luke . . ." She cradled his head tenderly against her breast and rocked back and forth, back and forth, sobbing. "Don't you dare die on me!"

11

—•◆❧◦ ◦❧◆•—

"Luke."

He wasn't moving. No matter what Hannah did, Luke didn't move.

Oh, God, what if he's dead, she thought. *Oh, please, don't let him be dead.*

There was blood on his face, his back, and on his side. Rolling him gently onto his back, she peeled away his torn shirt. Rain streamed into her eyes, and she brushed it away resentfully.

Along his hairline near his temple was a deep gash. She laid her ear against his chest and listened. When she detected a heartbeat a moment later, her eyelids sagged with relief.

Drawing a deep breath, she made herself think. Luke was unconscious and seriously hurt. She had to get him out of the rain, get him dry, and do what she could for him. But how? How could she

194

move him? He was so much bigger than she. Tears threatened again, but she fought them back.

Hannah, you're not to cry. For the first time in your life, you are going to do something to help another person.

This man cannot die. He just can't. And the only way he's going to live is for you to get your wits about you and do something to save him.

But what? What can I do? I don't know how to do anything!

First, you must get him to shelter. To the small cave he mentioned earlier.

She laid his head gently down on the ground and stood up, then limped quickly back to the campsite for a blanket.

Minutes later she returned and tucked the wool tenderly around him. The blanket was damp, but it would help shield him from the rain.

She leaned over to pat him on the cheek, then lurched up again and scurried off in search of the overhang Luke had mentioned.

She found it quickly. The overhang was large enough for two and, thank goodness, it was dry. The wood Luke had gathered earlier and left there was still dry, if she could just find a way to light it.

She stood for a moment, hands on her hips, thinking. How was she going to move him?

Scrambling back down the hillside, she ran to kneel beside him. "Luke," she called softly. "Luke, you have to wake up now."

"Luke," she said more loudly, patting his face, "you've got to wake up and help me. You're too heavy. I can't lift you."

His eyes remained closed.

Hannah refused to consider how serious his injuries might be. "All right," she said, "it looks like you're determined to be difficult." She rushed back to the camp and untied the horse, then she got the rope off Luke's saddle and the knife out of his scabbard. After what seemed like hours, she managed to saddle the horse and lead it back to him.

Working quickly, she tethered the horse to a limb, cut two holes in two corners of a blanket, and tied the rope through them.

Rolling Luke over onto the spread blanket, she looped the rope around the saddle horn, praying it was secure enough to hold.

"I hope you realize that I wouldn't do this for any other man," she muttered breathlessly.

A renewed sob caught in her throat as she looked at Luke. "Trading me away for a piece of land . . . that wasn't very nice of you," she scolded. He couldn't hear her, but talking to him kept her from crying. She'd cry once he was safe and talking to her again.

Rising, she coaxed the horse forward, watching to see that Luke remained on the blanket. The blanket eased across the wet ground, carrying Luke with it.

It seemed to take hours, but she finally guided

the horse to the cave entrance. The space wasn't high enough for the horse to enter, but she managed to maneuver the animal close enough so that she could painstakingly roll Luke inside.

She left him momentarily to unsaddle the horse and tie it to a nearby limb. "Stay there," she warned the animal. She knew they would be completely helpless if the horse decided to leave.

Picking up the corners of the blanket, she grunted, groaned, and strained as she dragged Luke's heavy bulk deeper under the overhang.

She ran back to their camp and gathered up the rest of the supplies. She was cold now and soaked to the skin, but fear was making her shiver as much as the elements. She was wishing she'd paid more attention to how Luke had started a fire.

She spied his saddlebags where she'd dropped them nearby, and she ran over and rummaged through the pockets. "Matches!" she cried out with joy when she discovered the little box wrapped in oilcloth. There were six matches left, so she knew she'd have to learn fast.

She rushed back to him and laid her ear against his chest once more to assure herself that he was still alive. He was, but his breathing was shallow and his face was an ashy gray. The gash on his forehead had stopped bleeding, but it looked bad. She pulled the wet blanket up closer around his neck. "Now, don't worry. I'll have a fire going very soon," she promised.

She stood and walked farther back into the recess. She was relieved to discover leaves and dried grass scattered about. After she had gathered all of the debris, there wasn't much of a pile, but it would have to do.

With grim determination she struck the first match and held it to the precious pile of tinder. The match flared and smoked, then sputtered out. With trembling fingers, she lit the second match. "Catch, you ninny!"

The dried grass began to smolder, then flare as the leaves caught. Murmuring her heartfelt thanks, Hannah fed the tiny flame with twigs, then small sticks, then larger pieces of wood until she had real flames going. Relaxing a little, she held her hands out to the fire.

So there. You're not so dumb, Hannah Brewster.
Remembering to protect the remaining matches, she wrapped them carefully and stuffed them back into the saddlebag.

When the fire was crackling, she eased Luke closer to the warmth. He groaned, and she realized that he must be in pain, but she had to get him dry.

Taking a deep breath, she began to unbutton his tattered shirt. "Now you listen to me, Luke Kincaid," she said softly. "Don't you dare die. I may not be all that experienced, but I know what we shared that night was wonderful—and you know it too. It it weren't for the fact that I'm a Brewster and you're a Kincaid, you'd be looking at me the way you look at other women." A sob caught in her throat. "Why, you might even be looking at me a lot differently once I prove to you that I'm not all that bad even if I am Hamilton's Brewster's niece. Honestly, this silly feud has been going on long enough. I don't see why *we* have to involve ourselves in something *we* never started in the first place."

She carefully removed his shirt and examined his cuts and scrapes. Bruises were purpling his skin, especially along his left side. She sat back on her heels, thinking. What if his ribs were broken? What if one of them had punctured a lung?

She could remember hearing her grandmother talk about the man who'd lived down the road from her having had a punctured lung.

The man had gotten pneumonia and died.

Well, *this* man wasn't going to die. She ran outside again and back to the stream where she'd left her clothes to dry. Snatching her petticoats from the bushes, she raced back to the cave.

An hour later she had Luke's ribcage firmly bandaged with strips she'd torn from her undergarments.

No, he *wasn't* going to die. *She* wouldn't let him.

The rain finally stopped late that afternoon. A watery sun parted the clouds about an hour before dusk. Hannah checked Luke for the hundredth time to make sure he was still breathing. She knew that when he woke up, he would need food, but she didn't know how to shoot game.

She dragged the saddlebags back to the fire and began laying out the contents. She'd never fired a gun and didn't know the first thing about loading one even if she could fire it, so hunting was out of the question.

When the bags were empty, she surveyed the bounty. A straight razor, a knife, and some string wound together.

Her gaze centered on the string. A fishing line! Maybe the stream was deep enough to have fish. She remembered that there was a safety pin pinned to her petticoat that she could use for a fish hook.

Fishing had been Pike's pastime, not hers, but she'd heard him talk about it so much that she thought she could do it. She hurried to the pool and peered into the muddy water, hoping to see fish. Oh! Her heart raced faster. There were some!

What could she use for bait, she wondered. Glancing around, she spied a woolly worm. Grimacing, she began to have second thoughts. Luke might not wake up for hours, and worms were so *squirmy*.

But the memory of Luke, lying so still and dependent upon her, lent her courage. When he awoke, he would need food, and she would have it for him.

She went to work fashioning a makeshift fishing pole out of a tree limb, a length of string, and the safety pin. When she was finished, she felt quite elated about her handiwork. Squaring her shoulders, she drew a deep breath and marched straight over and picked up the worm.

Getting the bait on the hook was every bit as revolting as she had thought it would be.

It squooshed and she gagged.

She apologized to the worm profusely, then jabbed the point of the safety pin through its middle again.

Squoosh, gag. *Squoosh,* gag.

Finally she got the worm onto her makeshift hook.

Kneeling beside the pool, she cast the line out into the water and waited. After a couple of minutes there was a tug on the line. Excited, she jerked, but the hook came up empty.

"Damnation," she muttered. The *worm* was gone!

It took a few minutes to find another one. Hannah knelt beside the pool again, tense, waiting for the first tug on the hook. She wasn't going to lose this worm. She tried to remember everything Pike had told her about fishing, wishing she'd listened more carefully.

When a fish nibbled this time, she waited. When it nibbled harder the next time, she jerked quickly, setting the hook.

Delighted, she flashed a quick grin when a fine fish flopped onto the bank.

"Ha!" she yelled. "No more *rabbit!*"

Deciding she needed at least one more fish for a meal, she hunted up another worm.

201

By the time she'd caught two fish, she was exhausted. The method seemed to be: catch the worms first, then catch the fish.

She decided that in the future if she saw something she could use as bait, she'd catch and keep it until she needed it. She walked back to the camp, proud of her accomplishment.

Remembering how Luke had cooked dinner over the fire before, Hannah returned to the original camp and retrieved the three sticks he had used to spit the rabbits. Now all she had to do was clean the fish.

Hannah poked up the fire, added wood, checked on Luke again, and went back to the stream. She tried to recall how Pike had cleaned his catch. As the procedure came slowly back to her, she felt sick again.

Holding her breath, she managed to behead and gut the fish. After rinsing her knife and the fish in the stream, she returned to the cave.

Spitting the fish on a stick, she balanced it gingerly over the fire. One of the blankets was dry now, and she tucked it around Luke, hoping to make him more comfortable.

By the time the fish were ready, Hannah lay with her head on Luke's chest, sound asleep.

It was morning when she woke. Lifting her head, she looked around her, feeling disoriented.

Luke moaned and shifted, but he continued to sleep.

The fire had burned dangerously low. By the time she added wood and ate one of the cold fish, she realized she would have to begin the struggle for food all over again.

Trailing down to the stream, she took her coffee cup to collect worms in. She wasn't going to spend the whole day searching for bait.

As she rounded the bend, her footsteps faltered. The stallion was staring at her from the bend in the stream.

"Go away," she said crossly. She was angry with the horse for what he had done to Luke. He'd be getting no more tender shoots of grass from her.

As if sensing her displeasure, the horse began to walk slowly toward her.

"Go away," she said again. "You nearly killed a man."

The stallion moved closer, his warm, liquid eyes looking almost humanly repentant.

Hannah stood still as he clopped to within a few feet of her and stopped.

The rope still dangled loosely around his neck, and there was fresh blood where it had cut into his flesh.

Feeling her resentment begin to thaw, Hannah stepped forward to loosen the rope. Gently she slipped it over his head. "I'm really mad at you, you know. You had no right to hurt Luke the way you did. We *all* want to be free, but we have to be civilized about it. Look at me. Do you think *I* want to marry Edgar Huckett?" She shook her head sadly. "But I'm not going to trample him to death just because I'd rather marry Luke Kincaid." She paused, then smiled softly. "I would, you know. I'd much rather marry Luke."

At this moment, Hannah knew the reason why: She was falling in love with a Kincaid. It was simply deplorable.

The horse seemed gentle now. He nuzzled the palm of her hand in search of a treat. With a sigh, Hannah patted the stallion's neck, realizing that someone must have owned him once. He was truly a magnificent animal, and she was beginning to see why Luke wanted him.

The day passed slowly. She caught three fish and placed them on the spit to cook later. The wood supply was dwindling, so around dusk she went in search of more. Hoping to find pieces that might be larger and dryer, she went off into the small grove of scrub trees, pausing to gather small twigs in the cradle of her shirt.

When she located several large boughs, she dragged them back to the cave one by one. By the time she had a sufficient pile, the sun had set and she was weary. The coyotes' wails began to waver across the desert, and she crept closer to the fire, huddling close to the warmth of Luke's feverish body.

Suddenly she was overwhelmed by everything and quietly began to sob. She knew that Luke might never wake up, and she would be left out here alone. Completely alone.

Though he was in a dark, seemingly endless void out of which he could not find his way, Luke tightened his arm around her, trying to ease her agony.

Sobbing harder, she drew closer to him, willing her strength into him. He couldn't die; he just couldn't.

It was close to midnight when Luke stirred, then slowly opened his eyes.

His head pounded like an anvil, and each breath he drew was agony. As he groaned, memories of the horse came rushing back, and he silently cursed his stupidity.

When he attempted to roll to his side, his stirring brought Hannah upright.

"Are you awake? Oh, thank God, you are!"

"How long have I been out?" he murmured.

"A long time." She crawled over him, reaching for the canteen.

"Damn . . ." Luke recalled the horse's thrashing hooves and he tried to focus on Hannah. "Are you all right?"

"I'm fine," she reassured him.

"Where's the horse?"

"Forget the horse," she snapped. Lifting his head gently, she allowed a few drops of water to dribble onto his tongue. "Drink slowly."

The water began to spill out more quickly

nearly strangling him. Quickly, he averted his face.

"Oh, I'm sorry . . . I'm sorry," she murmured. She took the hem of her shirt and patted his face dry. "Oh, you look terrible. You need a shave."

He looked at her sourly.

"Are you in pain?"

"I've felt better," he murmured. "Where's the horse?"

"Where would you be if someone had thrown a rope around your neck and tried to strangle you?"

Luke swore, letting his head drop back to the blanket. "He got away again."

She stood, and he caught a generous view of her bare legs. "Are you hungry? I've prepared fish."

"Fish?" He winced. "How did you get fish?"

She smiled proudly. "I caught them. All by myself. Isn't that wonderful?"

"Wonderful."

"Here. See if you can sit up a little and eat."

To move was torture. Luke knew that his ribs were either bruised or broken, and his arms felt as if they had been torn from their sockets. His head was spinning, but he finally managed to sit up. He weakly accepted the plate Hannah handed him.

"Is there any coffee?"

"Coffee?" Hannah hadn't thought about coffee. "No, but I can make some."

He heard her rummaging until she located the coffee pot. "How do you make it?" she asked.

"You don't know how to make coffee?"

"No, I don't know how to make coffee," she mimicked. She did have her limitations.

Luke moaned as he shifted, trying to set his plate on the ground. "Fill the pot with water and throw in a handful of coffee."

Hannah ran to the creek to get water and returned. "A handful? Doesn't that seem like an awful lot?"

"Not a whole handful," Luke said shortly. "About four fingers. Here. Like this."

When he reached for the coffee, he caught his breath and swore.

"You really have a dirty mouth," she reminded.

"I really don't want to hear about it."

"You'd better be nice to me."

"Why?"

"Because, in case you haven't noticed, you're at *my* mercy this time." She sent him a smug smile. "Now, eat your fish."

She pitched a gob of coffee into the pot, then set it on the fire.

By the time Luke had finished eating, the coffee was boiling. Hannah had to admit it smelled delicious.

"How did the fish taste?" She watched him hopefully.

"Like hell."

She glared at him. "Don't you ever speak in whole sentences?"

He lay back and caught his breath in agony.

"Miss Brewster, I'm not in the mood to argue with you."

"My name is Hannah, Mr. Kincaid."

A smile creased the corners of Luke's mouth as he lay back, closing his eyes. "And my name is Luke."

Moving back to the fire, Hannah poured a cup of coffee. She didn't want to argue either. She would much rather have a normal, civilized conversation with the man, instead of all this bickering.

"Here's your coffee, Luke." She handed the cup to him.

He accepted it. "Thank you, Hannah." He glanced up a moment later. "Aren't you having any?"

"When you're finished."

"When I'm finished?" His eyes watered as he tasted the vile brew. It was strong enough to drive a man to his knees.

"Yes."

"Why?"

"Because my cup has worms in it."

"Worms?"

"Fishing worms."

Luke shook his head. Damn. Fishing worms. Glancing down, he noticed that his ribs were wrapped. "Did you do this?"

"Not a bad job, huh?"

Luke lay back again, settling his hat over his face.

"You're not going to say anything?" she prompted.

"About what?"

"About the way I wrapped your ribs?"

Luke could hear the disappointment in her voice. It wasn't hard to detect. Well, he did have to admit she'd surprised him. She had provided him a warm fire, food, dry blankets, and he was still alive. The little chit was not only beautiful, she had a brain after all.

"You did well, Miss Brewster."

"Hannah."

Luke smiled lazily. "You did well, Hannah. Now dry up so I can sleep."

Hannah went to the pool early the next two mornings. She unrolled her fishing line, chose a juicy worm from her loaded cup, and threaded it on the hook without one word of apology.

She caught fish with concise efficiency, cleaned them like a wizard, and carried them back to the camp, along with a coffee pot full of water.

Luke was sitting up a little more each day. He watched her go about her business with growing admiration. Gone was the spoiled little brat. In her place was a woman of substance. But he noticed she was saying little to him these days.

Shoving the coffee pot over the fire the third night, Hannah prepared the fish and sprinkled on a little of the salt she'd found in the saddlebags.

Her continuing silence was beginning to wear on Luke's patience.

"Aren't you going to talk to me?"

"Why should I? You don't answer."

"Just because I don't yammer every waking moment—"

Her eyes snapped up, halting him. "Do I need to remind you that I could have left you out here to die? I didn't *have* to stay around and take care of you. I *could* have left you for the buzzards to munch on."

"No, you don't need to remind me. If you've told me once, you've told me *thirty* times how you've saved my worthless hide."

"Well, I did."

"Thank you!"

"You're welcome! And what do you mean by 'yammer'?"

He shrugged. "Most women yammer."

"Strange, for a single man you think you're quite an authority on women."

Luke grinned, settling back against his saddle. "I'm no authority. You're the one about to get married."

Hannah glanced up resentfully. She'd almost forgotten about Edgar. "Thanks to you."

"To me?" His gaze skimmed her lazily. She was still wearing his shirt, and it was still driving him crazy. She was a mighty fine looking woman, even if she was a Brewster. "I thought you already had your heart set on marrying dear old Edgar long before I entered the picture."

"Well, I didn't."

"You didn't."

"No, I didn't."

"You said you did."

"Well, I lied."

She turned, snatching up her dress. "I'm going to the stream to take a bath."

She walked out of the cave, leaving Luke to wonder why she had lied about wanting to marry Edgar Huckett.

Luke tried to sleep while she was gone, but he tossed fitfully, his mind taunting him with pictures of her swimming naked in the stream.

He wanted her again. The urge was so strong, it was a tangible ache now. At night, when she lay across from him, he could hear her breathing, and his need grew into agony. He had long ago given up trying to convince himself that his thoughts would lead to nothing but more trouble. He had even given up trying to convince himself that she was no different from any other woman. She was, and he knew it. What he didn't know was what he was going to do about it.

If he let things be, the feud would be settled. Hannah would marry Edgar, and his life would go on as usual. But would it? What he had shared with her had been different. Luke wasn't a fool. He had been with his share of women, but he'd forgotten all of them by the next morning. But Hannah Brewster was different.

"Will you do up my hooks?"

Luke opened his eyes to find Hannah standing before him, holding her dress in front of her. Her hair was damp from her bath, and Luke could smell the sweet scent of her skin, scrubbed pink and rosy.

"No," he said, beginning to edge away from her. She had a dangerous look in her eye, and it made him uneasy.

Hannah's heart hammered against her ribs. He was edging away, but he was looking at her with a look that was all wanting and warm. His tormented gaze assured her that she had not been the only one lying awake long into the night.

"Why not?" she prompted softly. "Are you a coward?"

"I don't think your Edgar would appreciate what I'm thinking."

"Maybe not, but I do."

"Hannah . . ." Luke groaned as she let the dress slip lower.

"If I have to marry Edgar, then I will. But right now, you can't make me go away, Luke Kincaid. I want you," she announced.

The dress fell away, and he groaned aloud. She stood before him, naked and beautiful. *Beautifully* naked. Her young body was perfectly formed, inviting a man's pleasure. And Luke knew the Eden awaiting him. He remembered only too well.

"A man doesn't take what belongs to another man," he countered in a voice that had gone deceptively husky.

"Then I must tell Edgar he owes you an apology." Her eyes met his solemnly. "After all, I was yours first."

Dropping to her knees, she laid her head on his bare chest, her eyes closing with bliss. It felt wonderful to lie against him and know that nothing could hurt her while he was near. "Please . . . don't make me go away. I don't understand what's happening. I just know that every time I look at you I get all weak inside. I know I shouldn't . . . I know it's shameful, but ever since that night you made love to me, my body has all these strange, wonderful longings that ache to be fulfilled." She lifted her eyes, searching his imploringly. "Oh, Luke, you want it, too. I can see it in your eyes every time you look at me. You want to feel all those wonderful, exciting things, too, and I would gladly give them to you."

The feelings she was describing were her weaknesses. For Luke they were basic, fundamental needs, needs that taunted him constantly.

"Hannah, don't do this," he pleaded raggedly. This was the last thing he had expected or wanted her to do.

"No."

Threading her fingers into his hair, she pulled

213

his face down and her mouth took his hungrily. "No!" she murmured, returning his kisses with an unrestrained urgency. "I won't go away, I won't."

Luke felt himself responding, then checked himself. If he took her again, it wouldn't be as easy to walk away this time. "Don't you see how crazy this is? You're going to ruin any chance you have of marrying Edgar, and your Uncle Hamilton will be furious if I go back on my word to hand over that deed—"

Her searching mouth cut off his words as he groaned, desire driving him near the edge.

He was falling in *love* with her—no, he *was* in love with her, dammit, and the sudden realization jolted him.

"I don't care . . . Uncle Hamilton won't have to know . . . no one will ever have to know," she murmured, her mouth refusing to leave his. Her hands skimmed his body, arousing him to a fever pitch.

Their mouths came together in a long, soul-searing kiss.

"But I'll know," Luke argued. His mouth moved to press heated kisses along her satin shoulder. "And I'll feel like a—"

He tensed as her hand became bold and searching. "Hannah . . . dammit!"

Their breathing was coming in short, labored gasps now. Luke could feel his control slipping.

"A woman shouldn't be doing this to a man unless—"

"Oh, hush. It's 1879, Luke! Women are changing."

He groaned as she moved on top of him, her mouth relentlessly devouring his.

"Am I hurting you? I don't want to hurt you," she whispered. She kept most of her weight to the side until he invited her to do otherwise. But that didn't take long. Her mouth softened and opened, completely accepting his. A bond was forming between them. Hannah felt it, and hoped that he soon would be caught in the same revelation.

His mouth dropped to her neck, his breath growing shallow as he prayed for sanity. Passion weakened him, and he hated the feeling of helplessness she could bring upon him, yet he wanted her with the same relentless passion that she felt for him. "You're killing me," he said.

"Good," she lifted her head momentarily and grinned, feeling the throbbing proof of his compliance hard against her. "I can assure you, it will be a most pleasurable death."

As he pulled her closer, her smile melted into one of ecstasy, and when he slipped inside her, the world and all of its problems disappeared. *Aw, hell . . . you're mine, Hannah Brewster,* Luke conceded silently as he rose up to assuage the dark, sweet ache building inside him. *And you always will be.*

Like it or not, a Kincaid had fallen in love with a Brewster.

12

Friday was a perfect day for a picnic. Kamen and Ginny romped through the meadow where the scent of heliotrope was pungent in the air.

When Kamen grew tired of games, he spread their blanket in the shade of an old willow tree, hoping that Ginny would be ready to dip into the large wicker basket Consuelo had packed earlier.

"Race you to the fence line," Ginny called.

"Ha! That's no race," Kamen said as he took off running after her.

Before she'd taken a dozen steps, Kamen caught Ginny around the waist and swung her up in a wide circle. Laughing gaily, they collapsed in a heap, trying to catch their breath.

"What do I win?" Kamen challenged.

"A flower." She picked a star violet and tucked it into the buttonhole of his shirt.

She gazed up at him, and his heart battered loudly against his ribs. "I was sort of hoping for more," he confessed.

"Ahhh." She reached out and pinched his cheek. "And what more would you be wantin', Kamen Brewster?"

Kamen grinned as he reached for her, but Ginny rolled to her side, bursting into giggles. "Oh, no, you don't! I've already given you a kiss!"

"Just a small one," Kamen complained.

"And one small one is all you get until after our picnic."

Kamen sighed and removed his hat to run his fingers through his hair. Since Ginny Kincaid had come into his life, he was a happy man.

"It's going to get hot," he noted, glancing up at a flawless sky.

"Umhum," she murmured, fanning her skirt a little.

Kamen's gaze returned to her. She was small and delicate like a hummingbird. He felt he should treat her like some of his mother's fine china that was kept behind glass in a special corner cabinet. Her laugh made him as happy as a Christmas morning, and her smile warmed him like August sunshine.

Funny how things worked out. When he first came to Texas, he expected to spend the summer with Uncle Hamilton herding cattle. Not in his wildest dreams had he expected to meet a girl like Ginny.

Virginia. Even her name was special. He smiled to himself. The first time he saw her, he knew she was the one for him. A man just had a feeling about those kinds of things, and he hadn't been wrong. He was hers, all right. Trouble was, he didn't know how he was going to keep her.

It wouldn't be long before Luke would be back with Hannah, and Kamen wasn't looking forward to that time. With the Brewster and Kincaid families feuding the way they were, Kamen knew that he and Ginny wouldn't be allowed to see each other again. He didn't think he could stand that, and he knew Ginny felt the same way.

Kamen reached down and squeezed her hand as Ginny sent a pleased look up at him.

Ginny was in love with Kamen, too. She thought about how handsome he was and how good he'd been to her since her arrival at the Brewster ranch. Why, he'd spent all his time just looking after her needs, and she guessed that in the beginning, that was why she'd liked him so much. He'd nearly worn his feet out running to the spring house to fetch her buttermilk.

Now, she was just plain in love with him, and she couldn't bear to think about going back to *Esperanza*. *Esperanza* meant hope, but Ginny sure didn't have much hope that Luke would understand how she'd let herself fall in love with a Brewster.

Luke would never let her marry Kamen, and all

because of a silly piece of land that didn't mean a wit to Kamen or to her.

"What are you thinking?"

Ginny smiled. "I was thinking I don't want to ever go home," she confessed. "I want to stay right here with you . . . for the rest of our lives."

"Yeah, I know," Kamen said. "I've been thinking the same about you." Taking her hand, he pulled her to her feet, and they began to stroll back to the old willow tree.

"They won't let us stay together. You know that, don't you?"

"I know." Ginny sighed. "Don't hardly seem fair."

"Nope, but I'm noticin' a lot of things don't seem fair, once you're a grown-up."

Ginny batted halfheartedly at the tops of the orange coneflowers as they walked along. "I guess I just don't understand what all the fuss is about, do you? Seems to me that we've got plenty of water on the south range. I've heard Luke say so himself, but Papa just keeps insisting that we need that land, and that no Kincaid is going to kowtow to a Brewster."

"My uncle says the same thing. The men in the bunkhouse say the feud's just a case of old men's pride and bullheadedness. Thatcher Kincaid and Hamilton Brewster are only continuing a spat their grandfathers had over ninety years ago!"

"Well, I say it's twaddle," Ginny sniffed. "Plain old twaddle."

"I'd say that too." Only Kamen wasn't right sure what twaddle meant. But if Ginny thought the feud was twaddle, he did, too.

Ginny smiled, angling him another look. "Of course, if my father and your Uncle Brewster hadn't been feuding about the land, we'd have never met."

Her smile tied Kamen in knots. "Guess we wouldn't at that," he agreed.

When they reached the blanket, Ginny spread her flowers over one corner. "Are you hungry?"

"Sure am."

Ginny began to set out the meat pies, a small jar of pickles, some fruit, and sugar cookies.

"Ginny."

She glanced up. "Yes?"

"No matter what happens, I'm gonna tell Uncle Hamilton I'm takin' you to the fiesta in a couple of weeks, whether he likes it or not."

Her face brightened with a radiant smile. "You are? You'd do that for me—stand up to your uncle that way?"

"You bet I would."

The whole town always turned out for the fiesta. The citizens of Tribulation considered it a celebration of another year endured in the harsh west Texas–Mexico border country. The fiesta was a good excuse for everyone to get together and have a good time. Ranchers, their families, and their employees from miles around rode in for the day-long festivities and dance that evening. It was often dawn before the celebration ended.

"Ginny."

"Yes," she answered softly.

Kamen leaned toward her, brushing a tentative kiss across her lips. When she laid her hand invitingly on his shoulder, he moved closer, taking her gently in his arms. They kissed, their innocence making the embrace all the more fresh and exciting.

"Ginny."

"Yes, Kamen." Ginny grinned back at him. He seemed so shy at times that it endeared him even more to her.

"Will you be my girl?"

Ginny nodded and kissed him longer this time.

Being kidnapped hadn't turned out to be so bad after all. If she hadn't been kidnapped, she'd never have met Kamen, and meeting Kamen had been the best thing that had ever happened to her. The very, very best.

They shared the picnic, as well as occasional kisses between bites; then they waded into the stream and splashed one another like children.

Later, they lay on the blanket, and Kamen's hands grew bolder, but Ginny didn't discourage him. The feelings he brought alive frightened her a little, but they excited her, too.

As the sun turned into a round, orange ball in the west, they began walking back to the ranch. They'd be missed before too long.

"Wouldn't it be funny if your brother Luke fell in love with my cousin Hannah?" Kamen pondered thoughtfully.

"Oh, Kamen." Ginny's laughter tinkled over the meadow. "Luke fall in love with a Brewster? You're so funny."

"Well, it could happen. We fell in love, didn't we? Luke's out looking for Hannah right now, and once he finds her, why, it might be a few days' ride back to the ranch, and, well, my cousin Hannah—she's not bad—for a girl."

"Oh?" Ginny stopped, her hands coming to her hips. "For a girl?"

"Course," Kamen said, ruffling her hair playfully, "she can't hold a candle to you."

"Course not." Ginny leaned over and kissed him again. "But then, what Brewster could?"

Hannah whimpered, then collapsed against Luke. They lay tangled in each other's arms, spent from desire. Thunder rumbled outside the small cave, but the storm, for the moment, was over inside.

"Lord, woman. What am I going to do with you?" Luke grinned up at her. "You're a lusty little wench."

Hannah frowned, wrinkling her nose at him. "I know . . . do you suppose I might be turning into a hussy?"

Luke chuckled, drawing her back to him. *"Turning* into one?"

"Oh, you!" She pulled away, slapping at him when she saw that he was laughing at her. He'd teased her unmercifully about her 'yens.'

They had made love so many times in the past three days. Judging by his performance, Hannah knew that Luke was well on the mend, yet he hadn't mentioned starting back. She couldn't help wondering why, though she would be content to stay here with him forever.

Lying on their backs, they gazed at the firelight dancing on the cave walls. They talked, as they had for the past few days, about their lives before they'd met.

Hannah could lie for hours and listen to the sound of Luke's voice. It was deep and masculine with a rich, full timbre. He told her stories of his mother's people, stories that both fascinated and saddened her. She learned that he had taken a wife when he was fifteen, but the young Indian maid had died during the cold, hard winter.

"I guess you loved Morning Sunrise a lot," Hannah whispered. She was ashamed to feel so jealous of a woman who was dead now, but she did. She resented anyone who had lain in this man's arms and shared the intimacy they had just shared.

"We were just kids," Luke said quietly, "but a man's first love is hard to forget."

Hannah rolled onto her side, facing him. Her fingertips lovingly traced his strong profile. He had not once told her that he loved her, but she knew that he did. She could see it in his eyes and hear it in his voice when he was holding her in his arms and making love to her. "But a man's deepest love is his last," she prompted softly.

He caught her hand, and their eyes met in the firelight. The bond was there, strong and compelling, but their love was forbidden. A Kincaid could never marry a Brewster. Thatcher Kincaid and Hamilton Brewster would fight such a union with their dying breath.

"I have to take you back, Hannah."

"Oh, Luke . . ."

Hannah could see the answer to her silent plea reflected in Luke's eyes. "I gave my word to your uncle," he said softly.

"Isn't there some way you could let me go . . ." Her voice trailed off meekly when she saw his eyes darken with pain. "I'm as much to blame as you are for the mistake. If you'll let me go, I'll return to Iowa and . . . and I promise I'll never come back here again if only you and Uncle Hamilton won't make me marry Edgar. No one would ever have to know that you and I made love—"

Luke's hand closed over her mouth. "Hannah, don't. I can't let you go back to Iowa." Luke was torn. The thought of Hannah's belonging to another man sickened him, but hē had been taught by white man and Comanche alike that a man's word was his honor. His word had been given. He couldn't retract it now.

"This . . . the past few days have meant nothing?" she asked brokenly. She knew he had resented her at first, but the past few days—well, they had been different. Though he had been kind and good to her, he still refused to talk about the future. She didn't know what he was thinking, and that frustrated her.

"How can you ask such a question?" His eyes sobered as his hand slipped to her stomach to caress her bare flesh gently. He knew that it would be a miracle if she wasn't carrying his child. He had taken no precautions to prevent her from conceiving. "Are you still feeling all right?"

"Yes."

He leveled his gaze on her sternly. "Are you?"

Even if there had been signs that she was carrying his child, Hannah would have died before telling him. As far as she was concerned, if she were with child and he intended to stand by quietly while she was forced to marry Edgar, then he could just wonder for the rest of his life if the child was his.

Disappointment welled in her eyes as they gazed at each another. She prayed that he would tell her to stop looking at him that way. She ached for him to tell her that he loved her and that he'd put an end to the senseless feud. She longed to hear him say that they'd defy their families and make their own world.

But he said no such thing.

Instead, he merely said, "If I knew a way to solve this, I would. I just don't have any answers."

Rolling to her side, she stuffed a corner of the

blanket into her mouth to keep from crying. Biting down hard, she could feel her tears begin to roll down her cheeks, but she refused to let him see them.

She wasn't sure how she was going to live without him, but she would. It seemed to her she had no other choice.

The next morning Hannah was up long before the sun. After she'd caught her daily fish, she returned to the cave.

Luke was awake and waiting for her.

"I wondered where you were."

"Fishing." She held up her catch. "If we're starting back today, we'll need a hot meal."

Luke reached for his shirt and slipped it on. "I don't suppose you've seen the stallion?"

"I don't suppose I have." She put the fish on the spit, then stirred the fire.

Luke stood, tucking his shirttail into his pants. "He's probably twenty miles from here by now." He tried to draw a deep breath and winced when it caught midway.

"Are your ribs still sore?"

He glanced at her and winked gravely. "I think you've cracked another one."

"Very funny."

His brows lifted. "Are you mad at me again?"

She ignored his question, turning to hang the coffee pot over the fire.

"Hey, look at me."

Reluctantly, Hannah lifted her gaze.

"I don't want it this way," he said softly.

"Then change it."

"I can't change ninety years of hatred. Can't you understand that? My father is ill; your uncle is old —damn, Hannah, can't you see what I'm facing?"

"No."

"You're being stubborn," he said patiently.

"I am not. Somebody has to put a stop to this silly feud, and you should at least be trying."

"Me? How can I stop it? I've tried for years to convince Thatcher to give it up, but he refuses. If I walk in and tell him I'm in love with Hamilton Brewster's niece and—"

"You are?" Hannah interrupted.

Luke's brows rose again. "What?"

"You *are?*"

"*Are* what?"

"*Are* you in love with Hamilton Brewster's niece?"

Their eyes met and held.

"Tell me that you're not in love with me, Luke Kincaid," she demanded softly.

"You know that I can't tell you that."

Her gaze softened, and she ached to go to him. "Then tell me that you are in love with me."

"I won't tell you that. It would only make it harder for both of us."

"Oh, Luke"—she drew a ragged breath—"how can you let me marry Edgar Huckett when it's you I love?" She hadn't meant to make that confession,

227

but it was out now, and she didn't care. "Do you even know Edgar?"

"I've met him."

"Do you want me to spend my life with this man?"

Luke's eyes darkened, and she could see a muscle working tightly in his jaw. "No."

"Then, please," she whispered, "even if we can't be together, do *something* to help me."

They broke camp late that morning. Luke eased slowly onto his horse, then leaned over to offer Hannah a hand up.

"Wait a minute," she said.

Luke glanced up at the darkening sky. "We should be on our way. Rain will be moving in by night."

"So"—she shrugged—"we'll get wet."

Luke grinned at her. "You've sure changed from the prissy little nuisance you were a week ago."

She turned and disappeared into the thicket. Luke heard her rummaging around noisily as he reached into his pocket for a smoke. His face sobered as he thought of what lay ahead. He couldn't give her up without a fight. He knew that now.

A few minutes later she returned, leading the stallion.

The cheroot in Luke's mouth sagged as she stoically handed him the lead rope. "Here's your horse, Kincaid. I hope you treat him better than you treat your women."

Stunned, Luke stared at the horse. The magnificent animal's eyes were wide as it danced skittishly on the lead rope, but it apparently was going to allow itself to be led back to the ranch.

"My God . . . how did you capture him?"

Swinging into the saddle behind him, she adjusted her skirt over her bare legs. "It was simple. He loves me."

Luke turned to look over his shoulder at her.

"And when someone loves you that much, Mr. Kincaid," she said, meeting his cynical gaze calmly, "you're *supposed* to love them back."

13

Luke's horse topped the rise overlooking *Esperanza* late Sunday afternoon. Smoke curled lazily from the stacks of the *hacienda* as the ranch hands went efficiently about their work.

Removing his hat, Luke gazed at his home, aware that it was the first time in his life that he had not been eager to return to it.

"Well, there it is."

"Yes, there it is." Wistfulness filled Hannah's voice as she gazed at the peaceful scene below her. It seemed as though a hundred years had passed since Enrique brought her to *Esperanza* by mistake.

"Will you be taking me to Uncle Hamilton's right away?"

Luke settled his hat back on his head. "Not yet."

"Not yet?" She grinned. "I suppose it's because you can't stand the thought of losing me?"

"No, because the stallion likes you better than me." He leaned back, gave her a kiss, caressed her bare leg suggestively, then kneed the horse back into a canter.

Sighing, Hannah closed her eyes and squeezed him around the waist tightly.

He tensed, catching his breath painfully. "No squeezing."

"Oh . . . of course. No squeezing." Only this time she knew that his reluctance was only because of his sore ribs.

Pedro was waiting to meet them as they rode into the courtyard. *"Compadre!"* he called. "We have been *muy inquieto!"*

"Why would you be worried?" Luke grinned as he helped Hannah slide down from the horse before he gingerly swung out of the saddle.

With one hand protecting his side, Luke exchanged a poignant look with Hannah. *"Amigo,"* he said to Pedro, "this is the lovely Miss Hannah Brewster."

Noting the bittersweet look that Luke and Hannah exchanged, Pedro began to frown. *"Sí. . . . Buenos días, señorita."*

Luke handed Pedro the lead rope to the stallion. "Pedro, feed and water the horses, but watch this one carefully."

"Could it be, *señor?"* Pedro's voice was filled with awe. "Is this the wild stallion who dances in the moonlight and steals our mares?"

231

Luke nodded, acknowledging the legend that had been growing about the chestnut stallion.

"We have been concerned, *señor*. You are *no muy bien?*" Pedro asked.

"I'm all right. Just a few bruised ribs."

Pedro glanced at Luke, then back to the stallion. "So you have captured the wild stallion?"

"Yes, you'd better get a bridle on him."

Hannah could see that Pedro was reluctant to handle the animal. The horse was edgy, prancing and pulling at the lead rope.

"I'll do it," Hannah offered, afraid someone would get hurt.

"Muchas gracias, señorita," Pedro returned, swinging the large gate open. Smiling at Luke, Hannah stepped around the two men. They watched as the horse danced behind Hannah into the corral, wary of everyone but her.

Looping his arms over the top rail of the fence, Luke watched Hannah handle the stallion. It was unbelievable. A dozen men had tried to entrap the horse, and the horse had run for his life. But a tiny shave of a girl had walked up to the stallion, looked him straight in the eye, and he had fallen in love with her. Perhaps in some way the horse sensed Hannah had no desire to harm him. Perhaps it was her gentleness that had won him over. Whatever the reason, Hannah Brewster was the only human who had been able to tame his wildness. Affection creased the corners of Luke's eyes as he watched Hannah speak softly to the horse.

What are you laughing at, Kincaid? She's tamed you, too, he thought.

Pedro brought the bridle, and Hannah slipped it over the stallion's head. He shied and pranced nervously, but she spoke to him in low, persuasive tones and convinced him again she would not harm him. When she slipped the bridle over his head this time, he accepted it but still tossed his head.

Removing the rope from around the stallion's neck, Hannah handed it to Pedro. The little Mexican had brought a bucket of oats, which he dumped into a trough. Grasping the bridle, Hannah led the horse to it. After a few tentative sniffs, he began to eat, all the while keeping a wary eye on the men watching him while Hannah continued to speak softly to him.

Luke straightened, his hand coming back to shield his ribcage. "Pedro, I want you to send somebody over to Brewster's ranch. Tell Hamilton that I'm back and that Hannah is with me."

"*Sí . . . señor,* Brewster will be most anxious to know when his niece will be returned."

"Tell Hamilton that Hannah is exhausted from the long ride." Luke's gaze moved back to meet Hannah's. "Miss Brewster will be resting here at *Esperanza* for a few days."

"*Sí.*"

"Pick up Miss Brewster's valises while you're there."

"*Sí.*" Pedro eyed Hannah, feeling somewhat

233

confused. "Miss Brewster will be staying for a long while?"

Luke and Hannah exchanged another long look. "Just pick up the valises."

"*Sí* . . . I will send someone right away."

Hannah handed the reins to Pedro, who took them gingerly. Luke and Hannah turned, walking arm in arm to the back door.

"Luke," Hannah lifted her eyes to him. "You know as well as I do, I can't stay here. Uncle Hamilton will never permit it."

"I know he won't."

"Then what are you thinking?"

"Nothing. That's the point. I need a few days to think."

Even with all they'd shared, Hannah didn't dare hope that Luke was seriously considering backing out of his agreement. Yet she couldn't help feeling a glimmer of hope when he looked at her.

She knew as well as Luke what the ramifications would be if he dared to claim her. The feud would only deepen and lead to more disorder. But, oh, how she wished he would fight for her!

As they entered the kitchen, they found Luisa busy rolling out tortillas.

"Oh, *madre de Dios!*" Luisa murmured. She dropped the rolling pin, and rushed to the odd couple. "Where have you been?"

"Picking thorny roses," Luke said dryly.

Luisa's gaze swept to Hannah, who looked at least as bedraggled as Luke if not worse. *"Mio*

234

Dios, you look as if you've fought a war." Her worried eyes returned to Luke. "What happened to you, *señor?*"

"I had a little disagreement with a horse."

"Sí." Luisa stood with her hands on her hips, shaking her head woefully as she surveyed Luke. "The *caballo* won."

"Sí. What's to eat?" Luke sank into the nearest chair, drawing a deep breath as he eased his boots off.

Luisa's gaze returned to Hannah. "And what about you? The horse did not harm you?"

Reaching out, Luke drew Hannah onto his lap. "Strangely enough, the horse likes her."

Hannah felt Luisa's questioning gaze, but she was too weary to worry about what the housekeeper was thinking. The past few days had been dreadful. All she wanted now was a hot bath, fresh clothes, and a soft bed. She planned to sleep for days.

"Food," Luisa murmured. "What you both need is a hot meal."

"Thanks . . . oh, and Luisa?" Luke added, his eyes never leaving Hannah's.

"Sí?"

"Miss Brewster needs a large glass of milk." Luke studied Hannah closely. If she was carrying his baby, she was going to take care of herself. The smudges of fatigue under her eyes worried him. She looked as though she'd lost weight during the past week.

Wrinkling her nose with distaste, Hannah slid off his lap to help Luisa. "Luke, I hate milk."

"You'll drink it anyway."

Luisa charitably brushed aside Hannah's offer to help. "Sit down, sit down. No one is allowed in Luisa's kitchen unless Luisa says so."

"Oh . . . all right," Hannah murmured, dropping onto a chair again. She looked at Luke, and he winked at her.

"Where have the two of you been?" Luisa asked, unable to contain her curiosity any longer.

"Shortly after I located Hannah, I had a little run-in with the stallion, and we had to lay up for a few days."

"I see," Luisa said, cracking eggs into a skillet.

At the tone of disapproval in Luisa's voice, Luke winked at Hannah again.

"You were a *caballero* with Miss Brewster?"

Luke winked again. *"Sí,* I was a gentleman."

Hannah caught his eye and mouthed a silent *"Sí?"*

"Sí."

Noting the playful exchange, Luisa paused and Luke's face sobered immediately and he asked quietly, "Do you think you could get someone to haul in enough water for two hot baths? We're both in need of one. Pedro's sending someone over to the Brewster ranch to get her valises, but I want you to scout up something for Hannah to wear until he gets back."

Luisa slowly turned back to the stove. "Miss

236

Brewster will not be returning to her uncle's home?"

"Not immediately."

Luisa murmured something, crossed herself, then calmly flipped the eggs. "I will take care of your *chiquita*, Lucas."

"Thank you, Luisa."

"Your *padre* has been asking about you."

Luke sighed. "What have you told him?"

"That you have been very busy, but the excuse is becoming old."

"I'll go to him after I've eaten and cleaned up."

Luisa set the plates of food in front of them.

Both Luke and Hannah dug into the fare with relish. It was the first real food they had had in days. By the time they finished, wooden tubs were already being hauled upstairs and filled with hot water.

"After your bath, I want you to lie down and rest," Luke said quietly.

The idea sounded heavenly. Laying her hand on his, Hannah smiled. "Only if you promise to do the same."

Their eyes met and were reluctant to part. "You know we can't be together for a while," he said.

Living in the same house with her, yet not touching her would be a penance Luke dreaded. But he could not blatantly flaunt a Brewster in Thatcher Kincaid's home.

"I know we can't."

237

His hand closed over hers. "It doesn't mean that I won't be thinking of you."

"I know that, too." She felt bad that he would be the one who had to face her uncle's and his father's wrath.

"The next few days won't be easy." Luke had no idea how Hamilton would take the news that Luke had fallen in love with his niece. He knew how Thatcher would take the news. And there was Ines . . . she would have to be told. And Brewster was probably creating a holy row.

Luke and Hannah began to climb the stairs, arm in arm. "Will you speak with your father soon?"

"Yes. He has to be told what's happened and I'm not looking forward to it."

"Oh, Luke." She paused, love overflowing in her eyes. If she could only hold him, share in his blame. "I'm sorry I've caused you so much trouble."

"You should be, you're a pain in the—" He paused, grinning at her. "But a very lovely pain."

"Oh, you. You just love me because of my horse," she accused.

"*My* horse," he corrected with a teasing glint in his eye.

She shook her head. "No, my horse. The horse is my dowry."

"Oh, really?" His eyes ran over her lazily. "You think you need one?"

"With you I do."

Glancing down the stairway, Luke pulled her

back into his arms. She lifted her hands to his shoulders, her eyes meeting his. "I will miss lying in your arms at night."

"Not half as much as I'll miss having you there." He moved her closer, proving how much he already missed her.

"You have never told me that you're in love with me," she challenged.

"I haven't?"

"You haven't."

He kissed her softly. "I've never been too good at that sort of thing."

"But you're quite adept at other things."

She reveled in his sharp intake of breath as the feel of his desire grew more intimidating. A clatter from the kitchen made them jump apart guiltily a moment later. Reluctantly, they began climbing the stairs again.

Pausing before a doorway, Luke said quietly, "Your room is next to mine. If you need anything, I'll be close by."

She smiled. "Anything?"

He drew her back for another deep kiss as he fumbled with the doorknob. The door to her room swung open. "You're staying in here."

Hannah sighed, easing inside. The room was as Spartan as his, but she would welcome anything at this point. A tub filled with steaming water was sitting in the middle of the room.

"Take care, little one," he said, his gaze moving over her.

"You too, big one." She said, grinning.

Luke reached out to caress her cheek with the back of his fingers.

"I miss you already," she admitted, ashamed of the tears welling in her eyes. "I wish we'd never come back."

"I'll be here for you, Hannah. I just need time to work things out." He drew her close and held her.

"Oh, Luke. Do you think it can be worked out?" She lifted her eyes to meet his again. She could see how troubled he was, and it hurt her.

"I don't know," he said softly. "I just don't know."

After he left the room, Hannah began stripping off her soiled dress. The bed beckoned to her, but she was too dirty to crawl into it yet.

The tattered dress and underclothes dropped into a pile in the middle of the floor. She was testing the water with her toe when she heard the door open again. Startled, she whirled around.

Luke's eyes darkened as his gaze ran over her nakedness. "Sorry . . . Luisa thought you might need these."

"Th-thank you." Hannah accepted the stack of clothing shyly. Although he had seen her naked many times over the past two days, being here in his house seemed different. Improper—almost sinful now.

Luke grinned. He'd learned to read her expression like an open book.

240

"I'm not looking," he teased.

Her cheeks flamed as she lowered her eyes demurely.

Pulling the door closed behind him, he left her standing in the middle of the room blushing like a schoolgirl.

"Padre?" It was late afternoon before Luke rapped on Thatcher's door.

"Luke?" Thatcher's groggy voice came back to him. "Is that you, son?"

"Yes . . . are you awake?"

"Of course. I never sleep anymore. Come in."

Luke opened the door and entered the dimly lit room. "Damn, why does this room always feel like a dungeon?"

Making his way across the room, Luke swore again as he nearly tripped over a small footstool one of the *criadas* had left in the way.

"The light . . . it hurts an old man's eyes," Thatcher complained.

"How do you know? You haven't seen light in years. If you'd open those curtains once in a while, you might be surprised—"

"Where have you been?" Thatcher interrupted, switching to the subject that had been plaguing his thoughts. "I haven't seen you in days."

Easing into the chair, Luke winced as his hand moved to his side.

Detecting the small hissing sound, Thatcher cracked open one eye. "What's wrong?"

"Had a little accident."

"What kind of accident?"

"I two-stepped with a horse."

"That damn stallion again? He's gonna kill you, boy."

Thatcher's wished Luke would just give up on chasing that renegade. He was never going to capture him anyway.

Luke smiled. "He came near it, but I've got him now."

"The horse?"

"Yep. He's in the corral."

Both of Thatcher's eyes came open this time. "You don't mean it."

"I do mean it, but—Thatcher." Luke drew a deep breath. "We need to talk."

Luke never called Thatcher by his given name unless there was trouble. Big trouble.

"Oh, damn." He rested his head against a pillow. "Who have you killed?"

"No one. Why does everyone immediately think I've killed somebody?" Luke accused.

"Then what's wrong?"

"Well, it's a long story," Luke began. "Remember the night of my birthday party when Hamilton Brewster came here looking for his niece? Accused me of kidnapping her?"

"Yes—and you said she wasn't here."

"Well, that wasn't entirely true." Luke's hand shot up to block Thatcher's outburst. "At the time

242

I thought it was, but I found out later that I was wrong."

Thatcher eased up onto his pillow a fraction higher.

"Somehow when Brewster's niece got off the stage, she hooked up with Enrique, and he brought her out here in the mayor's carriage."

"Why in tarnation . . . ?"

"I have no idea what was going through Enrique's mind. Apparently, he thought she was coming out here. And I don't know why Hannah *thought* Enrique had been sent to take her to Hamilton's ranch, but the mix-up happened. Enrique brought her to *Esperanza* and left her in my room."

"Tarnation!" Thatcher muttered again.

"I'd had too much to drink at the party, and Ines sent me upstairs to sleep it off."

"Uh-oh." Thatcher pushed himself up straighter, his eyes growing round. Luke hadn't seen him looking this alert in years.

"When I got to my room and found the girl in my bed, I thought she was a birthday gift from the boys. Like last year . . ." Luke glanced at his father sheepishly. "I told you about that, didn't I?"

"You sure as hell didn't."

"Well, must have slipped my mind . . . anyway, one thing led to another . . ."

Thatcher's eyes narrowed. "I'm not sure I want to hear this, boy."

"I don't *want* you to hear it, but you have to."

Luke met Thatcher's accusing gaze apologetically. "I bedded Brewster's niece, thinking she was one of Bettianne's girls. By the time I realized who she was, it was too late."

"Tarnation!" Thatcher roared.

"There's more. Hamilton knew that his niece was here. Someone had seen Enrique bringing her out here and told him. So, sometime during the night, he had one of his men come in and snatch Ginny."

"Ginny! Sheep shit!" Thatcher was sitting straight up in his bed now. "Luisa *told* me Ginny was over at the Strickland place! Hellfire! Nobody ever tells me anything!"

"Luisa was just following orders," Luke said calmly. "Ginny would have been back by sundown the same day . . . if things had gone as planned."

"You mean there's more?" Thatcher asked incredulously.

"Yes. Hannah had come here to marry Edgar Huckett. . . ."

"Edgar Huckett! That simpering little burying man? Why would a woman still breathing have any use for Edgar?"

"She didn't want to marry Edgar. Apparently, the marriage had been arranged by her father and Hamilton."

Though the situation was far from amusing, Luke couldn't help grinning when he pictured Hannah and Edgar together. Hannah would have

244

the little undertaker laid low within the week with her lusty appetite.

His face suddenly sobered when he actually thought of Hannah with another man. He was likely to break *any* man's neck who came near her.

"Leave it to *Hamilton* to arrange a fool thing like that," Thatcher grumbled. At least Thatcher Kincaid wasn't so old he'd forgotten what love was all about. "Well, go on. What's happened because of all this tomfoolery?"

"The next morning I took Hannah back to her uncle's."

"Only sensible thing to do," Thatcher agreed. "Told him about the honest mistake, huh?"

"I told him."

"And he made a big fuss, bellowing and threatening all over the place."

"You could say that."

Thatcher grinned, visualizing the look on Hamilton's face. Served the old goat right. "So you got Ginny and got the devil out of there."

"Not quite."

The grin faded, and Luke saw a foreboding light enter his father's eyes. "You got Ginny and—"

"I don't have Ginny. I leveled with Hamilton. I told him exactly what had happened."

Thatcher's face suddenly lit with glee. "How'd he like them apples?"

"He was mad as hell."

"You *told* him you bedded his niece?"

Luke nodded. "I didn't see that I had any other

choice. Hannah was so mad she was certain to hold it over my head and cause more trouble than we had already."

"Yes . . . yes, I can see that. So what did you propose to do about the misunderstanding?"

"I promised Hamilton that if he would go on with the arrangement for Hannah to marry Edgar, without letting Edgar know what had happened, I would give him a legal deed to the disputed land.

Thatcher's face fell. "You what?"

"I gave away our part of the land."

The hurt that came over Thatcher's face seared Luke. "You gave away *my land?*" Thatcher murmured.

Leaning forward, Luke laid his hand across his father's. "I'm sorry. If there had been any other way, I would have taken it. I knew that Hamilton would accept nothing less in way of retribution for his niece's virginity. You would have done the same for Ginny."

Stunned, Thatcher lay back against his pillow. His face was drained of color. "Where is Ginny now?"

She's still with Hamilton, but I have his word she won't be harmed."

"And if a Brewster is carrying a Kincaid's child?"

Luke wouldn't meet his father's eyes this time. "That's been taken care of."

Thatcher was silent as Luke continued. "The

246

agreement is that if Hannah is carrying my child, Edgar will be made to believe that it's his."

The words bruised Luke even more deeply than the look of disillusionment on Thatcher's face.

"And the girl has agreed to this?"

"No," Luke said, resting his head against the back of the chair. "She was stung by my betrayal. She ran away and I went after her."

Thatcher sighed, remembering the ninety years of bitterness that had weighed heavily on his shoulders. Luke had done what he had to under the circumstances. Given the same situation, Thatcher knew he'd have been forced to do the same. "So, that's where you've been."

"That's where I've been."

For a long time the two men sat silently in the growing twilight. Sunset turned the room from muted shades of gold to topaz and then to blackness. The two men sat silently holding on to each other's hands.

Luke knew how hurt his father was over the odd turn of events. Ninety years was a long time to be carrying so much hate.

What he didn't know was how and when he was going to tell him the rest of the story. That he was in love with the woman.

Thatcher lay in his dreary, self-imposed tomb for another two days. He spoke to no one, and he refused to eat a single morsel of food.

247

Stretched out on his narrow bed, he lay staring at the ceiling, thinking.

He thought about what Luke had done. He thought about the feud, and the havoc it had wreaked upon innocent lives. He thought about his other children, Ginny and Pete, and the grandchildren he longed to hold in his arms.

But most of all, he thought about Rosy, and how much he had loved her.

On the third day, when Luisa entered the patriarch's bedroom, she found Thatcher sitting up in bed, waiting for her.

"Ay, Madre de Dios," Luisa murmured at what was a most unusual sight.

"Is that Brewster girl still in this house?" Thatcher demanded.

Luisa crossed herself. *"Sí."*

"I want to see her."

Moving lamely to the bed, Luisa nodded, positioning a tray in front of him.

Thatcher eyed the contents of the tray. "What's this you've brought me?"

"Only a small bowl of porridge and some dry toast."

"Sheep shit, woman." Thatcher shoved the tray aside irritably. "I want some real food! Bring me three fried eggs, a side of ham, and four or five of those things you call biscuits." He met Luisa's stunned expression evenly. "And open those damned curtains on your way out. Place looks like a blasted dungeon."

248

Luisa fled from the room a moment later, still making the sign of the cross.

"You wanted to see me, sir?"

That afternoon Hannah stood quietly in front of *Esperanza* 's reigning patriarch. When Luisa had told her that Luke's father wanted to talk to her, she had been surprised.

Now, coming face to face with Thatcher Kincaid, she felt her stomach was wrapped in knots. She was painfully aware of her sunburned nose and her boyish haircut.

"Come closer, girl."

Easing a step forward, Hannah hesitated again.

"Well, look at me. I won't bite you." In his younger days, he couldn't have made such a promise.

Slowly, Hannah lifted her gaze. She found a nice, warm pair of blue eyes awaiting her.

"Well, now, that's better."

"Thank you . . . sir."

"What happened to your hair?"

"Luke cut it," she replied softly.

"Damn. The boy better stick to ranchin'."

With the beginnings of a smile, Hannah drew a deep breath. Thatcher Kincaid wasn't so terrifying. She was actually warming to this crusty old man.

"So, you're Hamilton Brewster's niece."

"Yes. Hannah Rose Brewster."

Thatcher smiled. "Rose? That's a mighty pretty name."

"Thank you, sir. My father named me after my great-great-grandmother."

"Luke tells me it's possible that you could be carrying his child."

His abrupt statement caught her off guard. Hannah blinked, then drew another deep breath.

"Yes, sir."

Thatcher's eyes pinpointed her. "Well, are you?"

Dropping her head, she murmured, "It's looking more and more that way." She was to have begun her menses today, but she hadn't.

"Does Luke know?"

She shook her head, feeling the wetness begin to slide down her cheeks. "No, and I don't want him to know."

"Why not?"

She looked up again, her chin firming. "You know why not."

"The feud?"

She nodded. "The feud."

She was a pretty little thing. He suddenly found himself hoping that she was carrying Luke's child.

Rosy's grandchild.

"What's Hamilton saying about all of this?"

"I haven't spoken with my uncle since I got back. I . . . I hoped to avoid that until . . ."

Seeing her tears, Thatcher patted the bed beside him. "Come over here, *querida.*"

Hannah edged closer to Thatcher as he reached out and took her hand. "Do you want to marry Edgar Huckett?"

She shook her head, a sob catching in her throat.

Thatcher nodded. That's what he'd thought. "Edgar's a good man. Why, I hear that woman, Jane Bowling, would give her eyeteeth to snag him."

Hannah's shoulders lifted lamely. "It would please me to give him to her."

Thatcher's tone softened. "Look at me, Hannah Rose."

Hannah obediently lifted her eyes. "It's my boy, Luke, you love, isn't it?"

"Yes, sir. Very, very much."

"But you don't want to trap Luke into marrying you."

"No, sir." Another sob caught in her throat. "You see, in the beginning, I was determined to do just that because I didn't want to marry Edgar. So I thought if Uncle Hamilton would make Luke marry me, then I could be rid of Edgar and have my marriage to Luke set aside later."

"But instead, you fell in love with my boy."

"Yes," A long sigh escaped her. "Instead I fell in love with your . . . boy." It was hard for Hannah to think of Luke as a *boy.*

Thatcher chuckled, remembering the day Rosy was offered to him in exchange for five warm blankets and a string of horses.

"Oh, Mr. Kincaid, I've been so much trouble to

Luke already. I know he made the agreement with my uncle for the land because it was the only way to end the feud, but I hated him for doing it. I just . . . wanted to get away. But then Uncle Ham sent him after me. After spending a few days alone with him, I realized that he wasn't really bad, that he was only trying to do what was best for everyone."

"Then what are you crying about?"

"It's all such a mess! I love Luke but Uncle Ham would never give us his blessing even if Luke wanted to marry me. And I certainly wouldn't want him to ask me to marry him just because I might be having his baby." She glanced up accusingly. "He told me how much you want a grandchild."

Thatcher squeezed her hand. She reminded him so much of Rosy. His Rosy would have had the same concerns about such an arrangement.

"Has Luke told you that he's in love with you?"

"Yes, but"—she dropped her gaze in shame—"Uncle Ham has made it very clear that the Brewsters and the Kincaids have been at one another's throats for two generations. It's impossible. But with everything that's happened . . ."

"With all that's happened?"

"Oh . . . you know . . . we were alone for those few days and . . ."

Thatcher winced. "Oh . . . yes, I see what you mean."

And Thatcher did see. Only too clearly.

* * *

Hannah let herself out of Thatcher's room a half hour later. She started down the steps to find Luke just starting upstairs.

He paused when he saw her.

"Hi. Luisa said you were with Thatcher?"

"We had a nice, long talk."

"About what?"

"Oh, about the horse."

"The horse?"

"Sure. Thatcher wants me to push his wheelchair out to the barn so he can see him tomorrow."

Luke proceeded to climb the stairs until he was standing one step below her. It had been days since he'd held her in his arms. The nights had been the loneliest he had ever spent. "Have you missed me?" he asked huskily.

"A little."

Drawing her into his arms, he stole a brief but thorough kiss. "Are you feeling all right today?" Luke knew his time was running out. Hamilton was expecting him to return his niece within the week. But Luke had to know if she was carrying his child.

Hannah frowned, knowing exactly why Luke was inquiring. He had asked her that same question each morning at the breakfast table.

"Maybe, maybe not."

Lifting his eyes, his gaze held hers. "Are you?"

With a smile, she ran her fingers over his cheek lovingly. "Make love to me, Lucas."

"Hannah," Luke groaned softly, buying his face against her neck. "Don't do this to me."

"Do what?"

"Hannah . . ."

She caught his face, turning it up to meet hers. "I saw a nice, quiet hayloft when I was feeding the stallion this morning. No one would see us." She touched the lobe of his ear with her tongue.

"The men—"

Her mouth touched his lightly. "—Are just about to eat their supper."

Luke grinned, easing his hand over her bottom. "You little spitfire. You must have given this some thought."

She smiled, stealing another short but arousing kiss from him. "What do you think?"

Ten minutes later, they laughingly scrambled up the ladder into the loft. As they tumbled in the hay, they shed their clothes quickly.

"God, I've missed you." Luke's mouth was warm on hers, searching, demanding.

"I've missed you, too." Their hands were eager, resourceful, not daring to waste one single, wonderful moment.

Desire fed upon desire. They knew it would not be a gentle mating this time. Their need to be together was far too intense.

Hannah didn't question her need for him, and she didn't have the courage to think about what he was feeling for her.

She laced her fingers with his. Murmuring her name, he thrust into her.

Caught in the slanting rays of the sun, they gave themselves completely to the sweet, hot ache they'd so eagerly welcomed.

The sun was just setting as Kamen tapped on Ginny's bedroom door that same evening. She stood at the windows watching the last golden rays play across the mountaintop.

"Ginny?"

She turned and quietly went into his arms. "I don't want to leave you, Kamen."

Kamen closed his eyes and held her tightly. She smelled as sweet as roses after a summer shower.

"I love you, Kamen."

"I love you, too," he said, pulling her closer. "Don't you worry none. Nothing's going to keep us apart."

"I'm so afraid, Kamen. I heard the servants talking this morning. Luke and Hannah are back. Hamilton is raving like a crazy man, demanding that Luke bring Hannah back to the ranch. Hannah sent him a note saying she's all right, so she'll be back any day now."

"Well . . ." Kamen's arm tightened around her protectively. "So what if he does? That don't mean you have to leave."

Drawing back from him, she made him meet her eyes. "Yes, it does, Kamen. You have to realize that."

"Don't say that."

"It's the truth. Once Hannah is returned, I'll have to go back to *Esperanza*."

They gazed at each other. Their halcyon days of afternoon picnics and long, lackadaisical swims in the stream were coming to an end.

"I won't let you go," Kamen vowed. "I just won't! I'll go tell my uncle that I love you and that we want to get married. I'll tell him right now."

"You can't, Kamen. You're just sixteen and I'm only fifteen. Your uncle would send you back to Iowa, and we'd never get to see each other again."

Going back into each other's arms, they held on tightly. "Oh, Kamen, what are we going to do?" she lamented heartbrokenly. "What are we going to do?"

Kamen didn't know. But he was gonna do something. He couldn't let the only girl in the world he'd ever love go.

He'd die first.

14

When Luke came down the stairs the next morning, he found Thatcher sitting in the wheelchair, waiting for him.

"Good Lord." Luke stopped and just stared at his father. He couldn't believe his eyes. He and his father had fought about that chair since the day he'd brought it into the house three years ago, but it had always sat, unused, in a corner of Thatcher's bedroom.

Undaunted by his son's look of astonishment, Thatcher shrugged and straightened his blanket. "Don't look so surprised. I've been meaning to try out this blasted thing for a long time."

"What brought this on?"

"Well," Thatcher said, lifting his chin, "I've decided if the good Lord is bound and determined to keep me alive, then I might as well enjoy it. Besides, I'm not going to have my grandchild see me lying in that dad-blasted bed all the time."

Luke shook his head, grinning. "But *you're* fifty-two years old," he reminded. "You're old and sick and you can't get out of bed, least that's what you been saying."

"I'm only fifty-one." Thatcher's chin jutted out. "And I got a lot of years ahead of me. *And* I intend to spend them watching my grandchild take his first step, ride his first horse, and do all those things young-uns do."

Luke's smile began to fade. "And just where is this grandchild coming from?"

"Well . . . you know."

"No," Luke crossed his arms, "I don't know. Why don't you tell me."

"Me and that Brewster girl had us a long talk."

"And?"

"Well, she's carrying Rosy's grandchild," Thatcher said.

"Did *she* say that?"

"*You* said that. The night you come in and told me about the mix-up."

"*I* said she might be."

"Well, that's what *I* meant."

"That's not what you said."

"But it's what *I* meant," Thatcher insisted.

"And if she is?" Luke countered. He was more than interested in Thatcher's answer.

Thatcher knew he had to be careful now. He'd promised Hannah Rose that he wouldn't do or say anything that would pressure Luke into marrying her, but he couldn't stand by and take the chance of losing Rosy's grandchild. He wanted that child, and if it meant fighting for it, he would. That baby was going to be raised a Kincaid even if it did have Brewster blood. Besides, Hannah Rose wasn't so bad . . . right nice, actually. And she would be good for Luke. Settle him down a bit. "Well, if she is, then I intend to have her and Edgar out to the house quite a lot after the baby comes. After all"— he looked at his son innocently—"though your bedding a Brewster was a mistake, that don't make that baby any less *my* grandchild."

Luke's spirits suddenly lifted. Thatcher didn't seem to mind if it was a Brewster who was going to have his grandchild. "Are you saying you wouldn't mind if it was Hannah having my baby?"

"Oh, no . . ." Thatcher hedged obediently. He had to be very careful here. "I'd mind . . . but Edgar's a fine man, and he'll be a good provider for Hannah and the baby," he finished softly.

Damn! Luke swore silently. For one minuscule moment, he had actually thought Thatcher was going to relent and tell him that he should do his duty and marry the girl.

"Thatcher?"

"Call me Pa, son. You never call me Pa."

"Pa . . . do *you* want me to marry Hannah?" Thatcher leaned forward expectantly.

Luke straightened, holding his breath.

Seeing the anticipatory look on his son's face,

Thatcher let his shoulders slowly wilt. "No . . . course not. A Kincaid wouldn't marry one of those Brewsters . . . would he?"

Luke's body went slack with disappointment. "No . . . I suppose not."

"Well," Thatcher sighed, relieved to drop the subject, "guess we'd better get into the kitchen. Luisa's been yelling for the past twenty minutes."

"Yeah . . ." Luke murmured distractedly. "You need help?"

"Nope!" Thatcher beamed. "I'm coming to the dinner table tonight, too. I've already told Luisa that I don't want any more of those dad-blamed trays brought to my bed. I'm eating with the family from now on."

"You're spoiling him." Luke leaned over the rail to watch Hannah with the stallion later that morning.

"I don't care." She handed the stallion a carrot she'd stolen from the kitchen earlier. "Isn't he beautiful?"

"He's not half as pretty as you."

She wrinkled her nose at him. "Bet you say that to all the girls."

"Only to the pretty ones."

She rubbed the restless stallion's ears, smiling as he whinnied and shied away. He still didn't like all the fuss. "Oh, Luke. He is the most beautiful horse in the world."

260

"Yeah, you've got yourself a fine animal there," he admitted.

"Oh, he's not mine. He's yours."

"Mine? You'd better tell him that." The stallion still wouldn't let Luke or any other ranch hand come anywhere near him.

She sighed. "You'll have to see to his needs after I'm gone."

His gaze softened. "And just where do you think you're going."

"You know. And I don't think I'll be doing much riding where I'm going," she conceded.

Climbing through the fence, Luke grinned as he walked toward her. She recognized the hunger in his eyes, and it worried her.

"Luke," she warned, holding up a hand to ward him off.

"Luke," he mimicked.

"Luke," she repeated anxiously, "really, someone might see us."

"You know something. I just don't give a damn."

"You'd better. I think your father's peeking out the window at us."

"Then meet me in the loft in ten minutes."

"Ten minutes!" She stamped her foot irritably. Luke's brows shot up. He hadn't seen her act that way in a long time. "Yeah . . . you have a problem with that?"

"Yeah." She flashed him a naughty grin. "Make it five."

* * *

A knock sounded at Luke's office door later that afternoon. Luke glanced up irritably. He had left explicit orders that he did not want to be disturbed.

"Who is it?"

"Kamen Brewster . . . sir."

Laying his pencil down, Luke frowned. "Kamen?"

"Yes, sir," came the muffled reply.

"What do you want?"

"I want to talk to you."

Rising, Luke went to open the door. "Kamen, what in the hell—"

As the door swung open, Kamen brushed past Luke absently. "Don't give me no trouble. I got me a big problem, and you're the only one I know who'd understand. Me and you are gonna talk, Mr. Kincaid."

Mr. Kincaid? Luke closed the door hesitantly. Since when did a Brewster call a Kincaid *mister?*

A horse and carriage pulled into the courtyard a little before two o'clock that afternoon. Luke and Kamen were cloistered in Luke's office, but Hannah was unaware of the strange meeting.

She was busy currying the stallion. Distractedly, she glanced up to see a young woman striding toward her purposefully.

The woman paused at the fence and removed her gloves. "Are you Hannah Brewster?"

"I am."

Ines's eyes closed in distress. The girl was as lovely as she had feared. "May I speak with you?"

Laying the brush down, Hannah self-consciously wiped her hands on her skirt. "Yes, of course."

"Shall we walk?"

Hannah opened the gate, and the two women began strolling across the courtyard.

"Allow me to introduce myself. I'm Ines Potter." Ines paused for a moment, openly appraising Hannah. The girl was exquisite. She had a freshness and vitality about her that Ines both admired and envied. Her hair was cut in a boyish bob, but on her, the style was flattering.

Hannah was thinking Ines was the most attractive woman she had ever seen. With a sinking heart she wondered if the woman's visit had anything to do with Luke. Somehow, she guessed that it did.

"I don't suppose Luke has mentioned me?"

"No," Hannah returned honestly, "I don't think he has."

Sighing, Ines began walking again. "Why doesn't that surprise me?" she said more to herself than anyone else.

"You know Luke."

"I know Luke," she said softly.

It was Hannah who closed her eyes this time. Ines didn't need to say more. The reverence, the love, and the melancholy in her voice told Hannah all that she needed to know.

The women entered Luisa's rose garden and sat on opposite ends of a wooden bench. Hannah gazed at the lovely blooms, thinking how ironic it was that she should be surrounded by such beauty when she was losing Luke forever.

"May I be honest with you?" Ines asked quietly. Hannah nodded. "Yes."

"I'm very much in love with Lucas."

"Yes . . . somehow I sensed that."

"There's a rumor going around town"—Ines paused, drawing a deep, fortifying breath—"that you are carrying his child." The words tasted as bitter as the thought.

"I may be. I'm not certain."

"Does Luke know this?"

"He knows it's possible."

Ines placed her hand on Hannah's arm and implored her, "I beg of you, don't make him marry you."

Hannah met her gaze, her own eyes softening. "Do you honestly believe I could make Luke do anything against his will?"

"I know I have no right to make such a demand of you, but I have worked so hard to make Luke fall in love with me. So hard . . . and I really thought . . ." A sob caught in Ines's throat. Her voice broke momentarily, and tears welled in her eyes. Then, regaining her strength, Ines continued. "I thought I was making progress. I fully believe Luke intended to propose to me the night . . . well, the night this all began."

Drawing a handkerchief from her pocket, Ines wiped her eyes. "I know that you must have feelings for him—any woman would, but I want you to know that I would be good for him. We would have a good marriage. I know that I could make him love me. Our families get along well, and they're both pillars of the community."

Ines turned now, tears rolling silently down her cheeks. "Please, I beg you, marry Edgar and let our lives return to normal. I love Luke—more than anything on this earth. If he were to marry you, the union could bring nothing but a life of hatred and regret. The feud between the two families will never be settled." She broke down completely, and sobs racked her.

Wordlessly, Hannah drew her compassionately into her arms, not knowing how to comfort her.

What Ines said was true. She could make Luke happier than Hannah could. The feud would always be there . . . always.

Hannah stood at her bedroom window the following evening watching for Edgar's carriage. After Ines's visit the day before, she had gone to her room, packed her bag, and asked Pedro to take her to her uncle's home.

Since Luke had disappeared right after lunch, Pedro was at a loss as to what to do, so he consulted Thatcher.

Thatcher told him to honor the lady's request.

Hannah had ridden to the Brewster ranch in silent agony. She loved Luke more than her own life, but she knew that Ines could make him happier. A marriage between a Brewster and Kincaid would only bring about more heartache and despair, and there had been too much of that over the years. If she were carrying Luke's baby, she would raise it on her own. She wouldn't subject another innocent child to such hatred and bigotry.

Fighting back tears, Hannah watched the tiny speck on the evening horizon grow larger, and she wanted to cry again.

Long minutes later, she started down the stairway as Hamilton started up after her.

"There you are, my dear. Edgar is here."

She followed Hamilton into the sitting room. There on the settee sat a thin man with bony knees and thinning hair. Hannah's heart sank when she viewed her husband-to-be. This was the man with whom she would spend the rest of her life.

"Hannah Rose, may I present Edgar Huckett," Hamilton said civilly.

Edgar stood, clicked his heels together, and bent from the waist to bow to her. "Miss Hannah, I am *most* pleased to finally meet you."

Hannah reluctantly offered him her hand, and he took it. His palm was damp and soft, and his clasp was weak. He stood not more than an inch taller than she, his legs seeming inordinately long for his body.

His hair was thinning, a soft sandy color—blending with pale, nondescript brows.

His skin was fair, and unless Hannah missed her guess, extremely prone to sunburn. He spoke in hushed tones, a mannerism that she imagined was expected in his profession.

"Hannah, my dear, you sit right here," Hamilton motioned her toward a spot on the settee next to Edgar.

Hannah perched uneasily on the edge and folded her hands in her lap.

Edgar was everything she'd anticipated.

His cologne had a strange aroma, a pungent, almost bittersweet undercurrent that made her eyes water.

He was dressed in a conservative manner. The drab gray suit was not complimentary. His complexion was so pale she wondered if he had ever seen the sun.

Luke's bronzed skin, his strong body, his fiery touch, rose unbidden to her mind. Willing those thoughts aside, she tried to concentrate on what Edgar was saying.

"Hannah . . . I may call you Hannah?"

"Of course."

"Hannah, your uncle and I have discussed the . . . uh, wedding. I know you've had quite a disturbing week, but I trust you are willing to pro-

ceed with the agreement made between . . . uh,
your uncle and . . . uh, myself."

Forcing back rising hysteria, Hannah stared at
the floor. Maybe if she didn't look at him it would
help. "Yes, Edgar, I am willing to go on with the
plans."

"Excellent. Now . . . uh, what day might be
convenient for you?" Edgar pulled a small notebook from his pocket and opened it carefully. "I
have Thursday of this week open. And . . . yes,
Tuesday of next week. Either of those days would
do nicely . . . if that is your wish," he amended.

Hannah glanced at the notebook that Edgar was
studying so carefully. Each day of the week was
neatly penciled in with notations beside each. Apparently he had to work on Monday, Wednesday,
and Friday.

She felt panic crowding her throat again. He
was scheduling their wedding between funeral
services!

"Either day would do nicely, Edgar." She
smiled. "Perhaps next Tuesday,"

She would take all the time she could get.

"Very well," Edgar agreed, carefully penciling
in "Miss Brewster—Wedding" between a town
council meeting on Monday and a visit to the
prison compound at the fort on Wednesday. "Well,
this has indeed been a pleasure, but I must be on
my way now. I have to speak with Mrs. Grant
before evening." Edgar looked at his bride-to-be
knowingly. "Mr. Grant passed over this morning."

Both Edgar and Hamilton were looking at Hannah now, apparently expecting some comment from her. "Oh . . . no, I didn't know. I'm very sorry," she mumbled.

Edgar's glance was a little more stringent this time. "After we're married, Hannah, you will be going with me on these courtesy calls. Perhaps you can be of assistance to the grieving widows and children. You see, since we don't have a regular preacher in Tribulation, I quite often fill in as the pastor, speaking a few words of comfort, saying a few prayers over the deceased."

"Of course," Hannah murmured.

Her life stretched out before her on a trail of black crepe scented with funeral lilies.

"Well," Hamilton said, rubbing his hands together, "I believe we have a wedding date. That will work out quite well. You will be taking Hannah to the festival on Saturday?"

"Oh, my, yes," Edgar answered in his precise way. "Unless . . . well, unless someone needs me."

"Fine, fine." Hamilton beamed. "That will give you and Hannah an excellent opportunity to become better acquainted."

"And it will also give Hannah an opportunity to meet the townspeople and begin making friends. Making friends with potential customers is very important, Hannah," Edgar reminded her.

Hannah walked to the door of the parlor with Edgar. Leaning forward, Edgar aimed a smooch at her cheek but missed. The benign kiss just barely brushed the corner of her temple.

"You take care, Edgar. And Hannah Rose will be looking forward to seeing you Saturday night," Hamilton assured him.

Hannah stood beside Uncle Hamilton and waved as Edgar turned his carriage and drove away.

Hannah shook her head and murmured, "Did he smell like embalming fluid to you?"

Hamilton hooked his thumbs into his pocket, staring at Edgar's disappearing carriage thoughtfully. "Was that what that peculiar odor was?"

"I believe so."

"Oh . . . well, I suppose you'll get used to that smell."

Hannah turned and started back into the house. "I suppose I'll have to."

Hannah thought about dressing in black for the fiesta. Somehow the color seemed appropriate. But when she came down the stairs Saturday evening, she was wearing blue. A soft, demure blue.

Edgar commented that he had never seen her looking nicer.

But since he'd seen her so little, Hannah didn't put much credence in the compliment.

The fiesta was in full swing by the time Hannah and Edgar arrived. The schoolhouse seemed to be the hub of activity for the evening's festivities.

Hannah's eyes searched the crowd for Luke,

hoping he would be there, yet praying that he wouldn't. She had expected him to at least ride over to her uncle's ranch and ask her why she'd left so suddenly, but he hadn't. She hadn't heard one word from him in the past few days.

Not that it mattered. Edgar dominated her time now. She sighed. She had found it difficult, if not impossible, to discover a topic they could discuss mutually.

Edgar was totally involved in his work, and Hannah could hardly bear to think about his occupation, much less share it with any enthusiasm. They had spent most of the past three days in complete silence or with Edgar carrying on a narration about his prospective clients and appointments.

The schoolhouse was small, but it was centrally located on the main street, where dancing was already taking place. In preparation for the festivities, the street had been raked until it had a smooth surface.

A small stage had been erected on which an assortment of musicians were playing. Men dressed in their Sunday best and women in gay, colorful dresses were in the street, dipping and turning to the tunes played on guitars and squeeze-boxes.

Edgar directed Hannah to a table where a large bowl of punch and cups were laid out.

"I wonder if Jane has arrived yet?" he commented.

Hannah's cautious gaze swept the crowd. "Jane who?"

"Oh . . . er . . . Jane Bowling. She's new to Tribulation, hasn't been here but a month or two —oh, there she is now. Will you excuse me for a moment? I just want to make her feel welcome."

Hannah watched as Edgar scurried across the street to greet a small, dark-haired girl who was just slightly shorter than he and a little on the plump side. They began talking excitedly, and Hannah was amused to see a worshipful look appear on the girl's face.

"Where's Edgar?" Hannah glanced up to find her uncle standing beside her.

"Over there with Jane Bowling."

"Edgar's with Jane?" Hamilton peered through the crowd to see Edgar making his way through the crowd with Jane on his arm. "That don't hardly seem proper."

"Hannah, my dear," Edgar said as he arrived breathlessly. "May I present Jane Bowling. Jane is new in town and employed at the General Store."

"Miss Bowling," Hannah murmured as Hamilton bent over the young woman's hand.

There was an awkward moment as Edgar looked from Jane to Hannah while Jane gazed adoringly at Edgar. Hannah was sure she detected something more than just a casual interest between Jane and Edgar, but it could have been just wishful thinking on her part.

"I have to help serve the punch," Jane said, and

her gaze returned to Hannah. "I'm glad to meet you. I hope you and Edgar will be very happy."

As Jane walked away, Hannah was surprised to see Edgar's gaze follow the young woman almost wistfully.

"Uh, Jane is very involved in community affairs. She's already a member of the sewing circle, an officer of the women's club, and an active organizer for this celebration."

He was obviously smitten with the young woman. It was as plain as the nose on his face. Why then, Hannah wondered, had he agreed to marry her?

"How long has Jane been in town?" Hannah asked.

"Oh, just a month or so. She's made an attempt to get acquainted very quickly. A very nice young lady. Very nice."

That explained it, Hannah thought. Hamilton had already spoken with Edgar about marrying her before Jane had moved to Tribulation. Oh, *why* couldn't Jane have arrived just two months sooner! Hannah silently agonized. She felt so trapped. If she returned to Iowa, she would never see Luke again. Yet if she stayed, she could be carrying his child. How would she be able to bear seeing him with Ines . . . knowing how much she loved him, yet knowing that it would be Edgar who shared her bed?

"Edgar, I'm sure Hannah is just itchin' to dance," Hamilton suggested.

"Of course." Edgar offered Hannah his arm. "Shall we?"

The dance was a waltz, and Hannah moved into the steps easily. Edgar was not the smoothest dancer, but he was adequate. At least he didn't step on her toes. He held her loosely, with his hand touching lightly on the small of her back. He seemed distracted, which was fine with Hannah. She didn't feel like making even light conversation.

She was aware the moment Luke arrived. Wearing dark pants, a white shirt, a black vest, and a black hat, he took her breath away as he entered the town. His black boots gleamed in the afternoon sun, and he wore silver spurs that matched the silver discs lining his hatband.

She couldn't remember ever seeing him look so handsome.

Spotting Hannah, Luke dismounted, then made his way quietly through the crowd. As he reached her, they drank in the sight of each other for a moment.

"May I dance with your fiancée, Edgar?"

Giving Luke a disgruntled look, Edgar relinquished his hold on Hannah. "I'll be at the punch bowl if you need me."

"I won't need you," Luke said.

Finding the remark devoid of humor, Edgar ambled off.

Luke drew her into his arms, and his eyes met hers as he moved her out onto the dance floor. She felt lightheaded and giddy just being in his arms once more, and she had no intention of hiding it.

"What was that smell?" Luke asked.

"Embalming fluid."

Luke guided her away from the crowd. Drawing her even closer, he held her tightly, his breath warm against her ear.

"Why did you run away, sweetheart?"

She pulled back to face him, her happiness replaced now by a numbing fear. Fear that she had lost him forever. If there was ever a time for honesty, Hannah knew it must be now. "Because . . . I love you."

Their gazes held, refusing to part.

"I love you, too."

The music tempo picked up, and Luke moved with it gracefully. It was as if there was no one else in the world but the two of them now. Luke moved her closer, his hand at her back warm and controlling.

"I meant to tell you about Ines."

"But you didn't."

"No, I didn't. Actually, there wasn't anything to tell. I'm not in love with her."

"She said you were going to ask her to marry you."

"I might have." He gave her one of those smiles that made her weak in the knees. "But the good Lord sent you along in the nick of time."

"But she loves you, Luke. Almost as much as I

do. I left because I could see that you belonged with her, not me."

"Well, I don't like anyone planning my life for me, and that includes you, Miss Brewster."

The music died away, and Hannah felt bereft as Edgar moved in to claim her again.

"Come, dear, I know you must be warm."

For the first time, Hannah had to agree with him. She was very warm.

Her eyes refused to leave Luke as Edgar began anxiously to thread their way back though the crowd.

Luke stood watching Hannah. She glanced back over her shoulder at him. She couldn't attempt to read his feelings. But she knew her own.

Jerking to a halt, she nearly took Edgar down to his knees. She couldn't stand it anymore. If she couldn't have Luke, then she wasn't going to stay around and watch Ines have his babies!

"Wait a minute Edgar—wait a minute!" She jerked free of his hold just as Kamen and Ginny suddenly came bursting through the crowd.

Bright-eyed, Kamen climbed atop one of the hay wagons, a smile as big as Texas dominating his youthful features. Ginny stood by his side, blushing.

"Listen, everybody! May . . . may I have your attention." The youngster's voice broke with nervousness, but he straightened his thin shoulders and tried to get the crowd's attention.

276

"I have an announcement to make!" Kamen shouted.

"What's that fool boy up to?" Hamilton muttered.

"Just shut up, Brewster, and let the boy talk."

Hamilton whirled to find Thatcher sitting beside him in a wheelchair. Hamilton frowned. "What are you doing here, you old fool?"

"The same thing you are, you old son of a bitch. Now pipe down. The boy's got an announcement he wants to make."

The music died away, and a hush fell over the crowd. Luke calmly leaned against a post and lit a smoke.

Kamen faced the sea of inquisitive faces. Drawing a deep breath, he grinned proudly. "Me and Ginny just got hitched."

15

Wile Kamen was making his announcement, Edgar was trying to restrain Hannah.

"Let me go, Edgar. This is all a big mistake."

"Hannah Rose, what has gotten into you?" Taking her by the hand, Edgar led her behind the schoolhouse. It was quieter there, and they could talk.

"Is something upsetting you, my dear? If it's about Jane—"

"Yes, it *is* about Jane—and you and me—or don't you see that, Edgar? Our marriage would be a mistake! I don't love you, you don't love me, and neither one of us wants this marriage."

Edgar's eyes grew rounder. "But it's already been arranged—"

"Arranged? Well, we'll just unarrange it! I saw the way you and Jane were looking at each other."

Edgar flushed. "I'm sorry . . . Jane is—"

"Perfect—for you!" Hannah took Edgar's little round face in her hands, and gripped it tightly. "Listen to me, Edgar. It's *all right*. You don't need to apologize to me for falling in love with Jane."

"I don't?" Edgar's face brightened.

"No, you don't." Shaking his face gently, she smiled. "Be happy, Edgar. At least one of us should be."

"But your uncle and—"

"Let me worry about my uncle," Hannah murmured. "You just go find Jane."

"Kamen." Luke reach out to clasp the young man's hand.

Kamen grinned, returning Luke's grip firmly. "Don't know how to thank you, Luke. If it hadn't been for you driving Ginny and me to Falls River to get hitched, we'd never have been able to pull it off." Glancing at his new bride, Kamen grinned even broader. "Don't know how I'll *ever* thank you."

Squeezing Kamen's shoulder supportively, Luke smiled. "You can thank me by giving Thatcher four or five grandbabies as soon as possible."

Kamen's face turned at least fifteen shades of red. "Oh, don't you worry none. I can handle that." Kamen flushed again when it occurred to him that that might not be the thing to say to his wife's brother.

"You just take good care of my little sister,"

Luke warned, then winked and smacked Kamen playfully on the rump. "Or I'll skin you alive."

Kamen's smile began to fade. "You sure don't need to worry none about that, Mr. Kincaid. I love her an awful lot."

"Do me a favor, Kamen."

"Yes, sir?"

"Don't call me *Mister* Kincaid." Luke winked again. "It reminds me of how old I'm getting."

"Oh, yes, sir," Kamen winked this time, "but I bet this past birthday isn't one you'll forget."

The two men grinned at one another, a bond forming between them.

Ruffling his sister's hair, Luke said quietly, "You take good care of your husband. You've got a fine man."

"Luke . . ." Ginny gazed up at her brother worriedly. "You're not really going to let Hannah marry Edgar Huckett . . . are you?"

During the ride to Falls River that afternoon, Luke had filled Ginny and Kamen in on all the events of the past week—or most of them. He discreetly left out the part about bedding Hannah, but he sensed that Kamen and Ginny were smart enough to read between the lines.

Grinning, Luke shook his head. "No, Ginny."

Ginny glanced around, frowning. "Where is Hannah?"

Luke turned and scanned the crowd hurriedly. "I don't know . . . she was here a minute ago.

"Oh, Luke," Ginny began pushing him toward

the schoolhouse. "You'd better go find her. I think you've waited long enough to claim *your* bride."

Enrique was standing in the doorway of the Tribulation Livery Stable eating beans and meat wrapped in a tortilla. The sounds of the music drifted to him, and he tapped his foot happily. Enrique *liked* the fiesta. It was sooo much fun!

Humming, he was bringing the burrito back to his mouth when he suddenly tensed. The pretty woman was walking toward him.

Ay, madre de Dios. Enrique had hoped he'd seen the last of her!

"Oh, Enrique!" Hannah's face brightened when she saw him. "I'm so glad you're here. I need your help again."

Enrique began backing away slowly.

Hannah smiled understandingly when she saw the fearful look on his face. She knew that she deserved it. She hadn't been very nice to him in the past, and she was sorry now. "Enrique, don't be frightened. I apologize for being so rude to you." She paused and extended her hand to him. "Will you forgive me?"

Enrique looked at his burrito, nodding hesitantly.

"Do you understand what I'm saying?"

Enrique nodded again.

"Really? You really do understand?"

Enrique nodded a third time, extending his burrito to her.

281

"No . . . no, that isn't what I mean. I don't want your burrito." Sighing, she peered inside the empty livery stable. "Enrique, I need a carriage. I have to get back to my uncle's house right away."

Hannah planned to go after her clothes, then drive herself to Falls River. By the time her uncle missed her, she would be on a stage back to Iowa.

"Where is the livery keeper?"

Enrique shrugged.

"At the fiesta, of course." She answered her own question. "Then you will *have* to help me."

"Sí." Enrique nodded.

"I need to rent a carriage. Do you know if there are any for rent?"

"Sí." He nodded.

"May I see one?"

"Sí." Enrique gestured for her to follow him.

Hannah trailed behind Enrique as he led her through the livery. Out in the back, he pulled the cloth off to reveal one of the finest carriages Hannah had ever seen.

Enrique grinned. *"Bonito!"*

The carriage was pretty. Shiny black with brass trim, it was an open carriage with brass lamps mounted on the front. The seats were made of the finest black leather. The harness hung on a peg nearby was fashioned of black leather with gleaming brass buckles and trim.

"How much?" Hannah asked, hoping she had enough money with her to rent the carriage.

Enrique pointed to a list tacked to a post.

Squinting, Hannah tried to read the price list in the dimming light. Well, it would be expensive, but she could just barely manage the fee.

"I'll need a horse to pull it."

Enrique nodded, and came back a few moments later leading a tall chestnut gelding.

With amazing proficiency, he harnessed the horse and hitched him up. Stepping back, Enrique gazed at the carriage nostalgically.

"Enrique, why don't you ride with me?"

Enrique looked at Hannah, stunned.

"Come, ride with me?" She smiled, holding her hand out to him, beckoning.

Accepting her hand reluctantly, Enrique's eyes grew round as she led him to the beautiful carriage. *Madre de Dios* . . . the pretty woman was inviting Enrique to ride in the *bonito* carriage.

They climbed aboard, and Hannah picked up the reins. Turning back to Enrique, she grinned. *"I'll* drive this time."

"Sí," he murmured, so taken with his good fortune he could hardly speak.

It was a beautiful night. The stars were bright, and a large moon was just beginning to rise in the east. The sounds of the fiesta gradually faded as Hannah drove the carriage toward the Brewster ranch.

Tears suddenly began to roll down her cheeks. Her stomach cramped, and she knew without a doubt her menses had started. With all the excite-

283

ment of the past week, her monthly flow had only been delayed.

The tears rolled faster. She wasn't carrying Luke's child after all.

The revelation was heartbreaking. She had nothing left of Luke now. Nothing. Ines would have his babies, and Hannah would be left with only his memory.

Tears blinded her as she picked up the whip and flicked the horse across its enormous rump. Life as an old maid in Iowa stretched endlessly before her. At one time the thought hadn't bothered her at all. Now she wasn't sure she could live without Luke.

Enrique sat wide-eyed beside Hannah, grinning from ear to ear as the horse trotted down the road. He had dreamed of this day all his life. He was riding in the *beau-u-utiful* carriage. And it was a *wonderful* ride.

Enrique was *riding* in the carriage. *The* carriage! It was almost as good—no, it was *better* than riding on the Butterfield stage.

Enrique *liked* the pretty woman again.

No, Enrique *loved* the pretty woman.

Shifting to look over his shoulder, Enrique's eyes grew even larger when he saw that four horses were following them now.

Indians. He frowned, realizing that the riders were the same Indians who'd attacked them before.

Tugging on the sleeve of Hannah's gown, he

pointed to the braves, who were approaching quickly now.

Glancing over her shoulder, Hannah froze when she saw Stalking Horse urging his horse closer to the back of the carriage.

Whipping the horse faster, she watched with horror as Stalking Horse calmly rode to the front of the carriage and grabbed the horse's bridle.

The horse reared as the carriage came to a sudden clamorous halt.

Silence fell over the small group. Hannah and Enrique peered at the Indian anxiously. If he took one more ounce of her hair, she'd scream!

"Where is Eagle Who Flies Two Skies?" Stalking Horse asked.

Hannah blinked in surprise when the Indian spoke. "Eagle Who Does What?"

"Lu-kas," the Indian clarified in broken English.

"I don't know where *Lu-kas* is," she snapped. If it hadn't been for *Lu-kas*, she wouldn't be in this mess again!

Stalking Horse's gaze looked over her indifferently. He snorted. "His woman?"

Before Hannah could tell him that she wasn't, but that she wished she were, Stalking Horse swept her off the carriage seat and plopped her in front of him on his horse.

"Now just one minute!" she stormed. She'd had about enough of his barbarian tactics. His umpteen wives might let him get away with such shabby treatment, but Hannah Brewster was

285

about to put her foot down—square in the middle
of his backside!

"Quiet, woman!"

"Enrique!" Hannah yelled. "Tell this big bully to
put me down!"

Enrique's eyes were as big as saucers as he
watched the fracas.

"Crazy one, go!" Stalking Horse shooed Enrique
away like an annoying housefly.

Grabbing the reins, Enrique turned the carriage
in a wide circle and headed back to town at break-
neck speed. The dust rose, choking Hannah. She
just couldn't *trust* Enrique, she concluded. He
caved in under pressure every time!

Stalking Horse kneed his horse forward.

"This is an outrage!" She squirmed and wiggled
until he was forced to reach out and whack her
soundly across her buttocks. "Lu-kas woman talk
too much!"

"How dare you!" She reached up and slapped
him.

Stunned, Stalking Horse saw stars as the other
three braves burst out laughing.

Hoofbeats sounded in the distance as Hannah
braced herself for Stalking Horse's rage. She
shouldn't have struck him, but he had been asking
for it.

Stalking Horse drew his mount to a halt as the
rider approached.

Hannah nearly fainted with relief when she saw
Luke looking at her as if he could strangle her.

286

"Eagle Who Flies Two Skies," Stalking Horse greeted solemnly.

"Stalking Horse." Luke's gaze ran lazily over Hannah who was still draped unceremoniously on her stomach over the Indian's saddle. Lifting his hat, Luke added chivalrously. "Miss Brewster."

"I have woman again. She is much trouble."

"Yes, I've noticed that."

"You should beat her," Stalking Horse reminded Luke again. "She too hard to control."

"Yeah," Luke's gaze went back to Hannah lovingly, "I've noticed that, too."

"Stalking Horse would teach woman lesson."

"Oh?"

Hannah's eyes locked hostilely with Luke's now. "What would Stalking Horse do with such a woman?"

Stalking Horse looked down at Hannah's shapely backside. Not bad for woman who talked too much. "Stalking Horse not sure. Maybe Eagle Who Flies Two Skies should cut out her tongue."

Hannah was appalled when Luke appeared to give the suggestion serious consideration. "No, I don't think so. She would bleed to death."

Stalking Horse's face brightened at the unexpected but welcome prospect.

Luke nodded. "I'll take her off your hands now."

Stalking Horse handed Hannah over gladly. The imprint of her hand still glowed a bright red on his cheek.

Luke accepted his woman, who in turn immediately wrapped her arms around his neck tightly, burying her face in his chest. "No squeezing," he warned.

"I'm going to squeeze your head off," she warned irritably in a muffled voice. He would hear about his unamusing barter when they were alone!

Turning back to Stalking Horse, Luke noticed his flaming cheek.

"What happened to your face, my brother?"

Stalking Horse rubbed the side of his face resentfully. "Woman beat me."

Luke threw back his head and laughed.

Stalking Horse glowered.

The four braves wheeled their mounts and rode off.

As the horses' hoofbeats faded, Hannah collapsed against Luke and allowed the tears to spill over.

"Oh, Luke, I was so afraid!"

"You should be. You haven't got enough hair left to mess around with Stalking Horse," he chided.

Ignoring that jibe, she wiped her eyes, snuffled, and sat up straighter. "What are you doing here?"

"Looking for you again."

She looked at him peevishly. "Does Ines know where you are?"

"Does Edgar know where *you* are?"

"Yes, he does. I told Edgar that I couldn't marry him."

"You did."

"I certainly did."

"Well, how do you like that? I just finished telling Ines the same thing."

Hannah gazed back at him. "You didn't?"

"I did."

"Honest?"

"Do you want it in blood?"

"Maybe."

"Forget it."

"Kiss me."

"Why should I?" he inquired. "You're nothing but a peck of trouble."

Smiling, Hannah drew his mouth down to meet hers. They kissed ravenously as the horse clopped along the deserted road.

Their lips finally parted many long moments later, and Hannah gazed up at him. "How did you know where I'd be?"

"Edgar told me he had seen you heading toward the livery. You're not too hard to figure out anymore."

Their mouths drifted back together. It was sheer heaven to be in his arms again. Somehow, Hannah knew this time it would be forever.

"I love you, Luke."

"I love you, Rosy—did I mention that was my mother's name?"

"No—isn't that a coincidence."

Luke's smile was tender now. "Yeah, quite a coincidence."

"Did you really tell Ines that you couldn't marry her?"

"Have I ever lied to you?"

"I'm sure you have."

"Well, I'm not lying now. I told her."

"What did she say?"

"Ines said—" His voice lifted three octaves. " 'Lucas, you are making a terrible mistake. That Brewster girl will bring you nothing but trouble.' "

Hannah grinned. "And what did you say to her?"

"I said, 'Don't I know it, Ines, don't I know it.' "

"Oh, you." She punched him, then they kissed again, longer, sweeter, more deeply.

"Ines is in love with you," she murmured sadly against his lips. She took no joy in seeing Ines hurt by all that had happened.

"I know she is, and I feel bad about the way things have turned out for her. But, there are a number of other men who'll be real glad to have the chance to court her."

"Oh, Luke," she murmured, laying her head on the broad chest that had become so familiar now. "I know I shouldn't be so much trouble to you, but I couldn't marry Edgar, not when I love you so much."

"Do you really think I would have let you marry him?"

"Well—no, but I was beginning to wonder."

His eyes met hers lovingly. "I'm in love with you, Hannah. I wouldn't have let you marry Edgar. I was only trying to settle the feud with the least amount of pain and misunderstanding. It's all behind us now. You and I, and the baby—if there is one—can get on with our lives."

"Luke," Hannah closed her eyes, drawing a deep breath. He had to know that she wasn't carrying his baby. "I'm not going to have a baby."

"You're not?" He took the news as casually as he had accepted everything else surrounding the bizarre change of events since she'd come into his life.

"No." Her fingers toyed with the patch of dark hair peeking through the opening of his shirt. "Do you still feel the same about me?"

"Yeah, I still need someone to take care of *my* horse." He grinned, kissing her again.

"He's *my* horse," she snapped crossly. "Seriously, are you disappointed?"

"No, but Thatcher will be. I guess we have to devote a little more time to the project."

Lifting her head, she gazed at him. "That would mean you would have to marry me."

His brows lifted teasingly. "Change of policy?"

She nodded. "Change of policy."

"Well, you ran away too soon, Miss Brewster. You missed all the excitement."

"What excitement?"

"When Kamen announced that he and Ginny had run away this afternoon and gotten married."

Hannah caught her breath expectantly. "Kamen married your sister?"

"Yeah, I can't imagine how he pulled that off."

"But . . ." Hannah tried to absorb the glorious news. "Then that would mean that a Brewster *has already* married a Kincaid."

"Yeah." A smile touched the corners of Luke's mouth. "That's what it means, all right."

Hannah sat up straighter. "And that would mean that my uncle and your father couldn't say a whole lot more if another Brewster married *another* Kincaid."

"Looks to me that's how it'd work."

"Luke?"

"Yes?"

Her eyes sparkled dangerously now. "Are you thinking what I'm thinking?"

"If you're thinking now that Kamen and Ginny have broken the ice and that we can be married now without causing bloodshed, yeah, the thought has entered my mind."

"But how did your father and my Uncle Hamilton react when Kamen announced that he and Ginny were married?"

"You know, those two surprised me. They sat down together for the first time in years and discovered that they actually liked each other a little. They decided that they were sick and tired of their senseless feud, and they both agreed it was time it should end. When I left, they were talking about deeding the land over to their first grandchild." Gazing down at her, his eyes revealed all

Hannah had to know. He was in love with her. Deeply in love.

"So we'd better get busy, Miss Brewster, or Kamen and Ginny will beat us to the cradle."

Their mouths drew back together, and Hannah thought she would burst from sheer happiness.

His hand came up to cup her breast, caressing it lovingly. "The minister's at the fiesta. I told him to hang around—I'd have a little business for him when I got back," Luke murmured.

"Oh, really?" She pressed her forehead against his, looking him straight in the eye. "I don't remember Eagle Who Flies Two Skies asking me to be his wife."

"No? Well, he is now."

"Oh, no. I want to hear you say it. Say, 'Hannah Rose Brewster. Will you be my wife?' "

"Hannah Rose Brewster. Will you be my wife?"

"Maybe." She kissed him. "How does this sound," she began with a twinkle in her eye. *"Mrs.* Eagle Who Flies Two Skies With Many Papooses Tucked Under Her Wing?"

He winked at her. "I like it."

Hannah laid her head back on his shoulder, sighing happily.

"I like it, too. I will be your wife, Lucas Kincaid. What d'you think of that?"

"I like it." Luke grinned as his mouth lowered to take hers again. "I like it a lot, Hannah Brewster."

Reckless abandon. Intrigue. And spirited love. A magnificent array of tempestuous, passionate historical romances to capture your heart.

Virginia Henley
☐	17161-X	The Raven and the Rose	$4.50
☐	20144-6	The Hawk and the Dove	$4.99
☐	20429-1	The Falcon and the Flower	$3.95

Joanne Redd
☐	20825-4	Steal The Flame	$4.50
☐	18982-9	To Love an Eagle	$4.50
☐	20114-4	Chasing a Dream	$4.50
☐	20224-8	Desert Bride	$3.95

Lori Copeland
☐	10374-6	Avenging Angel	$4.50
☐	20134-9	Passion's Captive	$4.50
☐	20325-2	Sweet Talkin' Stranger	$3.95
☐	20842-4	Sweet Hannah Rose	$4.95

Elaine Coffman
☐	20529-8	Escape Not My Love	$4.99
☐	20262-0	If My Love Could Hold You	$4.99
☐	20198-5	My Enemy, My Love	$3.95